The White Spire

Corrupted Coil Series: Book 5

Theo Mann

The Invisible Publishing Company

Corrupted Coil Series

Contents

Chapter 1

"Run!" Yann Dilnao bellowed as a deafening crack split the ceiling of blue sky above his head.

He charged ahead, but he only made a dozen yards before the sky buckled and crashed down on top of him, Eliska, and Anríq.

The three friends tightened into a closer group, but the upheaval overtook them. There was nowhere to run as the whole upper Layer collapsed on top of the friends.

Anríq grabbed the giant battle axe off his back and spun backward to confront an incoming avalanche of Darklings and Dark forces breaking through from the wild Layers.

He couldn't defend himself or anyone else from all this. Darklings pitched through the breach roaring in fear and surprise as the collapse threw them into confusion, too.

They didn't have time to attack. They were as helpless before the Dark chaos as everyone else.

Yann dodged sideways to get closer to Eliska, but she turned back to help Anríq and Yann missed her.

Yann didn't even get a chance to raise his glaive before giant slabs of bedrock and enormous landslides of soil, lava, and water smashed into the ground all around the travelers.

The Layer in which the friends had just traveling collapsed around their ears, broke the earth beneath their feet, and sent them pitching into other Layers below.

The cascade spread through multiple Layers, each one collapsing on top of another.

Fire, ice, wind, cold, whistling missiles, and even helpless injured or dead Darklings struck Yann, ricocheted off, and wheeled away to nowhere before he even thought to defend himself.

A sudden sucking force squashed the three friends together and they collided inside one of Eliska's protective magical fields.

None of the friends had an instant's reprieve before another long, thin Dark vapor snaked out of the mayhem, struck her field, and shattered it.

The impact flung the three friends apart. She dove for Yann just in time and grabbed his wrist to pull him back. "Stay with me!" she yelled over the noise.

"I'm trying to!" He had to spin away from her and yank his hand free to stab his glaive at another Darkling that came tumbling too close.

The Darkling only made it a dozen yards away from the friends before a huge wall of lava swept across the Layer from Yann's right.

It came impossibly fast. It would have incinerated the three friends, but before anyone could stop it, it morphed into a gigantic shape.

It didn't look so much like a face as just some kind of grotesque shadow made entirely of flames.

The shadow rippled on the lava surface before whatever it was yawned open a huge mouth, swallowed the Darkling and a bunch of other crap caught in the chaos, and then turned on the three friends.

Yann stared up at a wall of fire and undulating lava coming straight for him. He couldn't move. His glaive wouldn't do anything to drive this thing off.

His brain registered one instant of clarity when he realized that the Dark lava actually did turn around to come after him and his friends.

The lava wall had been traveling from his right to his left. It swallowed the Darkling and then deliberately changed direction to target Yann, Eliska, and Anríq.

Yann didn't have time to mention it or even really to realize what was happening before the wall surged toward the three friends.

Shadows that might have been eyes migrated around in the flames. Searing heat blasted across the Layer and singed Yann's cheeks.

At the last possible second before the Dark lava attacked the travelers, Eliska cast another binding spell around them and reestablished her protective field.

She did something else to it and the ball blasted straight into the lava wall. The field lasted a split second before it evaporated again.

That field lasted just long enough for the three friends to break through into a different Layer behind the wall. The friends dropped into a landscape being torn apart by even more upheaval.

The Layer itself seemed like a relatively stable Island. The three friends crashed down on the ground outside what looked like a large city—maybe even the largest city they'd seen so far.

Paved roads passed through residential neighborhoods leading to larger, taller, more majestic buildings in the distance—or they would have if the chaos wasn't already tearing the place apart.

The chaos didn't destroy the Island. That was the strangest thing. The Darklings and Dark forces got trapped on the other side of the lava wall. They didn't break through to put this Layer in danger.

The Island was already in enough danger already.

Roads, houses, trees, hills, animals, people, and even vehicles that must have been using the roads before the instability hit—the Dark forces took them all and changed them in freakish ways.

The roads curled backward and whipped back down on the ground to strike at people.

Animals rushed in snarling and baring their teeth. Trees bent their crowns nearly to the ground and fired torrents of sharp needles at the friends.

Sections of sod peeled off the ground and tried to pummel the travelers as they passed.

Yann would have considered this particularly odd if this random stuff only attacked the travelers' party. He would have written it off as another deliberate attack by the Voyant Mendicat.

Yann couldn't assign this to any deliberate attack by anything—not a deliberate attack on the travelers' party.

All this stuff attacked everything else without exception, too. All these forces attacked each other with equal ferocity.

Roads, houses, trees, and vehicles didn't target the friends over any other target except that the friends just showed up in this landscape for the very first time.

That seemed to set off the whole Layer and everything came at the friends at once.

Eliska grabbed Yann even though he was already staggering to his feet. "We gotta move!" she yelled. "Come on!"

She pulled him closer to her and Anríq, flanked Yann on one side, and Anríq took the other side.

She kept firing magical blasts on her side while Anríq clubbed away objects, animals, and even people transformed by the Dark.

Yann couldn't even be sure it was the Dark transforming them. Did it really matter anymore if the Dark caused this instability or if it came naturally from the collapsing Coil?

The party set off for the city and ran through the outer neighborhoods. The buildings got progressively bigger heading for the taller towers a few miles away.

This was one of those cities with vehicles flying through the air. They flew wildly out of control and smashed into things. Yann even spotted some birds joining in an escalating air battle between the highest buildings.

In some cases, the vehicles picked up speed, charged each other, crashed into houses, trees, and even hillsides, and pulverized their targets.

Some of these insane vehicles survived the damage enough to pull their crushed bodies away and go after other targets—and then all those things turned on the friends, too.

The road slapped itself back down on the ground, but it never stayed in one place for long.

It kept swooping from side to side, curling up to strike at creatures and things, and then unrolling into a different position heading somewhere completely different.

In that moment, a bunch of random structures exploded out of the ground. These didn't belong to the same class as the houses and buildings the travelers had seen before.

Spiky towers stabbed through the sod and pavement of surrounding roads, sidewalks, and embankments. The towers barely took shape before they distorted into crooked, angled horrors and joined in the mayhem of attacking everything around them.

These structures kept growing, sprouting different side angles, and twisting their shapes. They extended wings and side turrets into structures that never would have been possible in normal reality.

Some of their pointed towers bent all the way over and stabbed down at the travelers.

The structures came from directly ahead of the travelers—right in front of Yann.

Eliska and Anríq were too busy defending the trio from behind and both sides.

Yann didn't have time to turn around even to alert them of the structures' attack. Yann was the only person facing in the right direction to see it in time.

He didn't hold out any hope that he would be able to stop them with just his glaive, but all three friends would be dead if he didn't do something.

He sprang forward and stabbed his glaive into the roof of a tower jabbing down at him from above. The roof even had shingles hanging off it.

His glaive crunched through the shingles and the tower reared back in alarm. Its sudden response tore his glaive through the roof a second time and ripped a bunch of shingles off to reveal the attic inside.

A shriek of what sounded like pain echoed through the hole. That sound set Yann's hair on end and the sound also set off all the other towers.

Someone fighting back infuriated the towers. A dozen of these misshapen buildings migrated across the ground to surround the party and the towers all attacked at the same time.

"We gotta get out of here!" Yann yelled over his shoulder. "You have to take us somewhere else!"

"There is nowhere else!" Eliska yelled back. "Nowhere is safe! The whole Coil is falling apart!"

"How can it be?!" Yann countered. "How can it just be falling apart this badly right this minute?!"

"It isn't! This has been coming for a long time! If I take us somewhere else, it would be just as bad!"

"Who the hell cares?!" Yann roared. "Take us—NOW!!"

He slashed his glaive at any building that attacked him, but they came too fast. One of them struck him backward and he crashed into Anríq.

The next minute, the whole Layer collapsed anyway. Yann didn't see if Eliska did it or if it happened by itself—or if another Layer collapsed on top of the friends.

It didn't matter anymore. They fell through another chaos Layer. Eliska cast a binding spell to hold the friends inside her protective field, and this time, it held.

"Where are we going?" Anríq panted.

Eliska shook her head and cast a frenzied glance around the Layer while all three friends caught their breath. "I don't know where we can go...."

"Take us to the White Spire," Yann told her. "If nowhere is any better than anywhere else, then we should go after it."

"We won't be able to break in without Marine's magic to help us out," Eliska told him.

Yann opened his mouth to tell her that they had to try again anyway, but right then, another Dark vapor came at the friends from directly in front.

This one may have just been traveling through the Layer with no direction in mind.

At that second, another Dark vapor—an orange-colored one—whipped out of nowhere. This one looked like it was moving randomly, too.

The two vapors collided and exploded the Layer. Eliska's field held and plunged through into a sky full of reddish-black clouds.

Her ball immediately started to plummet toward a torched landscape far below. This landscape didn't heave out of shape nor did anything change position to attack anything else.

Yann didn't see any sign of instability at all—not anymore. Whatever destroyed this landscape passed through long ago and left the area desolate.

Eliska used her magic to slow down the ball's descent. She would have floated the ball all the way to the ground, but she slowed it more and more until it stopped hovering a hundred feet off the ground.

"This doesn't make any sense," she murmured. "This Island should have suffered the same instability as all the others. It shouldn't be this stable."

"I know why it isn't," Anríq replied from behind her.

She turned around—and then she and Yann followed Anríq's gaze to the horizon in the opposite direction.

The wreckage of a destroyed city lay across one side of the countryside. This Layer might have been similar to the one the friends just passed through—the one with all the living objects and structures attacking each other.

Plenty of exploded vehicles lay in piles of cinders in the middle of the roads. Whole sections had calved off the buildings to expose decimated rooms and residences inside.

Nothing attacked here. Nothing so much as moved. Yann didn't see any people. They must all be dead.

The few buildings still standing extended their melted, scorched, blackened hulks to the gloomy sky. No vegetation grew in that landscape.

Only one building broke the skyline. It jutted its pointed turret above everything else around it. A building that tall and that solid didn't look right surrounded by all this wreckage.

A rim of spikes rimmed the building's tallest tower. Four windows looked out from a small room facing the four directions.

It was the White Spire—the Voyant's stronghold that the three friends had been searching for all this time.

Chapter 2

"Come on! Let's go!" Yann surged to the edge of Eliska's protective field, but he couldn't get out of it any better than all the Dark forces could get into it.

She shot out her hand to hold him back even though he couldn't go anywhere. "We can't, Yann. The Voyant has too many protections around the spire. We won't be able to go near it."

He looked around. "I don't see the river or the wolves."

"He's using different protections now—magical protections."

"We have to try something," he insisted. "We might not get another chance. We've searched all this time for any Layer where he might be hiding the spire. We have to strike now while we have a chance, even if we don't succeed. What will we do instead—just wander the Coil? If you're right, then everywhere will be as unstable as the Layers we've just traveled through."

"I agree with Yann," Anríq chimed in. "We're already here. We've tried so hard to get here. We should assault the spire...."

"*How* should we assault it?" Eliska countered. "I don't have the magic to break the Voyant's protections."

Yann's gaze migrated back to the spire in the distance. It wasn't white—not in this landscape. It looked as burnt and scarred as every other building around here.

Eliska really didn't want to go near it. Just looking at it made her sick to her stomach.

"What can you tell us about the defenses?" Yann asked.

She had to gulp to make herself heard. "I don't know what defenses it has. I don't want to check......I can only tell you that they'll be a hundred times stronger now than they were before."

"How do you know that if you haven't checked?"

She squinted at the landscape—the landscape in the other direction—away from the spire.

"I can't explain how I know.....except that maybe this power gives me a deeper connection to the Coil itself. The Coil will become increasingly unstable...."

"What could be more unstable than *this?*"Yann looked around even though this Island wasn't unstable.

It must have been unstable sometime. That's how it got like this.

"It will get more unstable," she repeated. "It might get so unstable that the Coil itself disintegrates. I don't know how far it could go, but we aren't anywhere close to that yet—but that doesn't mean anything. The defenses will get stronger the longer this goes on. Every day that passes before someone finds and takes the Shard of Hotha makes it increasingly difficult to find."

He gaped at her with his jaw on the ground. "Are you serious?! If we can't find it now, what chance do we have if it gets even harder than this?"

"That's what I'm telling you." She pointed at the spire and instantly regretted it.

Anríq read her mind. "Is the spire's magic Dark? Is that why you don't want to assault it?"

"No, the White Spire isn't Dark, but it does possess unbelievable power. That power is out of control right now......" Her eyes sliced back to the tower on the horizon. "The Shard is in there. I'm certain of it now—or it's in whatever magical realm the spire leads to."

"Then that settles it," Yann countered. "If the Shard is there, then we have to go. We have to find a way in—and we already know I can get the closest to the spire of all of us. You two will have to break the defenses so I can make it to the walls."

Eliska glanced at Anríq at the same moment he glanced at her. Assaulting the White Spire was the last thing she wanted to do.

That decision seemed to have been taken away from her now—by something other than Yann's determination to defeat the Voyant.

Yann's voice drifted into her ear from what seemed like a long way away. "You can take us there in this ball. That will be quicker than traveling along the ground. Get us as close to the spire as you can before you put us on the ground. Then you two can fight the defenses while I try to get to the spire."

She didn't argue nor did she tell him that she and Anríq wouldn't be able to defeat the defenses.

None of that meant anything to Yann anymore. It shouldn't have meant anything to Eliska, either.

It was already too late to pull out of this. The three friends lost Marine trying to accomplish this mission.

Now they had nowhere else in the Coil to go—and neither did anyone else. There was no other option. The Shard of Hotha was the only way out—for anyone and everyone everywhere in the Coil.

Thinking that drew her gaze back to the spire—and for some reason, her ball drifted there along with her gaze and her thoughts.

The ball floated lower and soared closer to the spire—and then she felt it.

She didn't detect any magical barrier. Maybe it happened the minute she decided to go near the spire.

Something snapped inside her. Her Dark poison reacted to the spire's magic in ways she didn't anticipate.

This never happened before, but her magic got a lot stronger all of a sudden. The two forces magnetized themselves to each other and she knew.

The Shard was definitely in the spire—and not in some magical other dimension or Layer. It really was in the spire itself—right in front of her.

An insatiable desire overwhelmed her to take the Shard into herself. She had to find it and take it. The urge became irresistible.

The feeling took control of her magic. Her ball flew faster and faster. She added more and more magic to make the ball fly faster and to increase its protective capabilities.

The spire's defenses reacted instantaneously—almost as if the spire itself knew that someone was trying to get inside.

Torrents of magic blasted out of the top turret. They erupted from the windows facing this way, but they didn't come from the Voyant.

Eliska wasn't sure he was even really in there, but it didn't matter. The defenses alone held the friends off—or tried to.

Each of those ejections bombarded the ball and tried to penetrate it. Anríq swung his club at the ball and timed his strikes for each blast smashing into its sides.

The impact unloaded his magic on the blasts and knocked them away to keep the ball intact.

Eliska stabbed her staff into the ball's outer rim and added more of her magic to it. She strengthened the ball and she also ejected her own magical bombardment from the ball's surface.

Eruptions of magic spouted from the ball toward the White Spire. She landed countless hits on that window, but she couldn't damage it.

Her ball shot across the landscape at mind-blowing speed. The bombardment from the spire escalated in intensity as she got nearer.

The spire pounded the ball enough to slow her down. The ball shuddered from her effort not just to keep it moving but to keep it airborne and finally just to keep it intact.

"I can't hold on much longer!" she shrieked.

"Put us on the ground!" Yann ordered.

She didn't have a chance to move before a brutal impact hit the ball and it burst fifty feet above the ground. She barely had time to cast a spell under all three of them to cushion their fall.

They all slammed down on the ground a hundred yards from the spire's walls. Eliska looked up and then launched to her feet when more defensive blasts belched from the spire windows.

She dove in front of the two boys just as they got to their feet, raised her hand, and blocked the assault back to the spire itself.

She added her magic to the blast—and then Anríq materialized at her side with his club in one hand and his axe in the other.

The bombardment widened to include both of them. He whirled his weapons back and forth as fast as he could to deflect countless shots bursting from the spire.

Eliska kept her staff raised in one right hand and radiated her magic in front of her to take the hellish barrage. She had to unload just as much magic from her left hand. She didn't dare to lower either of them.

She didn't try to hit every single bombardment. She wouldn't have been able to hit so many of them. Anríq had a hard time keeping up with them and she sensed him failing already.

Chapter 3

Yann darted forward to try to get past Eliska and Anríq, but another blistering torch of magic came perilously close to hitting him. Eliska had to dive out of position to protect him.

He immediately retreated behind her to get out of danger. He couldn't get near the spire without taking his life in his hands.

She considered just for a split second if she could advance across that space to approach the tower—and instantly knew that she couldn't.

She and Anríq together couldn't break these defenses. They couldn't even hold their current position. Forget about going any closer.

Right then, a particularly bright and much larger jet of energy shot from the spire's northern window. It torched across the landscape and hit Anríq in the chest.

It came so fast that it missed his axe and club completely. He was too busy striking away all the other blasts.

This one zoomed between his arms and his weapons, vaporized straight through his body, and hurled him backward to slam on the ground while the magical discharge kept going.

It shrieked upward in a howling curve to the skies, twisted around, and dove down for another pass. None of the spire's other defensive barrages did that before.

"ANRÍQ!!" Eliska roared and tried to get to him.

She couldn't move with such a vicious bombardment attacking her. Now she was the only person trying to get near the spire. All the defenses concentrated on her alone.

The assault built to a deafening thunder against all her effort to hold it off. She couldn't last much longer, either.

That one powerful torch of magic plunged out of the sky coming straight for her. If it hit her, it would take her down exactly the way it took down Anríq. Then Yann would be defenseless and their whole mission would be over in a matter of seconds.

She reacted instantaneously, fired two binding spells at both boys, and magicked all three of them away across the landscape to put as much distance as possible between herself and the spire.

Eliska set Anríq on the ground behind a hill. Blackened, twisted tree trunks covered the area. None of those trees had a single leaf of vegetation on them. Not a single living thing survived in this desolate wasteland.

She attacked Anríq with all her might and searched his body for any way to heal whatever was wrong with him.

She couldn't find anything wrong with him. That was the problem. She probed his body and even explored his magic. She didn't find any injuries, either internal or external. His magic was perfectly intact.

The fingers of both his hands remained clamped in a white-knuckle grip around the handles of his weapons. He didn't let go of them even when he fell unconscious.

"We should stay in this Island as long as we can," Yann murmured from not far away. "We don't want to get caught in another collapse until we have no choice but to leave."

She didn't turn around to look at him. She kept searching Anríq for any way to heal him.

She fought down panic when she probed his mind, all his internal organs, and everything else.

"What's wrong with him?" Yann asked. "Can you heal him?"

"I can't find anything wrong with him," Eliska muttered. ". Whatever hit him, it didn't leave any trace. It wasn't Dark. It just neutralized him."

"Does that mean he won't come back from this?"

She only mumbled, "I don't know," and prayed to High Heaven that Yann stopped asking questions.

He watched her for a minute. She struggled against the urge to give up. She had to bring Anríq back. She couldn't lose him.

She couldn't face losing him or Yann, but she had no way to prevent it, either.

A second later, Yann got to his feet. "I'm going to explore the area. I'll see if I can find anything....."

He wandered off and left her alone, but that hardly made her feel better.

She pried Anríq's weapons out of his hands, but his arms and fingers didn't relax at all.

She had to move one of his bags out of the way to get closer to him. He carried the tools of his trade in those bags.

She could have searched his bags and seen all the stones, shells, and trinkets he used for healing.

She pushed that idea away, and in her last desperate act, she planted her hands on him—one on his forehead and one in the center of his chest.

She shut her eyes and released her Dark power into him.

She didn't let herself feel this before, but the minute she tapped her Darkness, she found out what was wrong with him.

That shot from the spire left a trace of its own powerful magic in him. It wasn't Dark, so his own power masked it.

She flooded him with her Darkness to drive the spire's magic out of him. He shuddered, settled, and floated into an exhausted sleep. His arms collapsed at his sides and his head lolled sideways.

She withdrew her Darkness from him, but not before using it to check every part of him to make sure he was okay. He was. He was just asleep now.

Yann returned a few minutes later carrying an armload of wood. She didn't realize the sun was going down until he started building a fire.

He didn't try to talk to her while he lit it. Then he left again.

She didn't look up to acknowledge him. She hated to think she might be giving Anríq more attention. She would have been just as frantic to save Yann.

She took a long time before she satisfied herself that Anríq really was okay. She finally allowed herself to sit down by the fire. She added sticks to it while she waited for Yann to come back.

Yann was her brother—her only family. She couldn't lose him—but she would lose him.

Losing him would hurt worse than losing all the others—her mother, her father, her friends and companions.

He was different. She actually knew she had him this time. She lost her mother before she could remember. Yvan Dilnao died before she found out he was her father.

She knew about Yann. She loved him. The thought of losing him made her want to die.

The thought of losing him or Anríq drove her to some kind of insanity. Part of her wanted to trade one for the other, but she couldn't decide which she would rather trade for the other.

She would never trade either of them for the other. She only hoped she died first—but then she would inflict that devastation on them. She couldn't let that happen.

It would happen because none of them could defeat the Voyant.

She fell into gloomy brooding for a while before Anríq heaved a deep sigh in his sleep.

She turned around to face him. The fire cast a pleasant glow of light and warmth in the darkness.

She couldn't see the destroyed surroundings anymore. She could convince herself that she and the boys were just camping here the same way they camped everywhere else in the Coil.

Anríq opened his eyes and frowned up at the ceiling of dense cloud overhead. He didn't move for a minute. Then his eyes darted around the landscape and locked on Eliska.

"You shouldn't have done that," he murmured.

She didn't have to ask what he meant. "Yes, I should have. I had to save you. I couldn't leave you like that."

He pursed his lips and scowled. "Did you make yourself sick again?"

"No. The magic wasn't Dark. I just drove it out of you—but I would have done it to save you." She let her hand slip into his. "I can't lose you."

He raised one beefy arm, cupped her cheek, and held her there while his eyes bored into her. "I don't want you to risk yourself—not even for me."

"I have to. What good am I without you? What good is this power at all if I don't use it to help you—and Yann? He's the one who keeps saying it's a good thing. There's no reason for me to even have it if I don't use it for this." She gulped down a lump in her throat. "What else would I use it for if not to heal you? No one else could do it."

She couldn't stand the painful concern in his eyes. Her connection with him told her exactly what he was thinking and feeling.

He didn't want to lose her, either. The idea of her dying first stabbed him in the guts. He couldn't decide whether he would rather lose her or Yann first. Anríq would rather die himself first than face life without them.

She crumbled onto his chest and shut her eyes in the safety of his arms. She didn't have to do or be anything else as long as she was with him.

He sighed and pressed his lips to her hair. "Thank you," he whispered.

She wrapped her arms tighter around him. She didn't want to let go, but he pried her head up to force her to look into his eyes.

She realized a second before he did it what he planned to do. She froze and then melted into his hands when he pulled her toward him and kissed her.

That kiss settled deeper into her soul than the kiss they shared in the Dark Layer. This was the first time he'd kissed her since then. They'd only just talked about their relationship since then when they did anything about it at all.

They both knew it would happen—it would happen for as long as it lasted until one of them fell in this war.

That could happen tomorrow. It could happen next week.

She drifted into that kiss and let this feeling sweep her away. She gave over her entire self to this feeling of being with him.

She just had to feel this even knowing the outcome.

She wouldn't come out of this with any kind of prize or victory. That wasn't possible.

She just had to feel this. This was the only reward—for something she couldn't even define.

It wasn't a reward because it hurt worse than any torture. Kissing him—loving him—aching for something that could never be.....

The torment she endured from the Keepers of the Dawn had been child's play compared to this.

She wrapped her arms around his neck and kissed him back with all her heart and soul. She poured every trace of emotion into that kiss.

She hoped it never ended, but of course it had to. She sank into his arms, stretched out on the ground with him, and floated in a world where tomorrow didn't exist.

Chapter 4

Yann headed back through the trees toward the campfire in the distance. It guided him through the darkness to where he left Eliska and Anríq.

Anríq better be okay. If he wasn't, Yann might have to convince Eliska to give up this quest. He and Eliska wouldn't be able to go after the White Spire or the Shard of Hotha on their own.

They would need to retreat to some other Layer while they decided what to do.

The best decision might be to do nothing—or to travel somewhere else until they found someone strong enough who could help them go after the Shard.

He stopped among the trees when he saw Anríq and Eliska together. Anríq lay on his back on the ground by the fire.

He cupped her cheek with one hand and stared into her eyes. Yann heard them murmuring to each other from this distance. He didn't try to hear what they said.

Then Anríq pulled her down to kiss her. Yann only had to see the way they both enveloped each other in that kiss.

He turned away and took off walking through the trees. He could give them their privacy while he made himself scarce.

He didn't find any source of food or water when he explored the area. This Island had neither.

He wandered around in the dark for what he hoped was a long time. He had no way of telling the time out here and nowhere else to go.

He was just considering sitting down somewhere and maybe trying to get some sleep when he saw a light glowing in the distance.

It came from the opposite direction from the campfire and the White Spire.

This glow was much too big to come from any campfire. The glow lit up a rim of the sky over there.

Yann should have been able to see it from among the trees. The friends should have been able to see it from their camp spot. They should have been able to see it even from the White Spire.

They didn't see the glow because it hadn't been there before. He headed for it, came to the edge of the dead tree trunks, climbed another hill, and stared across the landscape at another city in the distance.

Something must have happened to this Island because that city definitely wasn't there before. All three of the friends would have seen it when Eliska's ball first entered this Layer.

She hovered high enough above the landscape while the friends talked about going after the spire.

All three of them surveyed the rest of the Island to every corner of the horizon. There had been no other city—in that direction or any other direction.

Deafening booms echoed across the landscape from an unholy bombardment against the cloud ceiling above this Layer. Yann, Eliska, and Anríq would have heard that noise from the other side of the trees.

Blazing fireballs smashed through the Layer above the city. They rained hellfire on tall buildings, fighting vehicles Yann didn't recognize, and detonated whole neighborhoods to smithereens.

As soon as those projectiles broke through the upper Layer, a constant deluge of all those burning torches hammered all over the city.

The city must have been relatively intact right up until the bombardment. Yann could even see glass in some of the windows.

It all shattered out of its frames when the fireballs hit—and then he saw Dark forces up there beyond the breach.

They weren't Darklings. They looked more like indistinct shapes of some kind of misshapen creatures.

They emerged from a combination of Dark vapors and more lava masses, hurled all those projectiles down on the city, and set it ablaze.

A long line of refugees snaked out of the city. They followed the roads leading away to the north—or what Yann thought must be north.

Thousands of people filed out of the city carrying bundles, children, and pushing handheld wheeled trolleys piled with the refugees' possessions.

Yann watched from a distance trying to understand. Those Dark forces up there breached the Layer to attack this city, but the city Island still didn't collapse.

The Voyant must be doing something to stabilize this Island—now that he finally found somewhere to put the White Spire. Of course he must not want to keep moving it around all the time.

The glow in the sky came from all those catastrophic fires and explosions laying waste to the city right in front of Yann's eyes. This must have destroyed the Island in the first place—so why didn't it destroy this city the first time?

Yann couldn't help those fleeing people. They were already escaping their city by the only route available.

He started to turn back. He planned to go get Eliska and maybe Anríq, too. They could use their magic to help these people if anyone could help.

Right then, something shot out of the ground next to the column. The thing looked like a house from this distance, but it couldn't have been. There hadn't been any houses in that part of the countryside before now.

Whatever it was had a cube shape with four walls holding up a pointed roof. The house-thing turned on the refugees to attack them. Then the thing turned into some kind of creature.

This wasn't a Darkling, either. It looked more like some kind of giant misshapen organism that might have been living underground until just this minute.

Yann didn't hesitate. He took off at a sprint down the other side of the hill and veered up the column getting closer to the thing.

The refugees reared away from the creature. Screams echoed out of the crowd.

The creature dove to snatch up as many people as it could catch, but the refugees dodged just in time—just long enough for Yann to get there.

He took a running leap for the house-thing or whatever it was. He would have landed on its roof, but it lunged for the refugee column right then. He landed behind it and stabbed his glaive into it from behind.

It roared and spun around to confront him, but he only darted around its other side. He stabbed and slashed at it again and again from all sides.

By that time more bizarre shapes, creatures, and objects came out of the unstable landscape.

They only attacked the refugees for some reason. None of these things attacked Yann, not even when he attacked them first.

His glaive damaged the house-thing. It wasn't really a house because this thing actually had a body his blade glaive could penetrate.

His blade sank into its skin and came away bloody. The thing wasn't made of boards and shingles.

He didn't take the time to consider what these things were or what they were made of. He charged between them stabbing and swiping at everything in sight.

"Keep moving!" he yelled to the refugees. "Get away from the city!"

They rallied, especially when his assault distracted the creatures away from them.

All these things took a long time to turn away from the column. Fireballs and raining flames kept pouring through the breach in the upper Layer, but the collapse concentrated on the city itself. It didn't follow the column out into the wilderness.

The instability kept spawning these strange shapes and creatures, but they concentrated around the city, too.

Yann didn't understand this. He fought his way to the end of the line and hacked his glaive at anything that threatened the refugees.

He pivoted between them and the attacking creatures. The creatures didn't follow.

One by one, the creatures turned their attention back to the city, lost interest in the refugees, and fell farther and farther behind as the column moved away.

None of this made sense based on Yann's previous experience in the Coil, but at least these people weren't in danger anymore.

He climbed another hill and surveyed the landscape to the south and east. He should go back to Anríq and Eliska now, but he wanted to make sure he got these people to some kind of safety.

Nothing would be safe, but at least no one attacked them in the wilderness—not until the next collapse.

Three or four thousand people marched in a long line moving away from the destruction. Their route led them straight out into the torched landscape leading to the farthest horizon.

He was just thinking about how they would find food and water when a group of refugees came up to him.

They wore very nicely tailored clothing but in a much more modest and understated style than he'd seen in Tenby and Savaré.

Four men and an older lady came up to him and shook hands all around. "Thank you so much for your help." A tall man with shoulder-length straight brown hair glanced down at Yann's uniform. "Who are you? Where do you come from? Do you belong to the Army or something?"

"You don't know what the Black Watch is?" Yann had to check himself. He'd never met anyone who didn't know about the Black Watch.

The people in front of him exchanged glances. "I've never heard of it," the same man replied. "Should I have?"

Yann waved that away. "Never mind. These people will need food and water soon—not to mention shelter."

"We brought supplies with us," the woman replied. "We're traveling to our sister city fifty miles away. We'll make it as long as the landscape doesn't fall apart again."

"Would you come with us?" the first man asked. "We can't defend ourselves."

"I'm afraid I won't be able to do much." Yann waved over his shoulder. "I have two friends back there. I can go get them. They'll be able to help you better than I can."

"Don't leave us alone!" the woman insisted. "What if something happens?"

"I wouldn't be able to help you if something happens. These two friends of mine are magic-users. You'll be better off with all three of us than just me."

Right then, a deep rumble shook the nearby hills. They morphed out of position and started to change shape along the column's route.

They took identifiable forms similar to those that attacked the refugees closer to the city, but these shapes didn't attack. They stayed in the same line as the hills they grew from. The shapes menaced the refugees from a distance.

He set off striding forward and positioned himself between the column and the hills, but the shapes still didn't attack.

They roared, thrashed, and grimaced. Yann swiveled his glaive between them and the refugees, but he couldn't be certain these Dark shapes even were roaring and grimacing at the refugees.

The shapes didn't seem to be aware of the refugees. Maybe this was just random instability—so why didn't it take the rest of this Island?

Yann strode down the column to escort the refugees past the shapes, but the instability kept following the column all the way up that line of hills.

The instability always stayed with the column and never came any closer. The landscape settled back down as soon as the column passed. The new instability tore the countryside apart ahead of the column when the refugees drew level with the hills up there.

Yann frowned at the situation. This instability focused on the refugees. It followed them—and yet it still didn't attack.

Did this instability have something to do with the refugees themselves? Did something about these people cause the instability? Was that the reason the Dark forces attacked and destroyed their city?

If it did, why didn't the instability strike the column? That was the strangest part. The instability always stayed the same distance away. It left the land clear and solid for the refugees to travel on their way.

He couldn't answer any of those questions. He kept his glaive pointed at the hills as more gruesome shapes took form over there. They reared, bellowed, bared their teeth, and made horrible faces at the refugees.

People kept screaming, cringing, and sobbing in terror, but at least those Dark forces didn't attack.

Yann didn't dare to leave to go get Anríq and Eliska now. Yann glanced over his shoulder. He couldn't even be sure anymore where they were compared to the city where he helped the refugees escape.

Eliska would be able to find him. Then she and Anríq would be better able to protect these people and get them to some kind of safety.

Chapter 5

Eliska rested her head on Anríq's bicep and traced her fingertips over the Servant's mark on his chest. "You're so lucky you have this," she murmured. "I'm jealous."

He lay on his back with his eyes closed. He didn't open them when he answered.

"You have nothing to be jealous of. It's just a mark like any other tattoo. The mark that really counts is the one on the inside and you already have that."

She looked up at the side of his chiseled face. He still looked like a boy at the right angle.

She sank back into the crook of his arm and went back to tracing every part of him with her fingertips. "It's the greatest compliment of my life that you think that of me."

"Why should it be? You're more a Servant than I am."

Now it was her turn to clamp her eyes shut. She didn't want to believe that. "I could never be. I've only ever wanted to be a Servant as good as you."

He extended his other arm across his chest, clasped her by the head, and kissed her on the temple. "You are. Your heart is pure. I know it i s."

She settled deeper into this feeling of burying herself in the connection between them. Nothing existed outside this little halo of blissful togetherness. She didn't have to think about or even know about anything that happened outside this glow of happiness.

The instant she thought that, her eyes snapped open in the dark. She stared at nothing—and then shot up into a sitting position.

Anríq's hand trailed down her back. "What's the matter? There's nothing here."

"That's the problem. Yann's gone." Eliska scrambled to her feet. "Something's wrong. Something happened to him."

Anríq's eyes widened and then he sat up, too. He frowned at the area around them.

Yellow-orange firelight formed a circle around their campsite. Neither of them could see anything in the darkness beyond.

Eliska didn't have to see. "There's something over there." She nodded toward the west. "He went that way."

She grabbed her staff—and then looked around again. The three friends didn't bring any other baggage apart from Anríq's bags and his weapons. He was still wearing them.

"He took his glaive," Anríq pointed out. "Maybe he found something dangerous."

"No, it wasn't that." Eliska turned away. "Come on. We have to find him."

She kicked dirt on the fire to put it out, waited just long enough for Anríq to stand up, and set off through the trees.

She only let herself stay connected to Yann long enough to see him watching her and Anríq. He walked away to avoid seeing the two of them together.

He put them out of his mind and she did the same thing. She paid attention to Anríq. She didn't let herself keep track of where Yann went or what he was doing.

She kicked herself for that, but it was too late.

She opened her Coil projection on the way through the trees. Yann's line passed through these twisted trunks and ended near some hills in the distance.

She and Anríq came to the edge of the trees and climbed a low run of hills. It blocked them from seeing the countryside beyond.

She expected to see more scorched wilderness without a blade of grass anywhere.

These hills formed some kind of borderline or demarcation zone between the burned-out area close to the White Spire and everything beyond it.

The countryside beyond these hills rolled away in a low, dry prairie of short grass and a few scattered bushes. None of the vegetation grew above Eliska's knees.

A long line of people wound through the countryside heading northwest.

"Can you tell who they are or where they came from?" Anríq glanced behind him. "Their direction seems to indicate they came from the White Spire. Did they escape from the city when the Voyant brought the spire here?"

"I can't tell anything about them. That's the strangest part." Eliska frowned when she extended her power toward the column. "I can't pick up anything about them—no memories, no fears—not even any thoughts. There's something wrong with them."

"How is that possible? How can they be alive without thoughts and memories?"

Eliska consulted her projection. "Yann is definitely with them—and he's moving away with them. Come on. Let's go find him. Maybe he can explain this."

Anríq set off down the hill by her side. "How *could* you explain this? These people would have to be dead not to have any thoughts."

"Maybe they have magic-users who are blocking me from sensing anything."

Anríq compressed his lips, narrowed his eyes, and shot a hard glare at the surrounding countryside.

Eliska looked away from him. She didn't believe her own explanation of why she couldn't detect any thoughts coming from these people.

Picking up people's memories, fears, nightmares, and every shade of their emotions and reactions had become her everyday reality now.

She wasn't exactly getting used to it. The tide of human experience invaded her mind whenever she went near someone and even when she didn't.

She could sense the memories of people hundreds of miles and dozens of Layers away. Memories from people long dead plagued her at the worst possible times.

How could an entire host of thousands of people have no thoughts, emotions, memories, or nightmares at all? It made no sense at all.

These people didn't even seem to be alive, but they were. They kept walking on and on and on heading northwest.

How alive they were became obvious when she and Anríq drew level with the column. Men, women, and children marched in that column. Parents even carried their children in their arms.

None of those people saw or spoke to Eliska or Anríq. None of the refugees turned their heads at the travelers' arrival.

Eliska checked one person after another. Their memories should have assaulted her mind just from standing this close to them.....but she sensed nothing at all.

Her skin crawled when she looked at the empty outer husks of these people. They weren't alive—not in any way that counted.

They lurched one stumbling step after another. Their glazed, haunted eyes registered no flicker of recognition or awareness of where they were.

Anríq and Eliska stood back and watched them for a minute.

"Can you tell where Yann is if you don't sense him?" Anríq asked.

Eliska shook herself back to reality, opened her Coil projection, expanded it, and zeroed in on the line that traced Yann's route from the campsite to here.

She followed it and located him stumbling along in the line with the others. He still carried his glaive and wore his uniform.

Other than that, he looked and acted exactly the same as everyone else in this column. She never would have found him without her projection.

She rushed him, planted herself in front of him, and yelled into his face. "Yann! Look at me! It's me—Eliska! YANN!! Wake up!"

He didn't even blink. He kept walking and bumped into her. He would have trampled her with the same slow, plodding gait.

She stumbled out of the way and Anríq stepped in. He grabbed Yann by both shoulders and shook him hard. "YANN!!" Anríq bellowed. "Yann—wake up! Look at me!"

Nothing. Eliska retreated out of line and watched in horror. Yann kept blundering past. He never looked at her once.

The absolute wrongness of this sent a chill through her bone marrow. Yann would never ignore her like this. He never left her alone from the minute they met.

He had acted the most concerned, the most attentive, and the most protective of her—even more than Anríq.

She was the only family he had left. He wouldn't turn his back on her like this.

Anríq tried again and again to get through to him, but Yann didn't respond to that, either.

Anríq eventually retreated out of line and backed away to rejoin Eliska. They both watched Yann pass them and keep on walking. He would keep walking forever.

"What do you want to do?" Anríq murmured. "What *can* we do?"

Eliska gulped. "Someone must have put a spell on these people. I'm going to go into him and use my magic to try to break the spell."

Anríq nodded. "I'll go with you."

Eliska only had to think about it to sense a halo of magic surrounding these people. It hovered over the whole column, but it didn't extend beyond that.

The Island remained as stable as ever. Whatever magic kept these people enslaved, it didn't affect the rest of the landscape. That magic didn't disturb even so much as a blade of grass.

Right then, Anríq extended his hand across the space between them and took hers. His touch hardened her resolve. She could defeat this spell.

She magicked herself and Anríq inside the spell. Walking over to those people and even getting in Yann's face didn't do it. Anyone could walk anywhere they wanted among these lifeless people.

Eliska concentrated on Yann and magicked herself and Anríq into the spell that surrounded him.

She crossed an invisible, almost non-existent shimmer of magic—and found herself standing in the middle of the road in a completely different Island.

Short green grass covered the surrounding hillsides and farmland. The road wound back and forth heading from east to west.

The road passed between a dozen small, cramped, quaint houses a hundred yards away.

She didn't see any other sign of human habitation, but she recognized the town instantly. She would never be able to forget it as long as she lived.

Livestock grazed in the fields. Women hung their laundry on the lines outside to dry.

Eliska's stomach plummeted into her shoes when she surveyed the whole area. Anríq wasn't here. He disappeared the minute she crossed into this world. No amount of glancing around would make him reappear.

She didn't see or even sense anything unusual or even magical about this place. No trace remained of Yann, the column of hypnotized people, or the spell that kept them entranced.

She set off toward the little hamlet. It was the only place she could get any answers, but she already knew she wouldn't get any answers there, either.

She recognized all the neighbors working, herding their animals, and going about their business—exactly the way they did the last time she came here.

She came here with the two boys. They would only be one place if they were here at all.

She stopped in front of the little house—the little house she knew so well.

This was her own house—her mother's house—the house where Alexiane LaFauve raised Eliska for a whole year before they both disappeared.

A confused tempest of emotion welled up in Eliska's being when she studied the house. She wanted to be here more than anything else in the world—and at the same time, she would rather be just about anywhere else.

She would almost rather go into the worst chaos Layer, fight Darklings, or even face the Keepers of the Dawn again than go into this house.

She could only be here *because* of this house. Whatever that spell was that held Yann in a trance, it brought him here. It brought both of them here.

She didn't see him anywhere in this landscape, but he would be here if he was even in this Island at all. He wouldn't come to this Island for anything other than whatever was in this house.

She strode up to the door and pushed it open. It swung inward on the same spotless, cheery, sunlit room.

The rocking chair and child's cradle sat next to the fireplace. Sunlight twinkled through the shiny windows over the sink. Golden beams lit up the wooden table and the polished floor.

She took a few steps into the room—and heard a child fussing in the cradle. Eliska stopped next to it and looked at a tiny little girl barely old enough to walk.

The child extended her chubby little arms and made a few squawking noises. Eliska bent over, picked up the baby, and sat down in the rocking chair.

The rest of the world disappeared in the child's deep brown eyes gazing back at her. The baby settled down as soon as she felt her mother's arms around her.

All the confusion vanished out of Eliska's mind. She was where she was supposed to be and doing exactly what she was supposed to be doing. She didn't need to be anywhere else.

Chapter 6

E liska rocked the baby to sleep in the rocking chair and then slowly lowered the sleeping child into the cradle.

She stood up, draped the blanket over the back of the chair, and cast one last loving look down at the child before she surveyed the room.

She would get her household chores done before Yvan came home. Then she wouldn't have to worry about all the tasks she didn't get done during the day.

She and Yvan would be able to spend their time just enjoying each other's company the way they always did in the evenings. The two of them would spend some quiet hours together before their children woke up and he had to go back to work.

She got ready to go to the kitchen to reheat his dinner for him, but she stopped when she saw the pictures on the mantel shelf.

The family picture looked the same way she always remembered it. The image showed her sitting on the chair with baby Eliska on her lap. Little Yann stood next to her hugging her arm in a death grip.

Yvan.....

Her eyes migrated up to the place behind Yann—the place where Yvan should have been standing.

The man in the picture wasn't Yvan. It was Anríq.

He looked exactly the way she remembered—tall, broad-shouldered, tattooed, and wearing the same combination of leather clothing, gauntlets around his muscular wrists, and beads, stones, and wooden decorations tied in his hair and to different parts of his clothing.

He even carried the same three shoulder bags slung across his torso. The same battle axe hung across his back. His club dangled from his belt on the right side and a leather thong tied his machete blade to his thigh on the left side.

He smiled out of the picture while he rested one hand on Yann's shoulder and the other hand on Alexiane's shoulder.

Anríq's blonde dreadlocks hung down his back....and then she saw it. His vest hung open just enough to expose the Servant's mark tattooed on his chest.

He was a Servant. He wouldn't be here, living in this house. He would be wandering the Col looking for anyone who needed his help.

He never posed for any picture, especially not with Alexiane LaFauve—and Eliska wasn't Alexiane.

Seeing him in the picture shattered the illusion. He wasn't Yann's father. Anríq would never have rested his hand on little Yann's shoulder like that. The baby in the picture was Eliska. She wasn't the mother at all.

Even if, in some distant fantasy, Anríq and Eliska wound up together, they would never stay in this house with these children. None of this was real.

She glanced around her one more time. The baby no longer slept in the cradle. A handsewn rag doll lay in the baby's place. The doll stared up at the world with huge, embroidered yarn eyes and a broad, smiling yarn mouth.

The whole disaster snapped into Eliska's mind in a heartbeat. The column of entranced refugees.....Yann trapped with them.....Anríq.....

Anríq was still out there somewhere. He was either trapped in this illusion along with her or he was alone in the Island outside the column.

She didn't know where either Anríq or Yann was. She only knew she had to get out of here.

She strode over to the door and yanked it open. The minute she did that, a sudden blast of magical power slammed into her from the front.

That blow must have come from the doorway. The spell tried to keep her inside the house.

The spell hit her hard enough to hurl her back across the room. She fell against the wall and stared at the doorway—her only way out of this enchanted house.

The doorway led to the outside—out into the road where all the neighbors went about her business.

Her powerful magic told her exactly what she would find out there.

She would have been able to leave this house as long as she stayed under the illusion.

She would have been able to visit anyone else in town, tend the livestock and the gardens, and even accompany her children to play outside.

The spell only reacted to keep her here because she opened the door to leave—to leave entirely.

The thought caused her own magic to erupt out of control. It flared outward trying to break the spell surrounding her.

The spell held for a second and then wavered. She couldn't break it. She was trapped here against her will.

Panic burst her magic beyond the bounds of caution. She unloaded on the spell in a brutal concussion. She never would have let herself go like this if she didn't feel herself imprisoned inside this spell.

The spell detonated and she reappeared back in the wilderness with all the mindless people walking westward exactly the way they did before.

The magic didn't let her go immediately, though. As soon as the illusion vanished, bizarre magical forces attacked her from everywhere at once.

Blinding streaks of light and energy whizzed between the entranced people and bombarded Eliska.

She blasted her magic outward again to drive them off, but they just kept coming. They didn't come from the people. None of these people even looked at her.

The magic seemed to come from the spell halo itself. Whatever held these people captive attacked Eliska trying to recapture her and force her back inside the spell.

She took the assault easily. Her magic had no problem protecting her from countless strikes, but she couldn't stay here. She couldn't risk getting trapped again.

She magicked herself away to a lonely hilltop miles away from the column. She got herself far enough away that the halo spell couldn't touch her.

The noise and blows of magic striking her stopped instantly and silence fell over the Island. She was back in the wilderness where she started—except that she was alone now.

She stared down at all those people walking one foot in front of the other toward the horizon. None of them knew she was here. None of them knew she had ever been one of them.

Yann was still down there, too. He didn't know she was here, either.

Anríq was gone, but her magic told her right away that he wasn't in the column.

She couldn't explain why she'd been able to magick herself inside the spell but she couldn't take him with her.

She didn't try to figure it out. She just had to find him so they could work on breaking Yann out of this trap.

She opened her Coil projection and located Anríq a dozen more miles out in the wilderness.

He walked straight ahead like he always did, but he didn't seem to be traveling in any particular direction.

He also didn't head for anyone he might be able to help. These entranced people were the only people alive in this Island apart from Anríq and Eliska.

She magick herself to a spot five hundred yards away from him and set off walking in his direction.

He saw her coming a long way off, turned, and picked up his pace to meet up with her.

He rushed the last few feet to her and caught her in his arms. "Thank Heaven I found you!" he exclaimed. "I thought I lost you."

She beamed at him. "I thought the same thing about you. Where were you?"

"I was right here. I've been looking for you."

"What's the last thing you remember—the last thing that happened after I tried to magick us into the hypnotizing spell?"

"Nothing happened," he countered. "You vanished into the spell and I wound up out here by myself. The column vanished with all of you in it. I tried to use my magic to find you, but I couldn't pick up any trace of you or Yann. I was going to spend the rest of today searching this Island and then break through to another Layer no matter how chaotic it was. I thought there was no point in staying if you two weren't here." He frowned at her. "Where have *you* been?"

"I've been inside the spell. It created the illusion that I was back in my mother's house."

His eyes popped. "Really? Did you....?"

"I got trapped by the illusion, but I got out of it—and I showed up right there in the middle of the column. It must have been an illusion. The spell doesn't take anyone anywhere. They think they're somewhere else when they're all still in the column."

"Is Yann still over there?"

She nodded. "He must be in an illusion, too."

"Was he at your mother's house, too?"

"No, he wasn't there. He must be somewhere else."

"How do we get him out, then?"

Her gaze migrated back to the horizon. "I'm not sure if we can. He might have to leave on his own." She took his hand. "Come on. Let's go back over there. We can observe the column from a safe distance so we don't get trapped in it."

She clasped his hand and magicked them both back to the same hillside. Her magic picked out Yann in the crowd. He never altered his position or his mindless stumbling gait.

"I wonder where he is," she murmured. "I might be able to help him get out of it if I knew."

Anríq didn't answer right away. They both stared down at the column.

"Why do you think *you* didn't get pulled into the spell?" she asked.

"I did," he mumbled.

She spun around to stare at him. "But you said you didn't. You said you got sent out into the wilderness away from everyone."

"I got sent out into the wilderness to look for you and Yann. Don't you see? I got what I wanted—the same way I got what I wanted when I left home to follow the Servant's path."

She frowned at the side of his head. "I don't understand."

"How were you able to leave the spell? How did you see that it was an illusion when all these people are still trapped inside it?"

"I...." She faltered over the words. "I remembered you. You weren't there—in that house. You weren't....." She gulped. She fought the urge to say the next words. "You weren't the father of my children and we weren't living there together as husband and wife. That never happened. I never wanted it to happen. I didn't want that. I didn't even feel tempted to stay in that world. All I want is to be out here w ith you."

He turned around immediately, folded her in his arms, and attacked her in ravenous kisses. "That's all I want, too," he panted between kisses. "I don't want to be anywhere but out here with you."

She collapsed into that feeling. "Is there any way?" Her voice cracked. "Is there any way we could do it?"

He pulled back enough to stare down into her eyes. His gaze drowned her in meaning. "You would really do it, wouldn't you? You would become an aimless Servant wanderer with no home or destination, wouldn't you?"

"Yes!" she whispered. "I don't want anything else."

He fell on her again and she shut her eyes in the vastness of that kiss, but it was bound to end sooner or later. It couldn't last.

They both broke away and shared one last long moment of deep eye contact before they both turned back to watch the column of people in the distance.

Eliska swallowed down a lump in her throat. She and Anríq would never get to be together as wandering Servants. That would never happen—not with the Voyant still wreaking havoc on the Coil.

One of them would fall. That wandering life would remain a distant fantasy even more elusive than the blissful life in Yvan's and Alexiane's house.

"I know what's happening here," Anríq murmured. "These people—their Wishers."

"What's that?" she asked. "I've never heard of it."

"The magic grants wishes. It takes each person where they most want to be and gives them the life they most wish to live. In exchange, it traps their body here. The spell drains their magic if they have it. If they don't have magic, the spell feeds on their energy and keeps them walking around all the time until they die. No one notices when they fall."

"How do we free Yann, then?"

"It's like you said. He might have to leave on his own the same way you did."

"I had to break the spell with my magic," she pointed out. "I couldn't leave on my own."

"Then we have to help him. You have to go back into the spell and convince him to leave."

"I don't think that's possible. The only way would be to convince him that he doesn't want this life—which he obviously does if he's still trapped in it. He would have to give it up."

"Then you have to convince him to give it up for something else—something more important to him than whatever dream life he's living. Wherever he is, he must be extremely happy. You have to convince him that something means more to him than that."

"What could be more important than that?"

"The Servant's path," Anríq replied. "He was willing to give up any chance at happiness to becomes a Servant and a man of the Black Watch. That's where his heart lies—not in whatever comfort and happiness this spell is giving him. You have to remind him that he already made that choice. Then he'll make it again."

Her eyes darted down the hill to the column. "I would risk getting trapped again if I went in there."

"You can handle it," he told her. "You know it's an illusion now. You would be alert to any inconsistency. The spell matched us together before. It probably will again. The memory of me will bring you out of it the way it did before."

"If you're right, then I could be going around and around in circles. I could wind up in my own wish and never get through to his."

"You can only try it." Anríq squeezed her hand. "I'll stay close to the column from now on without putting myself in danger. I'll be here when you come out."

She would have liked to squeeze his hand back, but the thought of going back into the wish spell gave her the shivers.

She had to be strong for Yann. She had to get him out. She couldn't leave him like this.

Chapter 7

Yann yawned, stretched, and immediately stopped when he felt a woman lying in bed next to him.

She tightened her grip around his ribs, buried her head in his chest, and groaned in her sleep when he disturbed her.

He fought his brain back into gear enough to realize that she had long black hair and a slender body hidden under her thin white night-gown.

He wasn't wearing a shirt. Her arms felt blissful around his torso—and then he smelled her. The scent coming off her hair and body told him instantly who this was.

He wrapped his arms tightly around her, shut his eyes, and hugged her with all his might. Marine. Marine was back in his arms—where she belonged.

She sighed again when he hugged her. Then she rolled away from him and her hair fell aside enough to reveal her glowing, angelic face.

He had to kiss her. He drowned in the feeling of belonging with her for all time. He would never let her out of his grasp again.

She softened against him, wrapped her arms around his neck, and melted into his kiss—but right then, a high-pitched scream echoed through the walls.

Yann barely had time to register that he was lying in the bedroom of a house before the door blasted off its hinges.

Three young children charged into the room, pounced on the bed, and started climbing all over Yann and Marine.

A little five-year-old girl tugged Marine's arm away from Yann. "I'm hungry, Mother! You have to get up!"

"Don't listen to her," a seven-year-old boy interjected. "She spent the last hour eating everything in the pantry. Now Mother will have to spend all day making more."

Yann looked around—and knew instantly that these were his and Marine's children. He knew everything about these children, including their names.

"Artur Comenceau is looking for you, Father," the oldest boy told him. "He says the Corsairs are making forays into the area again—and he says they wouldn't do that if they weren't planning another attack."

Yann pried himself out of bed. "I better go see what's happening."

The littlest, three-year-old boy clambered over Marine and even stepped on her in his haste to get near Yann. "Can I come, Father?"

Yann picked up the boy, kissed him, and held him on one arm while Yann walked over to the chair to get his uniform.

"You can join the Black Watch when you get old enough." Yann put the boy down on the chair and picked up his shirt. "For now, I need you and Bennot to guard the women and children and keep the enemy away from the door."

The older boy laughed. "That's silly. The enemy isn't at the door."

"They aren't at the door because we have strong, hearty boys like you defending the place," Yann replied. "You keep an eye on your mother and sister."

He pulled on his jacket and straightened his uniform and hair in front of a mirror on the wall.

He adjusted the gold oak leaf on his collar. The Commander of the Black Watch had to look right before he set foot outside the house.

The window of this bedroom looked out on a yard full of poultry and garden beds behind the house.

The children ran off. Their yelling voices echoed through the house getting farther away down the stairs to the lower stories.

Marine slipped out of bed, came up behind him, and wrapped her arms around him from behind. "Come home early tonight," she murmured. "I hate it when you're away."

He twisted himself around, drew her to him, and kissed her deeply for a long time before he broke free. "I'll never be far away. I'll come home as soon as I can."

He had to field a bunch of assaults from his children on the way out of the house. By the time he shut the door behind him, the sun was already shining down on Middleborough from high in the sky.

He shouldn't have let himself sleep in so late, but the feeling of Marine lying next to him and melting into him proved too strong a temptation.

He set off for the wall surrounding the town—the town where he'd lived his whole life.

Everyone he passed nodded, greeted him by calling him, "Watch Commander," and wished him a good morning.

He found himself surveying this town with a critical eye. Everyone in it lived and died by his command of the Watch.

Pride surged in his heart when he thought of his position in this town, but it also laid a heavy responsibility on his shoulders.

Two dozen uniformed Watchmen waited for him at the wall. He gave orders to them all before he climbed up the wall to look out over the countryside.

Artur pointed to the north. "We spotted a sortie of ten Corsairs coming out of the river bottoms over there. They cut east and then south. There's no question they were reconnoitering for another attack."

"Contact Linné at the apothecary to scry the area and see if she can see their movements," Yann ordered. "Then go through the men and make sure they all double up on weapons—even if you have to reforge new ones."

Preparing for the Corsair attack took the rest of the morning. The Corsairs launched attacks against Middleborough every now and then.

The Black Watch repelled them each time with the help of four local magic-users.

He snuck away at lunchtime to return to his own house, but when he walked in, he found the house deserted.

He went from room to room calling everyone, but no one answered. They must have gone out.

He stopped in the middle of the living room while he decided if he should go back to the wall or not. He would go back soon, but he decided to wait a little longer in case his family came home in time.

He glanced around the living room and spotted the row of family photographs on the mantel shelf above the fireplace. Some of the pictures moved around, but others stayed still.

He gazed at the largest picture of his family. Marine sat on a chair and held their youngest son on her lap. Yann stood next to them with his arm around Marine's shoulders.

Their oldest son stood in front of Yann. The boy wrapped his arms tightly around his mother's arm. The girl stood on Marine's other side resting her head on Marine's shoulder.

Yann frowned at the picture. Something was wrong with it. He couldn't pinpoint exactly what it was. The picture always looked exactly like this for as long as he could remember.

Marine's hair looked a little too dark in the picture—and there was something wrong about the children, too. What was it? They looked perfectly fine.

Something was wrong about the image of Yann himself, too. He studied every detail of his face, hair, and uniform, but he couldn't see anything out of place.

Right then, the door opened behind him. He turned around expecting his children to rush in all yelling and talking.

He froze when a stranger stepped into his house. He knew everyone in Middleborough and he'd never seen this person before in his life.

She was a short, wiry young woman of about sixteen. Long, dark hair draped a gaunt, haunted face drawn many years beyond her age.

She wore a strange collection of patched garments with a black traveling cloak over everything—and she carried a staff in one hand.

He could barely make himself heard. "Who are you? What are you doing in my house?"

She walked right up to him. "You have to get out of here, Yann. You're trapped in a magical spell that makes you think this is all real. You don't live in Middleborough anymore." She held out both her hands to steer him toward the door. "Come with me. I'll help you...."

He swatted her hands away and would have retreated from her, but he forced himself to stand his ground.

Something about her repelled him—and yet some kind of fascinated horror made him keep staring at her.

"Get your hands off me!" he fired back. "Who the hell are you? I know everyone in this town. The Watchmen shouldn't have let a stranger into town without checking with me first."

She let her arms fall to her sides and her lips tightened into a scowl. "You don't know me, do you?"

"Of course not!" he countered. "I've never seen you before in my life."

"I'm Eliska," she told him. "I'm your sister. We met in Middleborough weeks ago—and then Darklings destroyed the town along with the Black Watch. We wandered in the Coil together with your father and the surviving Watchmen. Don't you remember when we met Marine at the Dark river?"

"Marine! She's right here! She's been here for years." Yann waved at the picture on the mantel behind him.

Eliska barely looked at it. "You aren't married to Marine, Yann, and you don't have any children with her. That's part of the spell. It makes you think you have all those things—and you aren't Commander of the Watch, either. You couldn't be. The men of the Watch are celibate. A member of the Watch couldn't be married with a bunch of children."

He gasped in horror and gaped at her. "You can't be serious! Look at me! I'm wearing the Watch Commander's uniform! I wouldn't be doing any of this if I wasn't Watch Commander."

She passed him and pointed at the picture. "That picture was on the mantel shelf of our parents' house—our parents, Yvan Dilnao and Alexiane LaFauve. In the picture, he was a normal working man and I was the little girl sitting on our mother's lap. You were the little boy standing next to our mother with our father standing behind you."

She turned around and looked up at him with those haunted black eyes. They made him sick, but some other part of him wanted to believe her.

He summoned all his effort to push that thought away. He couldn't walk away from Marine and their family. Protecting them and Middleborough meant everything to him.

"We're Servant's, Yann," she murmured. "You, me, and Anríq. We dedicated ourselves to finding the Shard of Hotha and saving the Coil. We have a mission to fulfill. This spell is stopping you from doing it. This might even be one of the Voyant's defenses to trap us somewhere we can't get out of."

Yann gulped hard. He didn't want to listen to this, but some inner voice in his gut told him she was telling the truth.

Right then, the door burst open a second time and Marine and the children all flooded into the house.

They surrounded him. He scooped up his daughter, and when he turned around the next time, Eliska was gone.

Chapter 8

Yann woke up when sunshine flooded his bedroom. He blinked toward the window and then immediately shut his eyes when he felt Marine touching him.

He clamped his eyes shut against the overwhelming intensity of emotion that welled up in his being when she glided her hands over his bare chest.

Something distracted him, though. That bizarre visit from Eliska yesterday wouldn't leave him alone.

He forced himself to open his eyes and turn his head. Marine leaned over him propped on her elbow. Her dark hair spilled onto his chest.

Her dark eyes sparkled when she smirked at him with all her old mischievous charm. "Are you trying to pretend I'm not here?" She gave him a dig in the ribs. "I'll make you pay attention to me."

He burst out laughing. "You don't have to because you're impossible to ignore."

She gasped in mock horror. "How dare you insult me like that?!"

"Quit clowning around." He glanced toward the door. "Where are the ravagers?"

Now she was the one to laugh. "They're playing outside—just long enough to give us some time together."

She leaned in and kissed him, but only for a second. She leaned back and grinned at him again. "So? What would you like to do first—hold the tickling championships?"

"Didn't I already win that one last time?"

"You could have won because I'm not ticklish—unlike you." She grabbed him and tried to dig her fingertips into his ribs again, but he caught her wrists and held her.

He found himself falling into the depths of her eyes. He hadn't felt this way about her since......

He had a flashback of the time they spent in Savaré. The illusion slipped, but just for an instant before it reasserted itself and took over his whole awareness.

He pulled her in and kissed her again. "I'm so glad you're feeling better."

She laughed at him. "Was I sick?"

"Your magic made you crazy. Don't you remember?"

She snorted at him. "I was never crazy—unless I was falling crazy in love with you. Does that count?"

He froze staring at her—and all the memories came back. As good as this moment felt—as good as this whole life felt—he actually liked her better when she was crazy.

Eliska was right. Marine never lived in Middleborough and she absolutely had never been married to him.

His old angst about not being good enough for her—it all came back with a vengeance.

She noticed the change right away and frowned. "What's wrong? You know I love you, right?"

"You don't remember, do you?"

"Remember what?"

"Savaré?" he asked. "You don't remember Laval.....and Eliska.....and Brother Matherus?"

She frowned even deeper. "What's Savaré?"

He pushed her off and stood up, but he found it hard to decide where to go or what to do.

She wasn't real. Marine wasn't real. His children weren't real. His whole life here in Middleborough wasn't real.

She sat on the bed and watched him pace around the room. "What's wrong, darling?" Her voice trembled. "You're scaring me."

"Do you know who Rainier Terriau is?" he asked.

She furrowed her brow. "Who? I don't know anyone by that name."

"No, of course you don't." He crossed the room to the chair and started yanking his shirt on.

"Where are you going?"

"I have to get out to the wall right away," he mumbled. "I'm already late."

"Don't you want to eat breakfast? The children will be sad if you don't say goodbye to them."

He stared at her holding his jacket in his hand. The children wouldn't be sad because they didn't exist.

He had another flashback to the joke he made about her marrying a prince, having a bunch of children with him, taking all their children to church, and making the children sit through a five-hour service the way her mother made her sit through it.

That memory stabbed him in the heart when he remembered where she really was right now and what she really was right now.

She was out there somewhere, out of her mind and lost in the Coil. He really hoped he never saw her again.

This....this thing in front of him right now.....this was no more the real Marine than that lunatic animal out in the Coil right now. She was dead.

A rising surge of fury boiled out of his soul. Who in the holy hell conjured up this image of Marine to torment him? How dare they?

He could kill whoever did this. He would have tried to kill her, but she wasn't even real enough to do that.

He took his glaive and his jacket outside without even looking at the children. Who in the name of God had the nerve to make him think he married Marine, had a bunch of children with her, lived in Middleborough, and served as Commander of the Black Watch in this town?

Eliska was the only person who told him the truth.

He gulped down despair when he remembered what she said about the men of the Watch being celibate. How could he not listen to her and believe her?

He didn't know what to do, so he went up to the wall. The men treated his arrival as the non-event that it was. He spent every day on the wall.

The sight of the men gave him another brutal stab of grief, rage, and longing. None of these men were real. None of them had been the real Watchmen in Middleborough. None of these men really died in Middleborough or afterward.

What an insult this whole illusion was to their memories. Who the hell could be so callous as to throw this in his face after all he'd lost?

He clamped his eyes shut when he remembered his father. Yvan served on the wall for decades to defend the real Middleborough. He would gladly have given his life to defend that town. He only survived because of some cruel twist of fate.

Artur broke in on Yann's thoughts. "Commander? There's something moving out there."

Yann's eyes snapped open. He went over to Artur's post and followed the man's gaze into the surrounding farmland.

A dark figure moved in the trees out there. It reminded him of the times he'd seen Marine lurking in the landscape outside Laval—and other places. Was that her? Was that the real Marine?

He grabbed his glaive and sat down on the wall. "Defend the town no matter what," he barked over his shoulder. "Don't let any strangers come near the walls without challenging them." He pushed off and jumped down onto the ground outside the wall.

"Hey!" Artur yelled after him. "Where are you going?"

"I'm going to check it out." Yann almost said he'd be back in a minute, but he didn't want to come back. He never wanted to see Middleborough again, either.

Middleborough no longer existed. If he couldn't see the real thing, he damn sure didn't want to see some make-believe version of it full of make-believe people having make-believe relationships and telling him they make-believe loved him. To hell with that.

He set off walking for the dark figure. He got halfway there before he realized the person was walking upright.

They strode through the trees too directly to be Marine—and then the wind caught a torrent of black hair and a black cloak. The breeze blew both out behind the figure.

She turned toward him and set off at a fast pace to meet up with him. She rushed the last few paces and almost started to smile. Then she stopped herself when she saw his expression.

She pulled up in front of him and her mouth pinched. "I'm so sorry!" she husked.

He looked away. "Forget it. Let's get out of here." He looked around. "Where's Anríq?"

"He's waiting for us outside the spell."

Yann's head shot up, but he stopped himself from asking about that, too. Of course he must have been trapped by some kind of magic.

Eliska read his mind. He remembered everything now—everything right up until he met those fleeing people.

He remembered every harrowing ordeal he'd ever gone through with Eliska, Anríq, Marine, his father, and the Watchmen.

He actually appreciated the pain of those memories. At least he knew they were real. They were as real as Eliska standing right in front of him.

"We're still inside the spell," she explained. "I have to use my magic to break us out of it. Anríq didn't want to come any closer. He didn't say so, but I don't think he has the magic to get himself out of it. He stayed out so he wouldn't get trapped."

Yann didn't ask how she found him or how she got in and out of the spell.

She didn't hesitate to take his hand. She led him deeper into the trees, checked all around her in every direction to make sure no one saw them, and then turned to face him.

She took a firm grip on both his hands, clamped her eyes and mouth shut, and let off a brutal thump of magic.

It detonated from inside her and would have knocked him away, but she held him in place by clenching his hands in a bone-breaking grip.

The blast hit him and he slammed back against his arms and hers. The next instant, the illusion shattered and he found himself standing in the middle of some wide rolling grasslands.

He didn't see a single sign of the charred wasteland where he'd originally tried to protect the refugees.

A massive column of people lurched past him and Eliska. He recognized plenty of people from the Middleborough fantasy, but none of those people saw or recognized him. They looked straight through him.

The instant she shattered the illusion, dozens of magical streaks zoomed out of nowhere. They swooped between all the hypnotized people and rocketed in on Yann and Eliska.

She tackled him, strapped her arms around him, let off an even more crushing boom of magic, and magicked both of them far away from the column.

They reappeared on a hilltop a mile away. Both of them turned around to look down at the column.

No one looked up. No one even noticed the attack or Yann and Eliska magicking away.

All those people filed away toward the western horizon, each person lost in their own dream world.

They were all the same people who fled from the burning city. Some of them were the same refugees who asked Yann to help protect them.

He'd been on the verge of leaving them to go get Eliska and Anríq. Those upheavals that hit the nearby hills—the upheavals that threatened but didn't attack—those must have been part of the trick. He wouldn't have stayed otherwise.

Now the illusion was gone—and so was Marine. What a heartless trick—making him think he had her back. He hated whoever did this to him, but he couldn't hate those people down there.

Heavy footsteps approached him and Eliska from the other side of the hill. Yann caught sight of Anríq out of his peripheral vision.

Yann couldn't look at him. Yann couldn't look at either Anríq or Eliska—not after what he just went through.

Eliska knew. She saw the whole imaginary world. She knew the secret desire of his heart, but she didn't say a word.

She touched his elbow and murmured, "Let's go."

Yann followed them down the other side of the hill. They passed into a different part of the Island where he couldn't see the column anymore.

Chapter 9

Yann looked around at the grasslands—or he would have if the firelight let the three friends see more than the immediate circle around their camp.

Pitch darkness blocked out everything beyond the rim of light. The heavy cloud hid the stars and any moon if there was one up there.

"Why do you think this Island is staying so stable for so long?" he asked.

"It might be because the White Spire is here," Eliska suggested.

"It can't be. We've seen Layers collapsing dozens of times even when they had the White Spire in them. We've seen them collapsing within minutes or even seconds as soon as the spire shows up in them. This is the longest any Layer has remained stable for this long."

She cocked her head to study him and then looked back down into the flames. "I wondered if that wishing spell might have been one of the Voyant's defenses."

Yann gasped. "How could it be? It was nowhere near the White Spire."

"He knows we're coming after him. He knows we're trying to take the Shards. What better way to stop us than by making us forget that we even wanted the Shards?"

Yann looked away and snarled under his breath. "If he's the one who did this, then that's all the more reason for me to twist his ever-loving head off."

Anríq raised his hand and clamped it on Yann's shoulder.

Yann flinched at that touch, but he didn't shake it off. "I never should have left," he croaked. "I should have stayed there. I had everything I ever wanted. I could have lived the rest of my life in happiness. I never had to find out about any of this."

"You must have wanted this Servant's life more," Anríq suggested.

"And for what?" Yann spat. "So I can go off and get my head blasted off by some wizard who wants to kill us all?" He turned his head all the way away and squeezed his eyes shut tight. "I'm sorry. I shouldn't be talking like this. I'm grateful to both of you for getting me out."

Eliska didn't answer. She'd been suffering the secondary effects of Yann's turmoil ever since they left the Wishers' column.

She saw firsthand the life he'd been living in Middleborough. Of course he wouldn't want to leave that. She wouldn't have blamed him at all if he decided to stay even knowing it wasn't real.

He suffered worse from losing Marine this time than he did when he walked away from her at the Guardian Temple. This cost him more than when he told Anríq and Eliska to leave Marine behind in the Coil.

God, he loved her so much! Eliska never realized until right now just how much he loved Marine.

She felt his love before. She couldn't miss it when she relived his memories of Savaré and all the other places he and Marine spent together.

She even felt the torment of him begging Marine outside the walls of Laval for just one look—one hint of recognition.

This pain obliterated all of that. He never let himself believe before. He never let himself hope he would ever feel what it would really be like to live with her as her husband—to build a life and a family together.

Now he had that. The Wishers branded the memory into his heart and soul. He would never be able to forget it.

He lost something more than a fantasy. It really had been real to him. He suffered just as deeply from losing that as if it had been real.

He might have lived with her for thirty years and watched their children grow up. He and Marine might have grown old together before one of them had to suffer the ordeal of putting the other in the ground.

At least he would have those years to sustain him. Now he lost the whole thing without any of the foundation to keep him going.

Eliska didn't say anything to make him feel better. Knowing she understood actually made it harder for him.

He'd avoided eye contact with her all day on their way here. He might never get over this, but that was okay.

He'd helped her through far worse. She could give him this one. She could give him a lot more.

She glanced over at Anríq and read the heartfelt concern in his eyes. Anríq couldn't read Yann's thoughts. Anríq couldn't see that fantasy memory imprinted on Yann's mind for the rest of forever.

Anríq must have sensed it, though. What other wish would the spell fulfill than the one Yann cherished about Marine? What else would he describe when he said the spell gave him everything he ever wanted?

She poked at the coals and added more wood to the fire. She prepared herself to drop the subject—maybe forever.

Right then, Yann's head shot up again. His hard eyes snapped right and left to both sides of the fire. "You two should take the Shards."

Anríq jolted. "What?"

"You two should take both Shards. You'll be together that way. If I take one Shard and one of you takes the other, you two will be separated. Anríq can become King and Eliska can be your Queen. It obviously works better if the King's affiliate is his Queen—not some stranger or a blood relative. The whole thing is supposed to be passed down through the bloodline. You two will be able to have children and pass on the Shards to your oldest son and whoever he marries. Then this won't happen again."

Eliska and Anríq exchanged a glance and both of them immediately looked away.

Eliska wasn't ready to start thinking that way—not when she and Anríq just started this....whatever it was they were doing.

Yann didn't seem to notice either of them being reluctant to talk about it. Yann turned to Eliska. "The landscapes we keep seeing the spire in must not be the same Layer where the Shard is located."

"What makes you say that?"

"Because they're all devastated, destroyed, burned landscapes. The pictures show the White Spire in a beautiful landscape. We also know the White Spire is in a city—a functional city full of prosperous people and commerce. We haven't seen that yet."

She looked back down at the fire. "No, it's there."

"How do you know?"

"I just know. The Shard was in the spire last time—this latest time when Anríq got hit. The Shard was definitely there."

"So....are you saying that we could have taken the Shard if we could have gotten into the spire?" His voice spiked with excitement. "We were that close and the Voyant knocked us back?!"

"I don't know if we could have taken the Shard. We still don't know how to find the Sacred Shrine. Maybe the spire itself has layers of protection inside it to deter anyone from finding the Sacred Shrine."

Yann's features hardened even more. "I want you to take us there."

Eliska's jaw dropped. "You what?"

"I want you to take us there—to the White Spire. I don't care what you have to do. We're getting into the spire, we're going to break into the Sacred Shrine, and we're going to take the Shards—both of them. I don't care if you have to unleash your Dark poison to do it."

She gulped—too horrified to speak.

"Wait a minute, Yann...." Anríq interrupted.

Yann spun around to confront him. "You're the one who keeps saying you would give everything, including your own life, to take the Shards and end this. You're the one who keeps saying it would be worth it to spare all these innocent lives. We have to stop this, no matter what it takes." He turned around to face Eliska again. "I know you don't want to...."

"We don't even know if Eliska has the power to get us into the spire—much less defeat the Voyant," Anríq cut in. "If he's doing all this, then he must be actively trying to stop us from getting near the Shard. We would need a magic-user powerful enough to defeat him and all his defenses. We don't even know if a magic-user that powerful exists anywhere."

"Well, she's the best we have, so we have to do it this way. We won't know until you try it. You have to unleash it. Who knows? Unleashing it in a worthy cause might heal you. Maybe the whole point of it is that it needs a channel to express itself—and what better way than this."

Eliska couldn't look at him. The wild glaze in his eyes made her tremble—but the idea of using all this Darkness for something scared her even more.

Anríq didn't argue anymore. Eliska couldn't look at him, either. She didn't want to see in his eyes that he really thought this might be a good idea.

She would see a hefty dose of concern in his eyes, too, even if he thought it was a good idea—or even a passable idea. She would see a hefty dose of concern in his eyes *especially* if he thought it was a good idea.

She couldn't release her Darkness—not even on the Voyant.

What would she become if she did that? She might turn into a Darkling—a real Darkling—not just the words people batted around when they didn't understand someone or wanted to insult them.

She might snap the way Marine did—or Eliska might go out into the Dark Layers and never come back.

She didn't want to think about that because there was no way in God's creation that she would ever unleash her Darkness—not the way Yann suggested.

She couldn't unleash it all—not completely. That was absolutely out of the question.

Yann waited for her to say something. "Well? What do you say?"

She looked up and opened her mouth to answer, but right at that moment, a brilliant halo of white light erupted in the darkness outside their campsite.

The Voyant materialized out of nowhere and threw the whole countryside into chaos.

Chapter 10

E liska shot to her feet just as the first wave of flying debris smashed her in the face. The two boys moved in on both sides—or she thought they did.

Anríq moved in, but Yann jumped in front of both of them and raised his glaive to threaten the Voyant.

"NO, YANN!!" Anríq and Eliska both bellowed at once.

The Voyant never moved. He didn't do anything before another curtain of rubble and razor particles swatted Yann away.

He hurtled backward and slammed down on the ground thirty feet from Anríq and Eliska.

She magicked to Yann's side in a split second, but she could barely see anything in the darkness.

Whirling shrapnel peppered her face and body and got in her eyes. She had to squint to see Anríq backing toward her.

He raised his club in one hand and his axe in the other, but the Voyant didn't hit him. Anríq never threatened the Voyant. Anríq guarded Eliska just long enough for her to touch Yann's arm.

He wasn't badly hurt, but she didn't trust him in the same Layer as the Voyant—not after the way he talked earlier about killing the Voyant.

She waited for Anríq to catch up with them. Then she extended a ball of protection around all three of them and let the ball sink through the ground into the next Layer.

Punishing hurricanes of shrieking wind tossed the ball in all directions. The friends pitched through dozens of Layers.

The Layers bombarded the field with boulders, lava flows, ice slabs as big as glaciers, buildings and trees torn out by their roots and foundations, giants, and grotesque Dark shapes.

Eliska looked around trying to decide what to do next, but before she could decide, Yann clambered to his feet. "Take us to the spire!" he yelled over the noise. "We have to end this now!"

"We just were in the same Island with the spire!" she hollered back. "The Voyant collapsed the Layer! We can't go back there now—and the spire won't even be there anymore. He'll move it somewhere else. We have to wait for it to settle somewhere before we can find it."

He grimaced and looked away at the turmoil outside the ball. "We shouldn't have waited. We should have gone right after we left the Wishers."

She opened her projection. "The whole Coil is collapsing. The whole thing is becoming unstable."

"Can you find another Island?"

"There are no Islands anymore. Some Layers that are less unstable, but that's no guarantee that they'll stay that way."

"Do what you can—and keep an eye out for the spire. As soon as it appears somewhere, tell us so we can go there."

She turned back to her projection even though she already knew what she would see.

She directed the ball through a dozen more Layers.

She shot it straight up to break through into a bouncy landscape. Creatures, Darklings, giants, and a few normal-sized people and animals sailed through the air, landed on the ground, and it swelled and stretched to bounce them into the air.

The creatures, Darklings, and giants tried to fight each other, but they floundered even getting near each other. When they did, they slashed each other with weapons or tentacles or teeth.

The landscape morphed again the moment the ball soared into the Layer. The ball paused at the height of its arc and plummeted toward the surface just as another wave of instability took hold of the Layer.

The ground flipped up like a sheet of fabric flapping in the wind. It didn't undulate and sink back into troughs or the same bouncy surface.

It snapped up too fast and sent Darklings, people, and a few houses flying across the countryside.

The ball landed hard enough to get thrown in the opposite direction. The ball flew toward a humongous giant zooming toward the ball just as fast.

He opened his mouth in a hideous roar. The ball was flying too fast to stop before it plunged straight down his throat.

At the last second, Eliska magicked the ball sideways through a sheet of molten silver into a completely different landscape.

This one started as a giant city getting pounded to rubble by boulders and brimstone pelting down from the sky. Eliska didn't see any breach in the upper Layers. The rocks and burning debris fell from the clouds.

They smashed buildings and blasted craters in the streets and surrounding countryside.

Just as fast, a wave of instability surged out of the distance, overtook the city, and erupted everything in a massive upheaval.

Eliska's ball got caught in the mayhem with people, cattle, horses, household pets, and random kitchen utensils spinning everywhere.

They all slammed into the ball as the chaos threw everything together in a jumbled soup. Bodies struck the ball, bounced off, and vanished into the confusion.

"You said you would take us to the White Spire!" Yann yelled into her ear.

"I'M TRYING TO!!" she roared back. "It keeps moving around too much!"

"Where is it?!" he demanded.

"How the hell should I know?!! I can't tell where in the Coil it is right now or if it even still is in the Coil at all!"

"What is that supposed to mean?!" he countered. "It must be somewhere."

"This crap happens every time it moves! It just completely vanishes out of existence until it comes back somewhere else. I would take us there if I could."

He clamped his lips shut, thank God. He scowled at the mayhem unfolding outside the ball.

He scowled like he actually doubted if she *would* take the friends to the White Spire even if she knew how to.

The ball soared from one scene of upheaval and chaos to another and plummeted through a dozen Layers, each one with a different landscape.

The chaos tore them all apart. Everyone and everything that had been living in those Layers got thrown into the mayhem along with Dark forces, vapors, and all the other debris from destroyed towns, cities, and entire Layers torn to pieces.

Eliska settled into just letting the ball fly through the Layers wherever the Dark forces struck it. What difference did it make where the three friends went?

Without warning, something switched in her mind. "I found it! It's back. Hold on!"

She anchored her magic into the ball and sent it whistling across their current Layer. The ball sailed through countless Dark vapors and broke through a curtain of crackling magic into another landscape burned to blackened cinders.

She slowed the ball as soon as it entered. The spire stood on the horizon, but she didn't dare to lower the party to the ground.

The three friends could see through the walls that this Layer was already falling apart, too. She kept the ball in the air. The friends were much safer here.

"I guess there's no point in assaulting the spire now," she pointed out. "It will only move again in a second."

Yann didn't argue to tell her to assault the spire right this minute the way he suggested before.

He frowned at the blackened countryside spread out below the ball. "This is strange."

"What's strange about it?" Anríq asked. "We've seen this before."

"Not like this. This Island wasn't a city before. Look. There are tree trunks all over the ground. They even surround the spire. This was never a city. It looks like it used to be a forest."

"The spire could have moved with the chaos," Eliska suggested. "Or the Voyant could be trying to trick us by moving the spire around so much that we can't find it—or we look for it in the wrong place."

"Can you keep track of it when it....?" Yann barely got the words out before the upheaval took this Layer, too.

She kept the ball where it was. The friends watched wave upon wave of treacherous commotion translate through the ground.

They converged on the White Spire—almost as if the landscape itself knew that this one building was causing all the problems.

Those waves smashed against the walls, tore up the ground all around the spire, dragged down what few poor scorched trees remained, and submerged them underground.

The waves threw tons of soil into the air, heaved bedrock out of position, and hurled everything at the spire.

The flying rubble smashed the walls to pieces and started dragging the torn sections down, too.

"My God!" Yann breathed. "The landscape actually seems like it's coming alive!"

"It's attacking the spire the same way it attacks us—and everyone else," Anríq pointed out. "The Coil is turning on itself."

Right then, another eruption hit some large hills underneath the ball. The same sprays of rock, sod, and broken tree trunks cartwheeled through the air and smashed the ball's underside.

None of the friends could deny anymore that the landscape was trying to attack the ball.

The waves reared out of the ground and didn't sink back. They shot towers of rock and twisted roots from underground that twined into tall extending columns to strike the ball.

They knocked the ball flying—straight toward where the spire just had been.

"Hold on!" Eliska yelled and braced her arms over her head.

The two boys didn't understand in time before the Layer directly above this one caved in.

A punishing avalanche of rock smashed down on top of the ball, pounded it into the cracks where the White Spire just disappeared, and the ball shattered as all that rock plunged down on top of it.

Chapter 11

Y ann heard Eliska yelling in the distance. He couldn't see a thing in the mass of Darkness and confusion.

Dozens of blows struck him all over, but he also felt plenty of open space around him.

Piles of rock and debris fell on him only for some mysterious force to yank all that stuff away.

She reestablished her protective ball around the three friends again and again. Its eerie light flashed outward in the Darkness only for the ball to get smashed in by another devastating collapse.

Yann couldn't see where the friends were. He didn't want to see. He just hoped Eliska's power held up long enough to get the friends..... somewhere.

If she couldn't find a safe haven, then maybe the three friends really were screwed this time.

Just then, another brutal impact crushed her ball again. The three friends twirled apart into a pitch-dark sea of mayhem ripping, hurtling, and pummeling them from all sides.

At that moment, another light cracked the Darkness apart. This wasn't Eliska's ball.

The Voyant materialized on Yann's left, but the Voyant's arrival didn't have the same effect as before. This Layer couldn't get any more chaotic than it already was.

Eliska snapped the ball around the three travelers in a heartbeat and magicked everyone away.

They smashed through one Layer after another. Yann couldn't keep track of them anymore. Some looked like giant nets of interconnected fibers crisscrossing everywhere.

Others would have resembled normal, stable landscapes. Massive human populations fled the widespread destruction of cities, towns, homes, and whole countrysides set on fire, flooded, or attacked by ice storms.

The friends lost sight of the Voyant in the confusion, but Yann couldn't hope the Voyant was gone. He wouldn't let the friends get away so easily.

The ball landed hard on the ground next to one of these fleeing populations and the ball exploded from the impact. That wasn't like Eliska. She usually lowered the friends to the ground more gently.

Yann picked himself up and crawled over to check on her, but he had to leap to his feet when another surge hit the surrounding landscape.

The ground reared upward in a towering wave of soil, trees, and animals caught in the upheaval.

The wave curved over the population to pulverize everyone into oblivion.

Yann did the only thing he could do. He raised his glaive, but before the wave could bury him, Anríq jumped forward and clubbed the wave away.

A boom went off from the point of impact. The wave evaporated, but the momentum of all the stuff inside it didn't stop.

It all hurtled toward the fleeing population. All that flying debris would have caused as much damage as the wave itself, but Eliska raised her hand and let off an absolutely bone-crushing eruption of magic.

She took a fraction of a second to erect the biggest protective shield Yann had ever seen. It covered thousands of people.

All the rock, dirt clods, dead animals, and torn vegetation hammered her field, bounced off, and whizzed off into the mayhem.

Yann spun around to try to help her. She never made it off her hands and knees before she saved all those people's lives.

He dragged her to her feet, but both she and Anríq had to continually counterattack all the forces moving in on these people.

"Can you transport them away?!" Yann yelled over the noise.

"Where would I take them?!" she fired back.

She barely got the words out before another tidal wave of confusion overwhelmed the Layer and it detonated in a maelstrom of whirling projectiles.

The countryside disintegrated if Yann could call it a countryside to begin with. What had been solid land for all the fleeing people to stand on evaporated into a churning hurricane of matter caught in catastrophic winds.

All those people went flying off to nowhere. They sailed into the Layers cartwheeling in every possible direction.

Eliska yelled out, "NO!!" before all those people became bodies caught in the tornado.

She unleashed an enormous binding spell to surround the population and all the land they'd just been standing on, but her spell didn't take hold in time before they all scattered to the winds.

She only succeeded in binding a bunch of rocks and broken building sections to herself. They would have crushed her, but she released them.

She didn't see the same blast send Yann and Anríq twirling away from her.

Yann had to fight off random forces coming out of the mayhem to attack him.

Anríq pivoted one way and another smashing things with his club and trying to defend anyone near enough to him.

Neither he nor Yann couldn't take themselves or anyone else through the Layers nor could they direct himself anywhere.

Yann got too busy fighting off Dark vapor. He didn't see Eliska when he tumbled past her.

She magnetized him to her and caught him by the jacket. "Stay with me! We have to stay together!"

He looked up—and then they both looked around and saw Anríq somersaulting through the mayhem a hundred yards away.

He wielded his axe to fight off the Dark forces that came near enough to threaten him, but he had no choice but to fall through the Layers. He was just as helpless as the rest of these people.

Eliska fired another binding spell at him and pulled him in until he slammed into her and Yann.

She cast a desperate, hopeless glance at the few other people nearest to the party. She might have been able to save them, too, but there was nowhere to go anymore.

Right at that moment, her head shot up a second time. "The White Spire! It's back! It's in another Layer."

"Is it near us?" Yann asked.

"No—not by a long shot—but it's all we have to go on."

She created another protective ball around the three of them and magicked them across Layers to the landscape in question.

The ball broke through into another torched wasteland of twisted, blackened trees and melted, imploded buildings.

The three friends surveyed the countryside from one horizon to another.

"I don't see the spire anywhere," Eliska remarked.

"What are we doing here if it isn't here?" Yann asked.

"You said you wanted to go to the Layer with the White Spire in it. I picked it up here, but it isn't here now. The Voyant must be tricking us somehow."

Yann gritted his teeth and looked around again even though there was nothing to see. "We have to come up with a way to overcome him."

"Maybe we should stay on the ground for a while," Anríq suggested. "We aren't accomplishing anything by flying around in the wild Layers." He turned to Eliska. "Set us down somewhere. Does this place have any water?"

"There's a river over there." She pointed.

She set the ball on the ground, but she took extra long checking and double-checking the surroundings before she released the ball. Yann read her mind. She didn't want to let her guard down.

"Thank you, Eliska," Anríq murmured. "Your magic is the only thing keeping us alive right now."

She looked away, but the landscape didn't offer any comfort. "I should have saved those people. I could have saved them all. I could have brought them all here instead of just the three of us."

"You wouldn't have been able to save them even if you did bring them all here," Yann told her. "We can't save anyone except by finding those Shards. If we ever see the White Spire or the Voyant again, I want you to attack right away no matter what else is going on. We can't keep letting him distract us."

"If I do that....." She tripped over the words.

"What's wrong?" Yann demanded. "You drove him away from that village. You don't know how much damage you could do if you really tried to fight him. Look around you. We have nothing to lose by trying."

"I'm just saying that.....if I attacked him while we were floating in the wild Layers, I would have to break the ball to do that. You two would be left unprotected. You might get killed. Then, if you're right that I even can defeat him, I would take the one Shard and I would become the new Voyant. Nothing would change."

"Then you can put us on the ground the next time we see the spire."

"And if we see the Voyant in the Layers?"

He started to say something, but instability seized the Island before he got the words out. The ground exploded underfoot and threw the friends in three different directions.

The bedrock ruptured under Yann's feet and a slab of broken soil tilted up into a vertical wall. It sent him pitching backward.

Chapter 12

Eliska used her magic to lift herself off the ground. At least she wouldn't get crushed or buried.

More slabs angled out of the ground to form walls. They connected themselves into a labyrinth. Some of the walls morphed into living shapes of monstrous faces or deadly creatures.

She retreated a little higher over the maze, but the walls or slabs or whatever they were kept rising. They formed a definite structure, but it didn't stay the same for more than a few seconds.

It kept rearranging itself as walls slid out of place and locked into different positions to change the route through the labyrinth.

The walls kept ejecting magical faces, shapes, and limbs from the surfaces that grabbed and tore at each other as much as anyone or anything else caught inside the maze.

Yann couldn't see Anríq anymore, but Yann had his work cut out for him defending himself against all these shapes and monsters coming at him.

He stabbed, slashed, and parried his glaive to deflect dozens of attacks from all sides. He held his own, but he couldn't anywhere to get himself out of this trap.

Eliska stayed where she was floating above the maze. She kept turning from side to side and looking downward in opposite directions. Could she see Anríq from that height?

Was she trying to decide whether to save him or Yann first?

Yann really hoped she would save Anríq first. Anríq would be much more help to Eliska to get all three of the friends out of here.

He had to turn back to fighting the shapes coming out of the walls. He didn't see Eliska until she plunged into the maze at a distance from him.

She vanished behind the walls, but he saw her again when the walls slid aside. They rearranged themselves to reveal her for a second.

She rushed him only to get cut off by another wall sliding across her path.

Hideous Dark shapes came out of the walls and backed him into a side passage he had to fight his hardest just to hold his position.

Another wall opened and she rushed to catch up with him, but the maze shifted too fast.

The walls closed to cut her off again, but a second later, a thump of powerful magic blasted the maze to its outer edges. Eliska dissolved all the walls to fine powder. The explosion didn't harm Yann or Anríq when the maze detonated.

The impact flung both boys away in the concussion, but she activated another binding spell and caught them both to pull them toward her.

All three friends landed together in a pile on what had been the maze floor. The dust from the walls kept whoofing outward. The breeze caught it and blew it away.

Yann pried her aching head off the ground to look around. Anríq got to his feet first and helped Yann and Eliska stand up.

The three friends looked around them in all directions. They weren't in the scorched landscape where she detected the White Spire. They weren't in any Island Yann recognized.

They stood on a lonely mountaintop in the middle of a vast mountain range spreading as far as the eye could see.

He didn't see a single sign of human habitation—or any other sign that anything lived here.

The mountains rolled, undulated, and heaved down in the valleys. The landscape swelled and rippled outward, back and forth, and even toward the mountaintop where the friends stood watching.

The upheaval didn't take this mountain for some reason. Everything about this mountain remained tranquil, silent, and perfectly peaceful.

Chapter 12

Yann inhaled a shaky breath. The landscape rippled all around the mountain where he, Anríq, and Eliska came to rest after their harrowing journey through the Coil.

He found it difficult to accept that the instability of this Island didn't touch this mountain. He struggled to hear some sound in the vast silence.

The wind murmured over the rugged peaks. Nothing else disturbed the glacial calm of this Island.

The instability didn't tear the Island apart. Those waves didn't seem to damage the landscape at all.

They passed through the surrounding mountains, rose, fell, and settled back into place before the next movement came along to do it all over again.

He could think of a lot of questions to ask Eliska right now—like where the three friends were and where they should go after this.

He didn't dare to say a word. One sound might trigger the whole catastrophe again. He wanted to cherish this silence and stillness for as long as it lasted.

Neither of his friends said anything, either. Anríq watched for a minute before he sat down crosslegged on the rocky ground. He didn't take his eyes off the landscape.

All the tension drained out of Eliska when she gazed into the distance. She didn't volunteer any information.

Yann let himself relax. He didn't want to leave this place to go back into the chaos Layers.

The Coil itself was trying to kill everyone inside it, including its own Dark forces. He'd seen too many features of the landscape attacking Dark forces, grotesque creatures, monstrous shapes, and even Darklings.

None of those forces came after the three friends—not specifically. Those forces didn't discriminate. They attacked anyone who came near them no matter who it was.

Yann couldn't assign any malice to these Dark forces. They were as likely to destroy themselves as they were to destroy anyone or anything else.

From what he'd just seen in the wild Layers, none of them could stop themselves from attacking or from getting attacked. The whole Coil was falling too far out of control. None of these things could control anything anymore.

The Voyant's presence increased the chaos and confusion. His arrival always caused a collapse of some kind.

His presence made the Coil more destructive, but Yann couldn't even be sure anymore if the Voyant could control it. Maybe nothing could.

For some reason, Yann turned away from the view first. He searched the mountaintop for some sign of food, water, or shelter the friends could use, but he didn't see anything.

He and his friends would have to leave this mountain to go search for resources somewhere else. Leaving the mountain meant going out into the instability. He didn't want to do that or to suggest it to the other two.

The three of them stood and sat around in silence for what seemed like a long time.

Yann couldn't wrap his head around a silence this deep. He kept trying to figure out what was wrong with the world that made him not be able to hear anything.

Just then, Anríq looked around and made eye contact with Yann. Eliska still stood there staring into the distance—probably trying to figure out what was wrong with the world that made *her* not be able to hear anything.

"I suppose we can't stay here, either," Anríq remarked.

"We have nowhere else to go," Eliska murmured without turning around. "It will be the same everywhere."

"So you can't reliably locate the White Spire anymore?" Yann asked. "That's what we learned the last time, isn't it? You might pick it up somewhere and we could go there only to discover that it isn't there at all."

She nodded still without turning around. "That's what I figured, too."

Yann looked around at nothing. "Then I guess it doesn't matter where we go."

"The Voyant will come after us eventually," Anríq pointed out. "If you're serious about Eliska attacking him to take the Shard...."

She came to life all of a sudden, spun around, and launched in with her old energy. "About that. I don't think that's a good idea, either."

Yann made a face. "We already know it isn't a good idea. The problem is that we have no other options."

"Just listen to me for a minute, will you? Let's say you're right and, by some miracle, I did have the magic to defeat the Voyant and take the Shard from him. If that actually happened, then I would become the new Voyant and you two would be left on your own to go after the second Shard. We already know Anríq doesn't have the magic to do that on his own." She glanced at Anríq. "Sorry. I don't mean that as an insult or anything."

He shrugged it away. "Not at all. We all know it's true—and you're right. If you took the Voyant's Shard, we would be in exactly the same situation. Yann and I wouldn't even be able to find the second Shard, let alone for one of us to take it."

"Me using my power to attack the Voyant won't get us anywhere," she went on. "Even my Dark power won't get us the outcome we want. We need to find both Shards at the same time so we can decide who takes them, when, and how."

"We might not have that option," Anríq pointed out. "If we defeat the Voyant—I mean if *you* defeat the Voyant—we might have to take the Shard right away. *You* might have to take the Shard right away. Maybe that's how it works. Maybe only the person who defeats the Voyant and takes the Shard by force can become the next Shard-holder—or whatever you call it."

"Then we can't attack the Voyant," she finished. "We need more information. We need some reliable way to access both Shards so two of us can take them. That's the only way we're going to bring peace to the Coil. Replacing the Voyant with one of us is the worst thing we could do."

Anríq nodded. Yann listened while he thought the whole thing over.

She was right. None of this meant anything unless two people took both Shards at the same time. The Coil would continue to collapse until that happened.

Eliska looked up at him. "Are you okay with this? You said you wanted me to use my Darkness to defeat the Voyant. I don't think we should—not yet."

He barely heard her. "Do you remember that the Voyant was originally a Barbarian?"

Anríq and Eliska both spun around to stare at him. "What about it?" Eliska asked. "How does that help us?"

"Maybe his people know something about this. He might have hidden the Shards with them."

"He didn't," Eliska countered. "We already know the Shards are in the White Spire."

"The Barbarians don't know anything about this," Anríq interrupted. "They're Barbarians. They don't get involved in this. Anyway, we don't know who his family is or if they're even still alive."

"We know who his family is," Yann replied. "He and Yimichi Ocuron both came from the Sirki Tribe."

"The Sirki Tribe comprises hundreds of bands all over the Sojourner's Sanctum and countless other Islands," Anríq pointed out. "We don't know if those Islands are even still intact or if anyone in those tribes is still alive."

"We could check," Yann suggested. "The Barbarians we negotiated with at Laval belonged to the Sirki Tribe. Morix even knew Yimichi and Noleron. He grew up with them."

Eliska gasped. "Why didn't you tell us before?!"

Yann shrugged. "I didn't think it made any difference. He couldn't tell me anything about the Voyant. Morix didn't even know about Yimichi becoming King in the White Spire or about him and his brother having a feud over a woman. Morix didn't have any clue about why Yimichi or Noleron left the Tribe."

"So what do you hope to accomplish by going back now?" Anríq asked.

"Someone else might know something that could help us get into the spire."

"Why didn't you ask them before?" Eliska asked. "You were right there talking to them."

"I didn't have time. I was too busy negotiating on behalf of Laval."

"We could have stayed," Anríq pointed out. "We could have stayed a little longer and questioned them further."

"I didn't think of it then," Yann replied. "Like I said, I didn't think it helped us at all—and it might still not help us. Besides, we had Aja with us then. I thought we had a better chance of all four of us getting into the spire."

Eliska looked away over the landscape. "Maybe there's some secret combination of spells or directions that you need to get into the spire."

"I don't see how it can be that complicated," Anríq countered. "The stories we've seen so far make it sound like the King can hand down the Shard to his son with no trouble at all. If the King has a son, the son just takes the Shard from the father and becomes the new King."

"We don't know that," Eliska argued. "Maybe the son has to go through the same quest and struggle. Maybe the stories just don't talk about it because the process is a secret and they don't want to give away too much."

"I think you're overcomplicating this whole thing," Anríq told her.

"If it's that simple, why haven't we found the Shards and taken them by now?" she demanded.

He shrugged again. Yann interrupted before they could say anything else. "So what do you both say to going back to Laval and questioning the Barbarians about it?"

Eliska's shoulders slumped. "I guess we have no reason not to. We don't have any other leads."

Anríq got to his feet. "The Voyant will come after us again like I said. We'll wind up fighting him either way. Any information we can get about his possible vulnerabilities will only help us."

Yann turned to Eliska. "Could you find this Island again if you had to? Could you bring us back here if we get into trouble?"

"I could if it's still here. We have no guarantee that the instability won't take the whole landscape while we're gone."

He nodded. "Let's do this."

The three friends moved closer together. Eliska established her ball of protection around all three of them and it shot straight upward.

It vaporized through the sky overhead and into a Dark Layer full of Darklings and dangerous vapors floating everywhere.

She kept flying upward and then zoomed sideways in different directions. Yann didn't pay attention to where she was taking the party.

He got fascinated by more scenes of Dark forces attacking each other, tearing their Layers apart, and even destroying each other.

Watching them succumb to their own violent impulses actually made him feel sorry for them. They were as much the Coil's victims as everyone else.

What would happen if the three friends failed to take the two Shards? What would the Coil become?

It might disintegrate into one giant tempest of storm winds and wild forces. The boundary between the Dark and everything else might cease to exist in a world of pure chaos.

The Coil sure seemed to be going in that direction. None of the three friends could stop it—not even Eliska.

The ball dropped through a few more Layers. Yann no longer even thought about trying to help all the people caught in danger. The friends could only help these people one way. The friends might not even be able to do that.

If Eliska fought the Voyant and lost, the three friends would be all out of options. If the Shards were in the White Spire and her Dark power wasn't strong enough to break in to take them, then what other option was there?

She broke through one last Layer and slowed the ball's descent heading for another burned-out landscape. Yann didn't recognize it until the ball got low enough to see a destroyed town in the distance.

Only a few charred frames of houses surrounded the crumbling wreckage of the Laval hotel. Yann never would have recognized the place if not for that.

He took one look at the ruined town and knew in his gut that there were no more people living there. He only prayed that some of them made it out alive.

The other side of the landscape didn't offer any more hope. None of the trees or grasslands remained. The friends could see all the way to the distant hills that once separated the Barbarian camp from Laval.

Yann, Anríq, and Eliska saw from a thousand feet up in the air that there was no one living over there anymore, either. Not a single tent, rope, or even a rock remained to show where the Barbarian camp had been.

Everyone was gone—from both sides. If anyone from the Sirki Tribe who knew the Voyant survived this destruction, they weren't here anymore.

Yann could have asked Eliska to track the survivors, but he didn't ask. What was the point? He never should have come back here.

She set the ball on the ground outside Laval. The friends surveyed the countryside in silence.

This Island seemed to be perfectly stable, too—apart from everything being burned to the ground.

The hotel was still there. Yann found himself migrating toward it. The other two followed him.

The steps creaked when he climbed up to the porch. The charred door hung off its hinges. He stepped into the central hall. The blackened stairs rose to the second floor, but he didn't go up there.

The hotel interior reeked of charcoal. What did he really hope to find in a giant pile of cinders?

Eliska and Anríq followed him into the building. He expected one or both of them to tell him how foolhardy he was for suggesting that they come back here.

Eliska broke the silence. "There is one other person connected with this."

Yann didn't look up. The smell made him sick. He really wanted to leave.

"Who is it?" Anríq asked.

"Hubua Ocuron—Yimichi's Queen. She came from the Hallowed Vales. She was born Hubua Aminato, the oldest daughter of King Reitor Aminato of the Verdant Gorges. King Reitor made an alliance with Yimichi and they sealed it by Yimichi marrying Reitor's oldest daughter."

Yann shrugged. "We might not find anything there, either. In fact, I'm certain we won't, but we have nothing else to do."

Chapter 13

Eliska sensed Yann slipping into despair. He really wanted to defeat the Voyant.

She made a conscious effort not to tap her Darkness when she freed the boys from the Layers and from that maze. She didn't need to use her Darkness.

The idea of using it against the Voyant was beginning to grow on her. Someone had to stop all this death and destruction.

Her only concern was taking the Voyant's Shard and becoming the Voyant herself. She would rather not take the Shard at all if there was any other alternative.

She created her ball around the two boys and transported them to the Hallowed Vales. She didn't hold out much hope of finding anything there—nothing apart from another burned landscape of charred trees and churning mountains.

The ball broke through into a clear blue sky. Fluffy white clouds raced across the ball's path.

It soared downward toward forested mountains, crystal rivers falling over waterfalls, and towering stone castles full of magnificent halls.

"Everything looks the same," Eliska remarked as the ball floated between craggy mountains carpeted in lush trees. "I don't see any sign of instability at all."

Anríq furrowed his brow at the surroundings. "I don't see any people. That isn't right."

She lowered the ball closer to the Royal Palace. The ball touched down in the center of a huge octagonal courtyard.

A massive stone cathedral occupied one side of the courtyard. Equally impressive buildings, castles, and towers sat all around the area with a beautiful garden blooming in the center.

A fountain bubbled there with the water spilling out of its basin into channels leading outward into the garden. Walkways from the courtyard's outer ring led inward to sitting areas where anyone could enjoy the flowers, trees, and the sound of running water.

"How is this possible?" Yann murmured. "This place looks completely untouched."

"Something's wrong," Eliska husked. "Anríq is right. The people are all gone."

"Should we find out?" Yann asked.

Anríq glared at the Royal Palace. It covered three sides of the octagon. A massive castle occupied the central section with high turrets, battlements, and flags flying from the parapets.

Two giant fortresses stuck out of the castle to form the other two sides of the octagon.

Anríq passed his hand downward through the air between himself and the palace. He opened a magical window that showed countless people going about their business inside the building.

All those wore splendid, colorful, elaborate outfits that must have cost a fortune.

"Something is in there," he murmured.

Eliska shuddered and looked away. "They aren't people. They're Darklings. The Dark took over the whole Vale."

"They aren't Darklings. They're only phantoms." Anríq took a few steps forward. "Come on. Let's see if we can find out anything about Hubua Aminato."

Eliska hung back. She didn't want to go into a castle full of Dark forces even if they were phantoms.

Yann advanced to follow Anríq, so she had no choice but to go with them.

She considered just for a minute if she should stay outside, but she wanted to be on hand in case something attacked the boys or they got into trouble some other way.

She realized in that moment that she would be able to defeat anything inside this castle. Her power exceeded anything in this Layer.

Maybe Yann was right about her being able to defeat the Voyant—but that didn't help the friends find the two Shards.

Her confidence rose after she made that connection. She was only here to help the boys—nothing else.

They entered a giant hall of carved timbers rising to the peaked ceilings. Countless carved figures of angels, creatures, and people in different artistic poses covered the beams.

The whole ceiling seemed to squirm with life except that none of it moved.

The phantoms sure were active. They crisscrossed the hall, passed into and out of dozens of passages branching off the central entrance, climbed the stairs, and held silent conversations with each other about whatever palace business the phantoms were supposed to conduct.

The boys advanced to the center of the hall and looked around at all the statues, tapestries, chandeliers, ornate carvings on the banisters, and doorways leading into every room.

The phantoms passed straight through the friends' bodies as these ghost people rushed back and forth in a flurry of activity.

The phantoms didn't see the travelers or try to interact. Passing through the friends' bodies made a slight chilly breeze sensation on Eliska's skin, but that was all. The phantoms didn't damage anyone.

The boys kept going to another enormous hall connected to this one. It looked more like a ceremonial gathering hall. The ceilings arched so high that Eliska couldn't make out the carvings up there at all.

Stained-glass windows lined both walls. The pictures showed different Kings and Queens of the Verdant Gorges and elsewhere in the Hallowed Vales.

Long narrow windows in the ceiling let heavenly streams of sunshine into the hall. They shone on the floor and lit up the hall with an angelic glow.

The ceiling angled halfway down the hall. The windows on both sides of that part of the ceiling shone on a colossal throne hewn out of black stone.

A giant stone crown had been carved out of the rock wall behind the throne. The crown hung over the seat to indicate that the King sat there.

The people of the Verdant Gorges had decorated this stone crown with colorful paints, gold leaf, and gemstones to make it look like a real crown only much, much bigger.

The sunbeams sparkled and reflected on the surface and scattered colored rainbows and flashes of light all over the hall.

Hundreds of phantoms packed the hall. Everyone here wore immaculate celebratory costumes. The women wore full-length gowns studded with diamonds and pearls, strings of gems in their elaborate hairdos, and the men wore fur-lined capes, jewel-encrusted weapons, and gold-trimmed jackets that shone in the light as much as the crown itself.

The courtiers milled around talking to each other, but none of them made any sound. Some bowed to each other. Some of the men kissed the ladies' hands and made room for their wide sweeping skirts so the ladies could get through the crowd.

The phantoms passed through Yann, Anríq, and Eliska here, too. The phantoms even passed through each other.

"They don't look so grand when they aren't really here, do they?" Yann murmured. "We can see straight through them."

"So what happened to them?" Anríq asked. "Did all these people die?"

"This Island reminds me of the Island of lost souls," Eliska pointed out. "These phantoms interact, but only with each other."

"Maybe they don't even do that. Maybe they're only an image with no substance at all." Anríq turned to Eliska. "Can you tell anything about what happened to them?"

"I can't pick up any memories from any of them. That's the strangest part. If I just happened to walk into an empty castle, I should have been able to pick up at least some residual memories from the people who lived there. I should have been able to pick that up even before I came here. Now I can't detect anything at all."

The three friends parted to search the hall. When they did, they saw a tall man with shoulder-length brown hair sitting on the throne at the end of the room. He hadn't been there before. He appeared just now.

He wore his beard neatly trimmed. An exact replica of the giant carved crown sat on his head.

All the phantoms bowed to him and then cheered silently. The scene didn't look right without any sound.

Eliska studied the stained-glass windows. Carved inscriptions lined the wooden paneling next to each window.

She scanned the first one with her magic to read the inscriptions. Some of the stories told the family lineages and marriage ties between different royal families.

None of them mentioned Marine—not that Eliska would have known. She didn't know which royal family Marine belonged to or even which Vale she came from.

Maybe one of these inscriptions would make the connection between King Reitor Aminato and Yimichi Ocuron.

Right then, Anríq called from somewhere behind her. "Over here! I think I found something!"

She turned around, but neither of the boys was still in the same hall. They must have wandered off to explore somewhere else.

She had to walk through all the phantoms to cross the hall. She followed the direction of Anríq's voice, but by the time she got there, she couldn't see which side passage the boys might have passed down.

The passages all looked the same with phantom servants and other dignitaries coming and going from every room.

She strode to the entrance of a random passage. Her magic didn't work to locate either of the boys. "Anríq!" she called. "Yann! Where are you?"

She heard them talking in a different passage, but they didn't answer. Was it possible they didn't hear her?

She turned down the passage and passed four rooms on the left before another slamming door made her turn around.

She didn't see anything behind her—not even any phantoms. The passage behind her echoed as hollow as the grave all the way back to the gathering hall.

She could see from here that the gathering hall was empty, too. Dust floated in the sunbeams coming through the ceiling windows.

She spun the other way, hustled farther down the passage, calling, "Yann! Anríq! Where are you?!"

She yelled into every room. When she didn't get an answer, she stormed back to the hall, turned into a different passage, and did the same thing.

She made it thirty yards before another door slammed. She whipped around fast, but she didn't see the empty gathering hall down there anymore.

Instead, she found herself staring into a completely different passage full of phantoms as expensively dressed as those in the gathering hall.

This passage must have been on the castle's outer walls because, instead of rooms on both sides, a line of tall windows covered the lefthand wall.

Those windows stretched from floor to ceiling and let more sunshine pour into the castle. The windows looked out over the expansive countryside with tall, jagged mountains leading away into the gorges.

The other side of the passage extended between columns to a high atrium. A garden covered the lowest floor with fountains and flowering trees growing under a high glass ceiling.

Phantoms meandered through the gardens down there, socialized on the balconies and galleries surrounding the atrium, and looked down on the delightful scene.

The sight of all these ghost people made Eliska's skin crawl. She turned back and set off at a fast walk to the other end of the passage—the end where she originally entered from the gathering hall.

She passed through a heavy wooden door at the far end, but it didn't lead her back to the gathering hall. Of course not. That would be too easy.

This door led into a long, tall library full of scholars, monks, and a bunch of other people.

They studied books at tables and lecterns, silently discussed things with each other, and climbed up and down ladders to retrieve and return books to the shelves standing all the way to the lofty ceiling.

Eliska took one look at the place and turned away a second time. Yann and Anríq weren't in here.

She used her magic to search the castle, but she couldn't find any trace of either of the boys. Their lines didn't turn up in any part of her Coil projection.

She could expand and map out every part of this castle. She might even have been able to scan some of these books for the information she wanted about Hubua.

Eliska didn't care about any of that.

She barged from one passage to another, from one hall to another, from one part of the castle to another. She didn't see any trace of Yann or Anríq.

She stopped when she came out in the entrance hall where she and the boys first walked into this castle.

She'd just been in a different corridor on the fourteenth floor—a corridor lined with the royal family's bedrooms.

She shouldn't have been able to get from that corridor to the entrance hall without going down multiple flights of stairs and traveling through a dozen other passageways.

This castle must be another maze labyrinth like the one where the Black Watch got trapped.

Now she was trapped here, which meant Yann and Anríq were trapped here, too.

She would be the best person to get the boys out of here. She just had to find them first.

She couldn't even be sure she really was in the Hallowed Vales anymore. This could be anything. It could be another trick the Voyant threw in the friends' path to stop them from finding the Shard of Hotha.

Chapter 14

E liska halted in the entrance hall and turned in a complete circle to examine everything around her. She had to think.

The phantoms kept going about their business as if nothing ever had gone wrong with their Island.

She did her best to ignore them. She found her way out of the maze Island. She must be able to navigate this, too.

She created her Coil projection and zeroed in on the castle's layout. She added more magic to it, but the boys' lines still didn't show up.

She couldn't trust her senses in this place. The boys could be right in front of her—or very close to her. The castle would change its configuration to hide them.

That would make this a more difficult puzzle than the maze Island. At least there, once she found someone, she could be certain they were real.

She shut her Coil projection feeling a sinking weight in her stomach. Searching the castle one floor at a time wasn't an option, either. The castle would just shift. She would probably die in here and so would the boys.

She set off walking while she considered what to do about it. If she made it back to the library, she would scan the books for information.

She couldn't retrace her steps, either. She just had to keep walking and hope for the best. This situation was no good at all.

She was just about to throw in the towel and use her magic to leave this Island when she opened one last door and walked into the library after all.

She thought she had been in a completely different part of the castle—and maybe she had been. She couldn't be sure anymore where she was or where she had been coming from.

The library looked completely different this time.

The high shelves loaded with books—the ladders and walkways crisscrossing all the tiers—the tables, chairs, and lecterns—they were the part that looked transparent now.

They wavered in Dark vapor. No monks, dignitaries, and scholars worked and studied in here anymore.

Darklings floated in the vapor between the shelves. They passed through the phantom images of desks and tables. The Darklings were definitely real.

They roared at each other and their tentacles hissed and whipped through the Dark Layer. The Darklings gnashed their fangs at each other and occasionally turned on each other, but mostly they just hovered there in the middle of the library.

The instant she saw them, she knew she had been right when she said outside that the castle was full of Darklings. Who would recognize the Dark better than she would?

Anríq was too good to see the Darklings for what they were. Every phantom in this place was a Darkling in disguise. This whole castle and maybe the whole Island were just one big trap.

The Darkness of this place wouldn't let Eliska retreat. It attracted her with an insatiable pull.

She took a few steps into the room. The Darklings didn't notice her. She was one of them. She belonged to this Darkness.

She drifted into the same blank quiet she experienced after she saved Symphorian.

She halted in the middle of the library—but it wasn't a library. It was a Dark Layer. The phantom image of the bookshelves barely existed for her.

Darklings and other Dark forces passed through the bookshelves as if they weren't there—because they weren't there.

She extended her power outside herself, took hold of those Dark forces, and directed them where she wanted them to go.

In that moment, she saw the Royal Palace of the Verdant Gorges for exactly what it was. She could find her way through the palace easily now. She knew all its Dark twists and turns.

She no longer cared to find her way through it. She wanted to stay here. Her Darkness could finally rest here. She didn't have to contain it or try to stop it from coming out in all kinds of ways.

She directed it into the nearby Darklings, turned them to her will, made them attack and stop attacking, and coordinated Dark vapors in their constant surges to different parts of the Coil.

She started to disappear into the universal dream of all the memories trapped in her head. They made sense here. They merged into one seamless whole.

The pain and tragedy of even the most horrific memories vanished under the tide of all the other memories.

She experienced a simultaneous flashback of her time with the Keepers of the Dawn. She found herself in the training hall with all the other initiates.

She unleashed her Darkness in a whirlwind bout of sparring, acrobatics, and magical bombardments.

A bunch of initiates attacked her and others fought on her side. The two teams assaulted each other and she let herself go in the delight of using her power on some target.

Overwhelming pride, admiration, and approval flooded her from the Rectors and watching students. They all appreciated her. They wanted her with them. She belonged with them in ways she'd never belonged anywhere else.

The feeling became intoxicating....and then she merged back into the awareness of being in this Dark Layer with all these Dark forces. She could be in both places at once.

The pleasure and rightness of all this started to get the better of her. She almost entirely forgot where she was and what she was doing here.

Right then, she caught another fleeting blink of awareness of the castle and its interior layout.

She wouldn't have noticed anything unusual about it—except that now she could detect where Yann and Anríq were.

She located Yann, but her awareness snapped to full focus on Anríq.

He'd somehow found his way back to the high gallery overlooking the atrium. A bunch of Dark forces cornered him against the door.

These weren't Darklings—not full-sized ones. These were smaller and looked more like the grotesque, mutated forms of people, animals, and objects that might have originally dwelt in this castle.

They lashed at him with different weapons clutched in long appendages made unrecognizable by twisting Darkness.

He fought back with his club and axe, but he couldn't fight so many. He didn't even have time to take his hands down to open the door to get away.

Her inner awareness showed her more of those Dark forces coming at him from behind that door. Escaping through it wouldn't help him at all.

There was only one way out. He glanced toward the columns leading to the gallery.

He could jump from the gallery and land in the gardens at the bottom of the atrium, but all the other phantoms down there would probably change into Darklings, too.

More of them went after Yann in a different part of the castle. Eliska didn't wait an instant even to check to find out where he was.

She transported herself out of the library without so much as a backward glance at the Darklings, the monks, the training hall, or anything else. The Keepers of the Dawn's approval meant absolutely nothing to her.

She magicked herself to Anríq's side in a split second, appeared right behind his shoulder, grabbed him by the vest, and magicked both of them away to a remote passage deep in the castle's upper stories.

His wild eyes darted every which way while he tried to understand what the hell just happened. He didn't lower his weapons.

"We gotta get out of here, Anríq!" she panted in his face. "This whole castle is a Dark trap."

"I know!" he gasped. "We have to find Yann—but he's probably lost in the maze somewhere."

"I know how to find him. Here. Take my hand."

Anríq hung his club from his belt, but he kept his axe out. He transferred it to his left hand and clasped hers with his right.

She smiled when she felt how strong and solid his hand was. She never wanted to let go of him.

She faced front to transport both of them across the castle to Yann's location, but just before she did it, she caught Anríq looking at her with the same glowing expression. They were together.

Chapter 15

Yann stabbed his glaive at a Darkling and made it retreat from him. He took that opportunity to dart into another side passage winding deeper into this haunted castle.

The doors, hallways, and rooms kept changing their position. He no longer tried to find his way out. He couldn't. He only hoped Eliska and Anríq found him before these Darklings got to him first.

They weren't the same kind of Darklings he remembered from his other encounters with them. These were smaller and looked more like something the people of this castle might have changed into when instability wiped out their Island.

That must be why the castle, the countryside, and all the Verdant Gorge's buildings and cities remained intact but none of the people were still here. The Coil must have transformed them all into these Darklings.

He charged into the side passage and slammed a heavy wooden door shut behind him. It wasn't strong enough to hold off the Darklings, but they didn't follow him.

He paused there and tried at the same time both to catch his breath and to hold it so he could hear what they were doing on the other side of that door.

He didn't hear anything. Did the Darklings just vanish? It wouldn't be the first time.

They'd attacked him twice before, only to disappear the next time he got away into a different side passage.

He rested his hands on the door panting hard. Sweat dripped from his eyebrows and glued his shirt to his back. He couldn't let himself relax even for a second. The next attack could come at any time.

He passed his sleeve across his face, turned around, and set off down the hall. This was another corridor lined on both sides with elaborate bedrooms.

Most of them had been empty or full of phantom servants straightening the furniture or putting laundry away in drawers and closets.

He didn't see anyone of any status who might have actually lived here—and he definitely didn't see anyone who might be real.

He barely looked into the rooms this time, but he stopped dead in his tracks when he saw a woman sitting on a chair in one of the rooms.

She wore an extravagant gown of deep magenta satin with creamy trim. Diamonds studded long lines of lace running down her bodice and then flaring outward down her skirts.

Her bust swelled over the top of her low-cut corset. A blood-red gemstone necklace surrounded by diamonds nestled right in the heart of her cleavage.

Her milk-white skin ran up to her long, slender neck. Piles of dark curls spilled around her aquiline features.

Bright black eyes sparkled out of her face and she smirked when she saw him gaping at her.

He took a second to make sure he really was seeing what he thought he was seeing. She was no phantom. She was very, very real and unbelievably attractive.

She grasped two handfuls of her skirts to lift them when she stood up from her chair.

She took two steps closer to the door, returned Yann's stare for a minute, and then gave a little scoffing laugh when she let her eyes dip to his uniform. "The Black Watch? What are you here for—to arrest me?"

He struggled to pick his jaw up off the floor. None of the phantoms had ever spoken to him or his friends since the minute they set foot in this castle.

This woman could definitely see him. She looked right at him. "You....you're real!" he gasped.

"What else would I be? How did you get into this castle?" She took another step closer. She kept surveying him up and down from his sweaty hair to his feet and back up to his face. "I've never seen a man of the Watch before."

He opened his mouth to tell her that he wasn't really a full member of the Watch yet, but the words died when she stopped right in front of him.

Her incredible beauty fogged his mind. He'd never stood this close to any woman dressed like this before. Her skin glowed with light. Every inch of her seemed to radiate some kind of magical power all its own.

"Who....who are you?" he stammered.

"I'm Acina....Acina Aminato." She snorted at him. "Don't you know? I'm the King's oldest daughter." She smirked in a wicked sneer. "You should be worshiping me on your knees, peasant."

Her manner remained him so painfully of Marine that he snapped out of it—and her name set his alarm bells ringing. "Are you in any way related to Hubua Aminato? She was the King's oldest daughter, too."

Her eyes darkened into a scowl. "Hubua is my great-great-grand-mother's name. She's been dead for years."

"The Hubua Aminato I'm referring to is the daughter of King Reitor—the King of the Verdant Gorges. He's the...."

"Reitor!" Acina exclaimed. She actually reared away from him. "Reitor is my younger brother! He's only five years old!"

Yann's brain went into a tailspin putting all the puzzle pieces together. Whatever this Island was, it had transported the friends to the time when Hubua's father was just a boy.

Yann wilted when he realized that Acina wouldn't be able to tell him anything about Hubua. No one in this place would be able to tell him anything about Hubua. She hadn't even been born yet.

He nodded more to himself than to Acina. "Thank you for your help. I really appreciate it. I have to go find my friends...."

"Wait!" she called after him and grabbed his arm to stop him from leaving.

"I need to find my friends. Two of them are lost in this castle somewhere...." he began.

She didn't give him a chance to explain. She took his hand, led him out of the room, and into the next room down the same corridor.

She opened a door that didn't look like anything special. She pulled him into a room full of people carousing on beds, couches, chairs, and even on the floor.

Yann stopped dead in his tracks. He couldn't move or even breathe when he saw what all these people were doing.

They kissed in deep, passionate embraces, tangled their bodies into all kinds of shapes of lust and excess, and their moans and sighs drifted through the door to the corridor outside.

His mind took one split second to register that all these people were just as real as Acina was. He could hear every ecstatic moan, every rustle of the ladies' skirts, and every growl of some man sinking his mouth onto his paramour's neck.

Yann's eyes skipped around the room trying to understand. How could these people revel in carnal madness like this when non-existent phantoms and Darklings roamed every other part of the castle?

He didn't get a chance to think it through before Acina rushed him, pushed him against the wall, covered his body with hers, and kissed him to the very bottom of his being.

He got lost in the magnificent sensation of her breasts crushing against his chest. Her mouth dissolved in sweetness when she kissed him—and then he smelled her.

The smell of her breath, her perfume, and some other pungent floral scent coming from her hair—they snapped him out of his trance in a fraction of a second.

His eyes flew open. She smelled, tasted, and looked too different from Marine.

He might have been able to forget her, but his recent experience with the Wishers brought all those memories slamming back to the forefront of his mind.

He pushed Acina away. She smelled, tasted, and looked hypnotically enticing—but not enticing enough to completely obliterate Marine from his mind.

He snatched his glaive and stormed out of the room without looking back. He had to get out of here.

This castle was a trap—a trap just as dangerous and tempting as the Wishers—but not quite tempting enough.

The Wishers gave him something he always wanted. They gave him a life with Marine.

This castle must have been bewitched to tempt him with something else—something on the opposite end of the fantasy spectrum from raising a family with Marine in Middleborough and serving the rest of his life as Commander of the Watch.

He didn't look into any of the surrounding rooms. He didn't want to see what was in them.

He didn't want anything but to find Eliska and Anríq and get the hell out of here. He wouldn't be able to get out unless he did find them.

He came to the end of the corridor, passed through another door, and stepped through.

He had no idea where he would wind up. He froze again when he found himself back in the ceremonial gathering hall.

The same phantom courtiers filled the room talking and gesticulating about something. None of them made any sound.

Yann set out to cross the hall heading back toward the castle entrance. Maybe he should just stay there.

Anríq and Eliska were bound to go back there eventually. They would find him. Then all three of them could leave this cursed place.

He couldn't even be sure they would be able to find him at the castle entrance. The castle might have a way to conceal one or all of them even when they were standing in the same room with each other.

He just had to put his faith in Eliska's magic. What if she really did have the power to defeat the Voyant? If she could do that, she could certainly get the three friends out of this castle.

Chapter 16

Y ann got hallway to the gathering hall doorway before a commotion went through the surrounding phantom courtiers. They all turned to the entrance, moved back to clear the way, and they all bowed.

Yann was the only person still standing up straight, but no one noticed him. He was the only living person in here.

He was still standing there like a dope when the same King he'd seen earlier walked into the hall wearing his splendid clothes and his crown gleaming on his head.

A tall, slender lady glided at his side with her arm through his. She wore a smaller, daintier crown and a long white gown decorated with diamonds and gold thread.

They passed down the hall to the throne where the King sat down under the carved stone crown over his head.

The Queen sat on a much smaller seat next to him.

All the surrounding phantoms stood up and cheered the King and Queen, but it didn't look right without any sound. The whole scene just looked creepy.

Yann studied the King and Queen more closely. This wasn't the King in the White Spire—or was it?

It might as well have been. For some reason, this King bore a striking resemblance to the Voyant Mendicat. Could this be Yimichi Ocuron?

Yann glanced at the queen. She resembled Acina in her facial features, but this young woman had deep chestnut hair slightly lighter than Acina's.

The Queen had deep hazel eyes instead of black eyes and her face seemed thinner and longer. Other than that, they could have been sisters.

They weren't sisters because Acina was Hubua's aunt—but the resemblance could have explained that, too.

These two couldn't have been Yimichi and Hubua because they were both phantoms, but they still fascinated Yann. Could they be carrying the two Shards of Hotha right now?

Neither the King nor the Queen had the Voyant's characteristic glowing halo—nor did either the King or Queen have the purple light shining from their chests the way they did in pictures.

Yann glanced around the hall trying to decide if he should leave or keep watching. Maybe these phantoms would tell him something he didn't already know.

He gave it up and turned away to go back to the castle entrance hall like he planned.

He happened to glance at the throne one last time—and the image changed. The King was the same man, but he no longer wore his crown and royal attire.

He wore the studded leather chest harness, gauntlets, and hair spikes of a Barbarian warrior. He stood nose to nose with another man wearing the same clothes.

They resembled each other enough to be brothers and they yelled at each other in silent fury while a completely different woman tried to pull them apart.

She had fair hair, light skin, and pale eyes completely unlike the queen who just entered the hall with Yimichi. That must have been Hubua—which meant this must be Teyama, the woman he and his brother Noleron fought over.

Noleron shoved Yimichi away and accidentally hit her instead. He sent her staggering and immediately corrected himself to try to help her.

The instant Noleron held out his hands to touch her, Yimichi attacked him, ripped Noleron away from her, and punched him hard enough to send him pitching onto his back.

Yann watched in fascination, but just then, a bunch of phantoms streamed across the room. They got between Yann and the two brothers, passed through Yimichi and Noleron, and when the commotion cleared, Yann didn't see the brothers anymore.

At least, he didn't see Noleron. The phantoms all stampeded to the other side of the hall on some emergency errand.

Yann didn't think too much about what they were doing. They left behind the same phantoms playing out a different scene.

Hubua sat on her seat next to the throne, but she wore a much plainer dress this time and no crown.

She smiled down at Yimichi who stood at the base of the throne. He didn't wear a crown or any of his official robes of state, either. He wore an understated version of the servant's clothes.

Pride and happiness transformed his face into a beaming ray of sunshine. He bent over and then went down on one knee when a little boy charged across the gathering hall and hurtled into Yimichi's arms.

Yimichi burst into a massive grin like he might be laughing in delight, scooped up the boy in his arms, spun him around, and kissed the boy on the cheek.

Yimichi set off across the hall toward the stairs outside. He carried the boy in his arms and bent low near the boy's ear.

Yimichi's mouth moved like he was talking to the boy and then the boy held up some stick he must have found. He answered and showed the stick to his father.

The truth hit Yann between the eyes in a sudden lightning bolt of understanding. Yimichi Ocuron had a son after all. He didn't die without an heir.

Who else in the world would the Voyant Mendicat be looking for if not the one person destined to take the Shard of Hotha? It all made sense.

Yann could finally put his own fears to rest. The Voyant wasn't looking for him. Yann already knew who his father was. Yvan Dilnao was no King.

The Voyant couldn't be looking for Eliska, either. He had to be looking for a man. Yimichi's son would be fully grown by now.

The realization exploded in his mind. He had to tell Anríq and Eliska about this no matter what. He turned around—and froze when a bunch of people came toward him.

These were more real people. None of them were the same people he'd seen upstairs, thank the stars, but they were very, very real.

They all wore the robes of state and they surrounded him. Two men took hold of his arms, lifted the glaive out of his hands, and steered him toward the steps leading up to the throne.

The sight of real people all of a sudden stunned him. He didn't realize what was happening until they parked him right in front of the throne.

They draped a gold-trimmed robe over his shoulders, pushed him down into the seat, and set a crown on his head. It was the same crown he'd just seen Yimichi wearing.

Yann's mind switched off. This couldn't be real. This was just part of the illusion. He wasn't Yimichi's heir. He couldn't be.

That phantom boy he'd just seen in Yimichi's arms was old enough to remember his father. Yann would have remembered Yvan ever standing with him and talking to him in a gathering hall like this.

As soon as the courtiers put the crown on his head, the crowd erupted in cheers. Their voices throbbed off the walls in a deafening surge of noise. This was all real. These people were hailing Yann as their king.

He shook that out of his mind. This wasn't real. None of these people were real. They weren't any more real than Acina had been upstairs.

He stood up, but before he could move, the crowd parted. A beautiful dark-haired woman glided down the aisle between all the dignitaries and courtiers.

She wore a pure white down emblazoned with sparkling gems. Everything about her gleamed with magnificence.

She floated up the steps, dropped onto one knee in front of Yann, and bowed her head while the nearby courtiers put a crown on her head, too.

She rose to her feet, her eyes drifted upward to meet his, and she eased over to stand next to him—right in front of the seat where Hubua had just been sitting.

Yann turned to stare at the woman—his Queen.

That one glance snapped him back to reality. She looked like Marine, but she wasn't Marine. It was Acina.

He didn't even take the time to explain himself—or to take off the crown—or to do anything. He only made sure to grab his glaive before he marched out of the hall heading for the castle entrance.

Chapter 17

Eliska glanced into the gathering hall. "Yann was just in here a second ago. I saw him. Now he's gone again."

"He isn't gone," Anríq told her. "He's right there."

He pointed up at the big throne at the end of the room. Yann sat there wearing magnificent robes and a crown on his head—the same crown Eliska had seen the King of the Verdant Gorges wearing earlier.

She couldn't speak from surprise. She could only follow Anríq into the gathering hall. They walked straight through the phantoms and halted in front of the throne.

The King wore a beard just like the other man, but this was definitely Yann. He looked older—and he was a phantom. Eliska could make out the detail of the carved stone seat behind his transparent body.

"What do you think it means?" she whispered.

"I don't think it means anything," Anríq murmured back. "Everything in this place is an illusion. The castle is showing us this to distract us from finding the real Yann. We know he isn't a King—especially not a King in the Hallowed Vales. He's a poor Watchman from Middleborough—just like his father."

Eliska couldn't stop staring at Yann. He sat so straight and proud on that throne. His eyes traced over all the phantoms in front of him—as if he really was their King and in charge of this ghostly realm.

A beautiful dark-haired woman sat on the seat next to him. She wore a long white gown encrusted with gems and gold thread. A dainty gold crown sat on top of her head.

She sure was beautiful, and in front of Eliska's eyes, he turned, clasped his Queen's hand, and smiled at her with a face shining with love and admiration.

Eliska gulped. Did this mean the real Yann was trapped in another illusion?

"We have to get him out of here," she decided and started to climb the steps. Anríq stepped up there, too, so he must have been thinking the same thing.

They got five feet away from Yann when a river of phantoms shrieked through the back wall behind the throne.

They vaporized straight through Yann and the woman sitting next to him. Before Eliska could think twice, all those phantoms changed into real, live, solid, breathing, yelling people.

Men and women wearing all the finery of the King's court attacked Eliska and Anríq, tackled both of them backward, bowled them down the steps, and all those people transformed into the same small, mutated Darklings that attacked Anríq earlier.

Eliska didn't have time to raise her staff or even to think about why this was happening. She unloaded an almighty blast of magic, hurled all the Darklings away from herself and Anríq, and launched herself to her feet just as the Darklings came charging back for a second assault.

That moment gave her one fleeting glimpse of the throne against the back wall. It was empty. Yann was gone.

She barely unloaded her magic a second time before the Darklings collided with her. They struck a field of magic between her and them, but they came too hard and too fast.

They knocked her back toward the exit—toward the castle entrance hall. They were trying to push her out of the room.

Yann wasn't here anymore, but she sensed him getting farther away from her. She panicked and unleashed an even more brutal thunderclap of magic against the Darklings in front of her.

She evaporated them out of existence, but the noise and commotion in other parts of the castle told her all she needed to know. More Darklings were coming after her and Anríq.

He grabbed his weapons and turned sideways to face the enemy on that side while he and Eliska backed toward the door.

She didn't know where she would go to find Yann this time. She would have to consult her projection to find him, but she had to keep blasting to her right and then again into the gathering hall to stop the Darklings from getting the better of her.

She glanced into the gathering hall to look at the throne one last time—on one last hopeless chance that Yann would still be there.

Instead, she saw dozens of Darklings streaming into the hall from both sides. They took the places of all the courtiers who had just been bowing to Yann's phantom.

She raised her hand and leveled all those Darklings in a heartbeat, but more came out of the woodwork. She and Anríq backed up a little more into the castle entrance hall.

"Take us out of the castle!" Anríq yelled over his shoulder. "We can't stay in here!"

"We are NOT leaving without Yann!" she bellowed back.

"We'll come back inside when we know where he is! You can track him from outside the castle and then you can magick us to wherever he is. You'll be able to find him without us getting into....."

He had to stop talking to smash more Darklings away with his club. He and Eliska couldn't talk for a second. The Darklings crowded too thickly for the two travelers to go anywhere.

There was only one place left to go—outside.

She lunged for him to grab him so she could magick both of them outside. Her heart bled to leave Yann behind even for a few minutes, but she had to do it.

She seized a fistful of Anríq's vest. He never stopped fighting the Darklings even to turn around to tell her that he was ready.

The instant she touched him, she activated her magic to send them out of the castle—and at the same moment, Yann darted out of a side passage, charged into the entrance hall, and barreled straight into the ring of her spell.

He was running so fast that he collided with Anríq, but it was too late. The spell blinked the three friends outside into the giant courtyard where they started.

She planned to stop there long enough for the three friends to regroup and maybe talk about where they should go next.

The instant the three friends set foot on solid ground, a deep rumble went through the castle behind them.

She glanced over her shoulder in time to see one of the high towers crumble from the top of its pointed roof all the way down the ground.

The mountains on either side erupted in mayhem and the upheaval took hold of every building in the courtyard.

She didn't waste her breath explaining what she was going to do. She dove for the two boys, grabbed them both, and magicked all three of them out of the Hallowed Vales entirely.

She didn't think about where she would take them. She only knew she couldn't stay here.

She surrounded all three of them in a protective ball and shot it straight up. The sky was the safest place in all this chaos.

The ball broke through another Layer and blasted into another clear blue sky full of clouds.

This one hung over an enormous city teeming with people and trade, but this wasn't one of the advanced cities of machines the friends had seen elsewhere.

This looked like another city like those the friends just left in the Hallowed Vales.

Everything about this Island looked stable, peaceful, and untouched by the chaos going on elsewhere in the Coil.

Eliska hovered her ball there for a minute before she lowered it to the ground.

Anríq stopped her. "Don't put us down here. This is another trap."

"How do you figure?" Yann asked. "It looks fine to me."

"That's the problem. The whole Coil is falling apart. If we see a stable Island, it's probably a trap." Anríq glanced at Eliska. "You're the one who said there were no more stable Islands. So what is this—another distraction?"

She scanned the surroundings. She didn't lower the ball.

"There has to be a way to....." She barely got the words out before the Voyant appeared in the air right in front of her.

She took one look at him—and knew. She could defeat him.

All her reservations about using her Darkness went out the window. To hell with it. What did she really have to lose? What did anyone in the whole Coil have to lose?

None of them would survive if she didn't destroy him.

She would never get to spend any time with Anríq—or get to know her own brother. They would all wind up dead if she didn't end this now.

Yann was right about that. Someone had to end it. She might be the only person left alive in the Coil who could do it.

She didn't explain to them what she was going to do. Yann told her not to hesitate and she didn't.

Chapter 18

Eliska released her protective ball, sent out one tiny tendril of magic to lower the two boys to the ground, and hurled herself at the Voyant with all her might.

She expected him to lash out and he didn't disappoint her. He struck her hard with a devastating blow, but she just kept right on coming.

She let her Darkness flow out of her—and once she started, she couldn't stop. She didn't try to stop. Yann was right about that, too. Using it for something felt unimaginably good.

She flung her arms out to both sides, bellowed at the Voyant, and let all her magic blast from her eyes, nose, mouth, ears, and skin.

It exploded her apart and smashed the Voyant's halo with brutal force. The collision of forces set off a catastrophic boom that ricocheted back and swatted her down hard on the ground.

She fell with bone-crushing force that stunned her just long enough for Yann and Anríq to get to her.

Anríq sprang in front of her brandishing his weapons at the Voyant, but Anríq didn't attack. He already knew he couldn't. Yann hauled Eliska to her feet. She couldn't think straight.

She blundered wherever he steered her....and realized he was running away into the Island landscape behind Anríq's back. They were running away from the Voyant.

The Voyant's arrival caused the same Layer collapse it always did. A breaking wave of chaos radiated out from his halo, tore the landscape to pieces, and demolished the glorious city in minutes.

Anríq retreated a dozen yards, turned on his heel, and took off running after Yann and Eliska.

She fought her brain back into gear trying to decide what to do, but right then, the instability overtook the party.

Chaos swept around them, brought the city crashing down in an avalanche of rubble and mangled bodies, and giant fissures cracked through the earth getting perilously close to the three friends.

Anríq fell farther behind. Eliska tried to turn back to help him, but Yann wouldn't let her. He kept half-pushing, half-dragging her forward to stay one step ahead of the upheaval.

A wall of disintegrating boulders pelted at the friends from farther north as whole mountain ranges erupted into millions of whizzing arrows.

All those particles came to life and went after the friends as well as everyone else who tried to flee the city before the Voyant completely wiped it out.

Eliska glanced behind her only once. Her stomach dropped into her shoes when she saw the Voyant soaring after the friends.

He completely ignored the city. Its destruction came as a natural consequence of his presence.

The wave of instability followed underneath him getting closer and closer to where Anríq hung back to protect Yann's and Eliska's retreat.

The instability surrounded Anríq. He clubbed it away again and again, but he couldn't keep up with it all.

The Voyant crawled up behind the party closing the gap by the second. Eliska couldn't deny anymore that he really must be trying to kill the three friends for real this time.

At that moment, at the moment when she turned back, an ejection of brilliant golden magic blasted out of the Voyant's halo. It couldn't have happened by accident.

It slammed Anríq down hard on the ground and knocked his weapons out of his hands.

She spun all the way around to go back for him, but Yann caught her and stopped her.

Time stood still as the Voyant came to a stop directly above Anríq. The Voyant's halo glowed brighter. That light cast an eerie radiance over the surrounding mayhem.

Eliska didn't hear the rumbles and explosions anymore. She didn't even hear Yann yelling in her ear.

Something snapped in her head. The Voyant was about to kill Anríq.

She didn't want to fight the Voyant anymore. She never wanted to see him again. She just wanted him gone.

She didn't even try to break out of Yann's hands before she unloaded her Darkness into the world.

The impact hurled Yann away and launched her toward the Voyant. She magicked herself instantaneously between him and Anríq just as another torch of power shot from his halo.

It would have pulverized Anríq to nothing, but it hit her instead. Another shattering boom went off, but it didn't flatten her the way this time.

She deflected all the Voyant's power back to him exactly the same way he deflected hers back to her.

He did the same thing this time, but she was all finished playing games—with everyone.

She didn't tap her Darkness or even try to use it. She just dropped the veil standing between her and the pure embodiment of Darkness that had been her true self all this time.

It started all the way back when she fell into the Dark river—back when she asked Wesh to use her magic to take the Darkness from Anríq—back when she healed Barsali—back when she saved Symphorian—back when the Keepers of the Dawn tried to use her for their own purposes.

All those moments gave her the power she needed. Yann proved himself right once again. Every awful thing that happened to her turned out to be a good thing. She wouldn't have been able to defeat the Voyant without each of those experiences.

The hellish bombardment of his magic against her only made her Darkness stronger. She released herself completely into the Dark and surrounded his halo in Dark power.

His halo throbbed faster and brighter trying to break the field. He couldn't even touch her. Whatever magic the Shard of Hotha gave him couldn't scratch the surface of how Dark she could actually get.

She didn't scratch the surface, either. She could squash him easily.

She started to strip away his halo to expose the man inside. Her many experiences with him in the past—all the information she'd gleaned from countless sources—her instincts told her the secret truth of the Voyant Mendicat.

He was an imp. Neither he nor Yimichi Ocuron had any magic—not until they took the Shards.

As soon as she destroyed the Voyant's halo, he would be nothing but a helpless man with no way to defend himself.

Then she would enjoy watching him writhe. Her Darkness could have all kinds of fun with a victim like that.

His halo started to flicker and diminish, but at that moment, another almighty blast went off somewhere.

It didn't come from the Voyant's halo. It seemed to come from everywhere at once. It might have come from the Coil itself.

A withering blow struck her hard enough to throw her off her feet, but her power caught her and held her up off the ground and free from the chaos tearing the landscape apart.

She saw instantly that she wasn't in the same Layer anymore. The Voyant might have destroyed the Layer completely.

She hung suspended by her magic in a whirling chaos Layer full of Dark vapors, enormous Darklings, and massive forces crashing, tumbling, and bombarding her at the same time.

Yann and Anríq weren't in the same Layer anymore. They weren't anywhere anymore.

The Voyant didn't wait an instant before he came after her. She took the space of one heartbeat to locate Yann and Anríq in the Coil. Her Darkness could read the Coil so much more easily than she ever could without it.

Both boys were in Dark Layers surrounded by deadly forces, but that wasn't the worst of it.

The Voyant had somehow divided himself into three. Three identical halos hovered in front of Yann, Anríq, and Eliska.

His magic broadcast across the three Layers to each of his three halos while he orchestrated those forces to attack the two boys from all sides.

Anríq held his own, but Yann was already starting to fail after only a few short seconds. He whirled and parried with his glaive, but he wouldn't last long in the wild Layers by himself.

Right at that moment, five massive Darklings moved in on Anríq. He destroyed one with a blow of his club before another hit him from behind.

It swatted its tentacle at him from behind, sent him flying across the Layer, and he slammed into a giant rock face that shattered from the impact.

He hurtled through it into a different Layer where even more Dark forces surrounded him. He wouldn't last long, either.

The Voyant went after him. The Voyant's halo affected the Dark Layers the same way it affected Islands and landscapes in the Coil.

His halo agitated the Dark forces to an epic pitch. They zoomed faster, struck harder, and each Layer disintegrated into a deadly churning grinder of debris, monsters, shrapnel, pieces of landscapes, Dark vapors, and elemental forces converging to annihilate the three friends.

The Voyant inflicted the same assault on Eliska, but her Darkness retaliated beyond anything she ever thought possible.

She didn't care about herself. She just wanted to protect Yann and Anríq.

All the memories of everyone in the Coil came back to her in the blink of an eye.

Each of these people deserved to live as much as the two boys. These people deserved to have her defend them with every ounce of her power even if it turned her Dark.

Most of those people were already dead, but plenty more survived in the Coil.

She extended both hands toward the Voyant, surrounded his halo with her magic, and ripped his halo the shreds. Her Darkness invaded him, found the part of him that had no magic, and demolished him to a pulp in seconds.

She stripped all his magic away from him and sucked it all into herself. It made her unimaginably powerful, but she just kept feeding it back to him no matter how hard he tried to defend himself.

He attacked harder and unloaded another equally brutal assault on her, but even that only made her stronger. She raised her hand, turned it palm downward, and swatted him downward with bone-crushing force.

Chapter 19

Yann picked himself up off the ground, dusted himself off, and looked around before he realized where he was.

A minute ago, he'd been trapped alone in a chaos Layer battling Dark forces with just his glaive.

The Voyant had been hovering a short distance away sending one Dark force after another to attack him.

Yann had been preparing himself to make his last stand when a devastating impact smashed him out of the Layer. He landed hard on the ground right here.

He blinked when he saw that he was back in the same Island where the friends first confronted the Voyant—the city Island the Voyant destroyed when he attacked the party.

The city lay in ruins, but Yann could already see people walking through the streets trying to put their lives back together.

No instability tore up the landscape now. The area sounded ghostly quiet after all that noise.

Anríq got to his feet next to Yann, picked up his axe, and both boys looked around.

Yann froze when she saw Eliska standing not far away. She kept her back to both boys and her head hung down.

Yann's blood burst into flame when he saw a man lying on the ground in front of her. It was the Voyant.

His halo no longer surrounded him and he no longer glared out at the world with his old expression of granite fury.

Blood saturated the white robe that covered his frail, bony body. He no longer looked strong, sturdy, or intimidating.

His features trembled all over the place and his whole body quaked. He tried to turn over, collapsed on his face in the dirt, and then puked right there in front of Eliska.

Yann's driving determination to kill the Voyant took over. Yann had been pushing himself all this time to stop this madness. Now he had the Voyant lying helpless right here.

Yann snatched his glaive off the ground, stormed over to the Voyant, and raised the weapon to drive the blade down into the Voyant's heart.

The Voyant saw him coming, tried to lean back to look up at Yann, and lost his strength again. The Voyant collapsed onto his back and sprawled there—right where his chest lay exposed for Yann to drive in the killing blow.

Yann tensed all his muscles to strike, but Anríq caught up with him a split second before Yann delivered the final stroke.

Eliska dove in front of Yann, too. She wouldn't have been able to stop him without using her magic, but she didn't have to. Anríq's strength overpowered Yann and held him back.

"Don't, Yann!" Anríq yelled. "He's helpless! Leave him alone!"

"Get your hands off me!!" Yann threw his elbows at both of them, but he couldn't break Anríq's grip. "Get off me! He killed my father!"

"Don't hurt him, Yann!" Eliska told him. "He's already dying."

"Do you think I care?!" he roared. "He wiped out Middleborough and he destroyed Marine! He's the one who has been doing all of this!"

"I know!" Eliska stood back first. Her presence did nothing to hold Yann back. Anríq did that by himself.

She turned to look down at the Voyant. "We have to heal him."

Anríq started to slacken his grip on Yann. Yann lunged forward again, but this time, Eliska held up her hand and stopped him with her magic.

Anríq jumped between Yann and the Voyant, and like something out of a nightmare, Anríq raised his axe and pushed it against Yann's chest to shove him away. "He's a human being and he's dying," Anríq snarled. "Lay one finger on him and I swear I'll kill you myself."

"This bastard destroyed my life!!" Yann raged. "You are NOT going to heal him!! We came here to kill him, remember?"

"We came here to defeat him," Eliska corrected. "He has been defeated. He's defenseless and broken. He'll die anyway. He might be able to tell us where to get the Shards."

"You can't be serious!" Yann countered. "He's the one who has been stopping us from getting the Shards—and you want to ask him for help?! You're insane!"

Neither Anríq nor Eliska answered him. They only gave him another hard look.

Yann's mind shut down when he saw his two closest friends glaring at him like that—as if he was their enemy instead of this villain on the ground.

Anríq turned away first, squatted down next to the Voyant, and laid both hands on him.

The Voyant tried hopelessly to turn onto his stomach and push himself up on his hands and knees.

His limbs failed and he fell into the dirt again. Blood and puke dribbled from his lips. Dirt stuck to his face, got in his hair, and smeared in the blood on his clothes.

Anríq placed his hands on the Voyant's back and shoulder. Yann didn't see what Anríq did, but the Voyant shrieked in pain as soon as Anríq made contact with him.

The Voyant arched back in an agonizing spasm, buckled onto his back, and lay there contorting in misery.

"I can't heal him," Anríq mumbled. "Help me, Eliska."

She turned her back on Yann. He seethed in fury, but he saw already that they wouldn't let him near the Voyant.

Anríq's threat carried more weight than anything. Yann would never doubt Anríq's word on something like that.

Yann wanted a lot of things out of life. Anríq as his enemy wasn't one of them.

Eliska walked around the Voyant to his other side and placed her hand on his forehead.

She didn't have to close her eyes. A bright glow radiated outward from her hand. Yann had never seen her do that before.

Anríq kept pouring his magic into the Voyant's body. He reacted so much worse this time.

He burst into excruciating screams of such obvious pain that Yann took a step back. The sound automatically made him feel sorry for the Voyant. He really was dying.

He thrashed so badly that both Anríq and Eliska had to back off. They stood up and watched the Voyant jerk back and forth on the ground.

His arms and legs twisted in hideous contortions—and then a strong purple-pink glow started to shine in the middle of his chest.

The process only seemed to wrack him with more brutal pains as the light shone brighter. It widened....and then all three friends stared as a glowing purplish gem appeared beneath his skin.

It covered most of his chest. It must have been at least a foot long and eight inches wide. Multi-faceted prisms of light flashed inside it.

It glimmered there beneath the surface and then emerged. It migrated through his skin, through his clothes, hung suspended directly above his chest, and then dropped into the dirt next to him.

It fell on Anríq's side of the Voyant's body. Anríq jumped back to get away from the Shard.

The sight stunned Yann so much that he didn't even hear the Voyant screaming anymore. None of the friends moved. They stared down at the Shard lying at their feet. It couldn't be this easy.

It wasn't. Anríq bent over to pick it up, but it vanished within two seconds of hitting the ground.

He closed his hands on empty air and then straightened up to stare down at the spot.

None of the friends moved. Yann couldn't even think. They came so close to getting one of the Shards only for it to vanish right out from under their hands.

A rasping croaky voice brought all of them back to reality real quick. "You can get it now......"

The three friends all looked up at the Voyant. He no longer thrashed and screamed nor did he try to turn over. He no longer seemed to have the strength for that.

He no longer seemed to have the strength even to keep breathing. Every breath cost him a massive effort, but he fought through it to choke out his dying words.

His eyes drifted partially shut before he dragged them open.....and he locked his gaze on Yann alone. "The King in the White Spire....." the Voyant husked. "Yimichi Ocuron.....he had a son......Oberion Oc uron....."

"Where is he?" Yann asked. *"Who* is he?"

"He loved a girl.....a princess....She was born an imp.....the daughter of imps.....She had a brother who was born a magic-user....he turned to the Dark......she developed a pathological fear of magic......." He gulped and his eyes rolled back in his head before he rallied enough to go on. "She refused to take the Shard.....so Oberion ran away with her. They vanished into the Coil......He took the name Yvan Dilnao.....and lived with her in a country town hoping no one would ever find th em......."

The world dropped out from under Yann's feet again. How many more of these blows could he really take?

The Voyant dragged his eyes open and glanced around to include all three of the friends. "Yimichi died.....and I had no one to take the second Shard.....I searched for Oberion everywhere.....The Coil became unstable. It separated Yvan and Alexiane and you were all lost in the chaos.....I searched for years....but the Shard.....it kills its host if one person carries it alone. No one can survive without an affiliate.....it's been killing me ever since....It's the only thing that has been keeping me alive.....I can die.....now that it's gone......You and your sister will take the Shards in my place.....There is no one else....."

He went limp on the ground and his eyes drifted shut.

"Wait!" Yann yelled out. "You have to help us find the Shards. How can we take them if we can't even find them?"

The Voyant didn't answer. His chest rose and fell a few more times before he lay perfectly still on the ground.

"So much for him helping us find the Shards," Yann grumbled.

He looked up at his two friends. They were no closer to finding the Shards now than they were before.

He really wished now that they had let him kill the Voyant. Yann could have lived his entire life without ever finding out that he was

Yimichi Ocuron's grandson—the one true heir destined to take the Shard of Hotha and rule the Coil.

At least he wouldn't do it alone. Eliska would be there with him.

He would just have to find another woman to marry. He really didn't care who it was. It could be anyone as long as she gave him an heir. Anything would be better than dying without an heir.

Dying without an heir meant the surviving affiliate would become another Voyant. The whole instability cycle would start all over again until the Voyant found another affiliate.

Yann couldn't let that happen. He would marry the first suitable woman who stumbled across his path. If she offered him some strategic alliance with the Kings in other Layers, so much the better, but that wasn't a requirement.

He would marry the kitchen maid if he had to.

He was just starting to open his mouth to ask Eliska to find the White Spire when the Voyant's body started to glow again.

This didn't come from any halo nor did it come from the Shard in his chest. The Shard wasn't there anymore.

The glow came from his whole body. Every pore of his wrinkled skin blasted out blinding light.

Yann squinted—and then the light flashed outward in a blinding starburst that transported the three friends away.

The destroyed city, the Voyant's body, and the surrounding mountains all vanished.

Chapter 20

The three friends appeared on a high hilltop miles outside of another wrecked city somewhere.

This one hadn't been destroyed by fire. It looked like it might have been pulverized by some kind of aerial bombardment.

A few buildings still raised their tattered, wrecked frames to the sky with mounds of rubble lying around their foundations.

This had been another city like the one the friends just left. Broken wagons, dead horses and oxen, and spilled cargo lay all over the streets.

Dead bodies of people lay mummified in the sun or stripped to skeletons. Whatever destroyed this city must have hit it a long time ago.

A prickle went up Yann's scalp when he saw the White Spire in the distance. It still looked blackened like it had been in all the burned landscapes where the friends had seen it before.

The four windows looked out to the four directions from the top turret, but the windows weren't empty anymore. The Shard of Hotha shone in the window and cast a bright purple-pink beacon all the way to the hilltop.

The sight of the Shard stabbed Yann in the heart. "This is it," he murmured. "This was the way. The Shard is ready for someone to come and take it. We just have to go over there and get it."

Anríq squinted at the surroundings. "I don't see the second Shard. How do we get both of them?"

"The Voyant is dead," Eliska pointed out. "Both Shards must be in the spire. If we go for one, we must be able to find them both."

"Why wasn't the second Shard there before?" Anríq asked. "I don't understand what was stopping him from just giving you the Shard."

"I don't understand it, either, and I don't really care," Yann interjected. "I'm going to get it."

"We all have to go," Eliska replied. "You'll need all our help to get into the spire."

"Make sure you get both Shards," Anríq warned. "Don't take one Shard and leave the other. You would become the new Voyant if you did that."

"I won't," Yann replied. "That's the last thing I want to do. Just remember what I said. As soon as we find the Shards, you two will take them. You two should be together. It's better that way."

"Then what will happen to you?" Eliska croaked.

He found himself smiling at her. "You don't worry about me. I'll be just fine once you two take the Shards and stabilize the Coil. Who knows? Maybe I'll even be able to come and visit you."

Her features pinched and she looked away.

He couldn't think about that anymore. His attention always migrated back to the Shard. It cast its light across the landscape.

That light called him to break into the spire, find the Shards, and finish this once and for all.

The Voyant's death didn't accomplish that, but at least he got them here.

The friends didn't have to worry about him anymore. This was between them and the spire.

Yann set off walking down the hill. He made it a hundred yards before he realized that he hadn't acknowledged to his friends that they would all go together.

They followed him anyway, but that didn't matter anymore. Nothing existed but him and the Shard.

The friends made it to the bottom of the hill. Nothing happened until they put their feet on level ground.

As soon as they did that, instability hit the city. The same combination of landscape upheavals, buildings morphing into monsters, random objects flying around, and deadly projectiles looping out of every surface came at the friends to stop them from entering.

The eruption started in the countryside outside the city before the friends got near the outermost buildings.

Grass sprouted out of the ground too fast and grew too tall. Pieces of sod blasted at the friends, tried to club them to the ground, and then changed into hideous shapes with fanged mouths.

Anríq and Eliska flanked Yann on a dead run for the city edge. Yann should have hesitated to go in there.

The same mayhem took hold of the entire city. The whole landscape seethed with life.

The forces in there attacked each other long before the friends made it to the city's outer neighborhoods.

Yann never stopped running. Only the Shard mattered.

The landscape didn't collapse and disintegrate. That somehow made sense to Yann now.

The Layer wouldn't collapse. This whole Layer existed so someone could get into the White Spire to take the Shard of Hotha.

The Voyant sent the friends here so they could take the two Shards. It was now or never. If not now, then when?

Yann sprinted between houses, dodged projectiles spinning toward his head, and dove into some tangled neighborhoods trying to get as deep inside the city as possible.

Anríq and Eliska flanked him all the way. They unloaded their magic on both sides, but not even Eliska's power could do much against this chaos.

She and Anríq carved a narrow path through the mayhem—just big enough for Yann to get through without losing his life.

Creatures, distorted animals, and fallen wagons came to life to assault the party.

Eliska erected a shield of protection around the three friends, but the continuous bombardment kept breaking it. She had to keep reestablishing it every few seconds.

"This way!" Anríq bellowed and veered to the left.

Yann followed him by pure force of instinct. He couldn't even see the White Spire or the Shard in the confusion. Were the friends even close to it?

Anríq dodged into one of the nearby buildings. It stayed remarkably intact despite the upheaval all around the friends.

For some reason, the buildings, streets, and overall city structure didn't change when everything came to life, moved out of place, and fell apart.

The buildings stayed in the same places and even mostly kept the same shapes even as the walls morphed and distorted in ever-changing waves of shifting faces, bodies, appendages, and objects blasting out of the surfaces.

The streets didn't change their layout, either. Piles of rubble, debris, and destroyed objects launched off the ground, joined the general whirlwind of stuff attacking and getting attacked, and then fell in different places.

All that stuff blocked certain streets and then fell somewhere else to block others and leave others clear. The route through the city changed, but not the streets themselves.

Anríq charged into one of the buildings. Its whole lower structure had been bombed out with half its tower blasted off.

Rooms and entire floors lay exposed to the outside world. Random twisted remains of furniture and carpet hanging off the obliterated floors.

All the windows, doors, and even the ground-level walls had exploded outward into the surrounding streets.

A dozen columns held up the rest of the structure and left a path through the building from one street to the other.

Anríq sprinted through the downstairs, came out on the other side, and turned to his right to continue on the way to the White Spire. At least someone in the group remembered where it was.

Yann and Eliska followed him into the building. A single intact wall section covered that side of the ground floor. They lost sight of him for a split second before they turned the corner, but he wasn't there anymore.

None of the friends could have seen what lay beyond that wall. Yann didn't see any way the area could have rearranged itself fast enough to hide Anríq from them.

Eliska spun in both directions looking everywhere for him. "Anríq!" she shrieked.

She turned back to dart into the building. Yann tried to grab her to keep her with him. He couldn't lose her, too.

She dodged too fast, came back, and then turned left trying to find Anríq everywhere.

Her voice spiked into the hysterical range when she ran all around the area calling for him. She came rushing back to Yann and opened her Coil projection.

"We have to find him!" she panted. "He could be lost in this city."

Yann caught her by the shoulders and pulled her up in front of him. "We can't! We have to go after the Shard. Use your head! Anríq is still in this city somewhere and he'll be heading for the Shard, too. We'll find him farther along. Come on! We don't have time to look for him now."

"No! We have to!"

Yann shook her a little too hard. "You aren't thinking clearly! He would want us to go after the Shard—and he'll go after it. He'll meet us there! Come on. Looking for him now will put all of us in danger. Let's go."

He didn't give her a chance to argue. He grabbed her arm and pulled her deeper into the city—away from the place where Anríq disappeared.

Chapter 21

Eliska glanced left and right trying to see Anríq anywhere in the mayhem. She kept getting distracted by fighting all the surfaces, shapes, creatures, Dark forces, and random objects that came out to attack her and Yann.

Yann fought back amazingly well considering he only had his glaive to defend himself. His fighting style had improved significantly since he left Middleborough.

He didn't hesitate to stab and even club anything that threatened him. He couldn't damage anything made of stone and sometimes even things made out of wood.

He inflicted plenty of damage on creatures and even managed to save Eliska from attack a few times.

The two travelers made their way onto what might have once been a main thoroughfare through the city. A strip of garden separated two broad avenues. Overturned benches, ruined fountains, flattened gazebos, and torn-up footpaths wound through destroyed flowerbeds and shattered trees.

All that stuff ripped itself out of place, came to life, and joined the upheaval. The whole area seethed with movement as everything out there attacked everything else.

Yann and Eliska battled their way up a side street getting closer to the thoroughfare. The noise coming from out there escalated to a deafening roar.

Eliska held back, but she had to keep going when Yann pushed forward. For an imp with the least ability to protect himself, he forged ahead much more enthusiastically than either Eliska or Anríq.

She and Yann drew level with two buildings flanking the side street. The two travelers looked out on a scene of chaos as deadly as anything she had seen in the Coil so far.

This Layer didn't collapse. She couldn't think the Voyant might have done this for some reason of his own. She understood him much better, now that she'd actually used her Darkness to defeat him.

He didn't do any of this for any reason of his own. His only aim in all of this was to find Yimichi's son.

When he couldn't, the Voyant went looking for Yimichi's grandson and granddaughter.

The Voyant already knew he was dying. He started dying the minute Yimichi died without an heir.

Everything else had been a result of the Coil's instability. Eliska couldn't hate the Voyant for that. She couldn't hate him for any of it.

Some bizarre aspect of the Shards' interaction must have arranged this Layer the way it was. This was the quest—to get inside the White Spire and take the two Shards.

This Layer—whatever it was—this was the obstacle a person had to overcome to take the Shard. How it worked didn't matter, but at least the Layer wouldn't collapse.

She, Yann, and Anríq would stay here until they either took both Shards or they all died trying. This was the final bridge the three of them had to cross. There was no other road to take.

The Voyant wouldn't have sent the three friends here for any other reason. He never had been their enemy.

He was actually her great-uncle. He'd been searching for her and Yann ever since Yimichi died. The Voyant spent his last years alive doing everything possible to save the Coil.

His final act in life had been to send the three friends here. He wouldn't have done that except to help them.

The Coil itself was their only enemy. The Coil's power was the only adversary the friends had to defeat to accomplish their mission.

She pushed forward to follow Yann into the thoroughfare, but right then, she passed another alley between two buildings.

She spotted movement down there and caught sight of Anríq in battle against a whole bunch of people.

He fought them single-handedly, swung his club at those closest to him, and set off deep booms of magic that shook the surrounding buildings.

He knocked his enemies back and then slammed his club down on the ground. It shattered the paving stones underfoot, created deep fissures, and all his attackers tumbled into the abyss below the surface.

"Anríq!!" Eliska yelled out and charged forward to intercept him, but he didn't hear her.

He sprinted away heading farther down the same street—away from Yann and Eliska. She barely made it twenty feet before he veered around another corner and disappeared again.

Yann caught up with her. "We gotta keep going! Come on!"

He grabbed her arm again. She dragged her heels and kept casting backward glances toward the place where Anríq disappeared.

He wasn't there anymore. She looked anywhere and everywhere for him, but she didn't see him. How could he just disappear like this?

He just didn't just run off. She didn't believe that for a second. He would have tried everything to find his way back to Yann and Eliska. Was this another mind trick?

She glanced around at the surroundings. Was this Island another maze—a vast, chaotic, city-sized maze? Was that the quest?

She had to put the question out of her mind when she and Yann got to the thoroughfare. Wagons, creatures, windows, and skeletons battled out there.

Trees uprooted themselves from the central garden strip. They danced around on their roots while their crowns and branches transformed into grasping arms wielding all kinds of weapons.

Some of those trees even used magic against each other and other living plants, objects, and Dark forces caught in the battle.

Eliska got distracted by the remains of a gazebo farther down the thoroughfare. It must have gotten pulverized in whatever cataclysm destroyed this city.

All the sticks, boards, and hardware that held the gazebo together lay flattened on the ground. Now all that stuff picked itself up, put itself together in a comic facsimile of its former shape, and bumped along the ground trying to attack anything that came near it.

The gazebo went after a distorted angel that tore itself away from a carved marble fountain nearby. The two magical combatants went at each other tearing, punching, and gnashing their teeth.

Right then, Eliska spotted Anríq running across the thoroughfare to the left.

He charged into the garden strip and attacked an enormous flower that had been growing on one of the trees.

The flower twisted itself off its branch, grew to an enormous size, and fluttered around in the mayhem getting batted here and there by the lashing tree branches.

Anríq ran over to the flower, clubbed it to the ground, and then went after the same tree himself.

Eliska whipped around and launched herself in his direction. "Anríq!!" she yelled out again.

Yann caught her and held her back. "Stop! That isn't Anríq!"

"What are you talking about?!" she bellowed. "He's right there! You're the one who said we had to stay together!"

"That isn't Anríq! Look around you! None of this is real! Anríq would never attack people like that. He wouldn't attack some random flower and random trees like that! This is totally out of character. That isn't him! He's lost in this city somewhere—and I guarantee you he's going after the Shard. Now come on! We can't keep getting distracted by these apparitions."

He didn't give her a chance to argue with that, either. He sure taking charge of this project.

He took her hand and pulled her the rest of the way across the thoroughfare. She couldn't tear her eyes off Anríq.

He was right there—less than fifty feet away from her.

Every instinct told her to rejoin him and to stay near him—but Yann was right, of course.

The longer she watched, the more she realized the awful truth. Whatever this was pretending to be Anríq, he didn't even try to get to the White Spire.

He stayed in the central garden strip fighting any random thing that came near him. He didn't even wait for them to attack him first.

That flower had been flapping along in the breeze minding its own business. It hadn't been attacking anyone or anything—much less him.

None of the stuff in this thoroughfare threatened him. He could have gotten across it easily without hitting much of anything.

He didn't even try to get across it. Yann had to be right. This wasn't Anríq at all.

Yann pulled her across the street and into another avenue heading west. Her heart sank when she lost sight of Anríq—or whatever that was.

She had to pay attention when they entered this street. The close walls put both her and Yann in more danger.

The walls had no one else to attack. They undulated, rippled, and shot out appendages to grab the pair from both sides.

Yann and Eliska turned outward to protect each other's backs. Yann stabbed his glaive at the wall on his side. Eliska fought back with her magic and the two friends made their way to the other end of the street.

It fed into another thoroughfare as chaotic and dangerous as the last, but from here, the two travelers could see the White Spire in the distance.

The Shard of Hotha gleamed as brightly as ever in its top windows. The sight cast a silent blanket of calm over Eliska's mind.

The Shard was waiting for her there. She could get it.

The iron certainty took root in her soul and her doubts vanished. She could get the Shard exactly the same way she defeated the Voyant. She just had to use this power that had been given to her.

She and Yann stepped out into the thoroughfare. Even fighting her way across the thoroughfare would be no problem for her.

Her magic told her in that moment where Anríq was in the city. She could find him easily, but she had to get the Shard first.

The Shard cast the same spell over Yann. Both of them stepped out into the open. The Shard attracted them with an unstoppable pull.

Right then, another building moved out of position on their right. This one uprooted itself exactly the same way the trees in the central garden strip uprooted themselves.

The building pranced around on its foundation trying to stomp on all the smaller combatants trapped around its lowest stories.

The building came out of nowhere and overtook the two travelers before either Yann or Eliska realized the building was there.

The building raised its right front corner to flatten both of them. Eliska reacted without thinking, seized Yann by his jacket, and magicked both of them across the thoroughfare to the other side.

They came to rest on a sidewalk next to another building—a solid one this time.

She turned to face him to tell him she would just take them straight to the White Spire. This business of traveling through the city on foot was becoming ridiculous—ridiculously dangerous.

She didn't get the words out before an enormous object barreled down on them from behind her back. The noise of so much commotion stopped her from hearing it in time.

Yann tackled her to the ground and rolled her back into the thoroughfare to save her from getting squashed.

Chapter 22

Yann and Eliska rolled and then stared at what looked like a giant bathtub with wagon wheels under it. Some kind of strange misshapen bird-creature sat inside the tub.

The creature couldn't have been steering the tub, but the whole bizarre contraption kept careening down the street, veering from side to side to go after different targets, and attacking combatants left and right.

Yann clambered to his feet and started to pull Eliska up when she spotted another flower coming at them from the garden strip.

This one didn't flap along minding its own business. It whizzed straight for the back of Yann's head, spread its bright blue and purple petals, and revealed a mouth full of fangs at the very center of the flower.

She lunged for him, grabbed him by the arm, and magicked both of them back across the street into another alley.

"Are you okay?!" she panted.

He nodded fast. "Yeah! Are you?"

She nodded back "I'm going to take us to the spire. This is getting silly. We don't need to waste our time fighting all this stuff."

"Good idea." He held out his hand. "Do it."

She took his hand, threw back her shoulders, and made eye contact with him once before she used her magic to transport both of them.

She froze and her heart stopped when she saw a glistening gem hovering in an alcove in the wall right behind Yann.

Her eyes fell out of their sockets when she recognized the Shard of Hotha. What was it doing down here?

He turned around to see what she was looking at. His jaw dropped when he saw it and they both stared at the Shard in silent disbelief.

Eliska had just been thinking about the obstacle course of dangers separating her from the White Spire.

She would have to fight her way through all of that just to get near the spire.

Then she would have to fight all the defenses the spire would surely throw at her so Yann could go inside and take the Shard.

No way could the Shard just magically appear in the same alley with them. That wasn't possible.

"It can't be real!" Yann whispered.

"What if it is?" she murmured back. "What if it knows we're looking for it?"

"We have to find both Shards. We already know that."

"So......you think we should just walk away? What if this is our only chance to get one of them? What if the Shard in the spire is the illusion? What if the Shards are hidden in the city somewhere?"

"Can you use your magic to find out? Is this the real Shard?"

She extended her magic toward the Shard, but she couldn't tell if it was real or not. It sure looked real.

The same overwhelming desire took hold of her. She stepped forward and raised her hand to touch the Shard.

Before she made contact with it, it rushed her and plunged into her chest—but the same Shard still hovered in the alcove in exactly the same position it had been before.

Before either she or Yann could move, the second Shard soared toward him and vanished inside his chest.

She glanced up at him. The purple-pink glow radiated out of both of them.

The two Shards matched each other. The glow of their combined magic radiated back and forth between them—and blissful, overwhelming joy and happiness flooded Eliska's being.

She burst out in a huge smile of pure ecstasy. She had never felt this much happiness in her life.

The Shard's magic wiped out all her Darkness in an instant. She was whole and healed the way she always hoped she would be.

The Shard healed all the hurt from getting separated from her family—and from growing up alone—and everything else that happened to her.

She still remembered everything from all the memories she'd absorbed. She could still understand and sense way too much from everyone in the Coil.

The Shard made it all okay. She could live with it now. She could actually appreciate it and enjoy it.

A matching smile of pure relief and happiness spread over Yann's face. All the care and exhaustion that hung over him since he left Middleborough—it all evaporated in an instant.

It left him whole, healed, and perfectly happy in ways Eliska had never seen him before.

She rushed him, threw her arms around him, and burst out laughing in pure relief and delight. Their Shards throbbed in harmony with each other. Nothing could ever be better than this.

That radiant glow spread outward from the two of them and swept through the city. The Shards' magic reassembled all the destroyed buildings.

All the skeletons put themselves back together, grew flesh, and went about their business carrying out a thousand jobs all over the city.

The trees, flowers, fountains, and buildings anchored themselves back in their old places. Everything returned to the way it was.

A wave of magic spread outward from Yann and Eliska, brightened the city, and made it shine with freshness and beauty the way the friends had seen it in the books.

A magical force surrounded Yann and Eliska. She found it hard to look away from the light shining in his eyes.

Aching love gripped her heart when she looked at him. He meant everything to her. The Shards bound them together more than she ever thought possible.

Their union erased the separation of years and the hidden resentment against him and their parents for not being there for her when she needed them.

None of that existed anymore. He was here and they were together at last—the way they should have been all along.

The magic flooding the city lifted Yann and Eliska out of the alley. They held each other's hands while the Shards carried up and over the buildings toward the White Spire in the distance.

It gleamed with blinding whiteness. Birds soared around it against a brilliant blue sky dotted with clouds.

Eliska could have laughed and cried and sang with joy at the sight of the magnificent city spread out below her. She was going home.

The war was over. The magic of the two Shards spread outward to the whole Coil, stabilized the Layers, and reestablished Islands where the survivors could rebuild.

The sense of relief and painful happiness became unbearable. She couldn't wait to enter the Hall of Light with Yann. Everything was going to be okay now.

They glided ten miles over the beautiful city until they got five miles away from the Spire. She and Yann kept glancing at each other and bursting into excited smiles. She had never seen him so happy.

She turned to hug him again, but right then, they hit an invisible barrier in the sky somewhere. She and Yann crashed through it and the illusion shattered.

That feeling of the Shard in her chest—its radiant magic consuming her and wiping out all her Darkness and care—it vanished just as fast.

It left her cold and plunged her back into despair. She never felt this awful since she left the Keepers of the Dawn.

The magic released her and Yann and they both plummeted out of the sky with nothing to hold them back.

The loss of the Shard's magic crushed her spirit. It couldn't be gone. The Shard couldn't be gone. She couldn't feel such overwhelming happiness and peace—only to lose it.

It *was* gone. The whole thing had been another cruel joke exactly like the Wishers tempting Yann with visions of marrying Marine.

She didn't think to break her own fall until the last second. She fought her way back to reality just in time to catch her and Yann before they splatted to their deaths on the pavement below.

They plunged back into the chaotic landscape of millions of monstrous shapes attacking each other and the travelers.

She and Yann crashed down on the ground among piles of rubble, burned-out buildings, and monstrous aberrations too horrible to look at.

The Shard didn't change anything because no one had taken the Shards yet. The chaos, destruction, and mayhem were all still here. The White Spire still towered black and menacing on the horizon.

The real Shard of Hotha still gleamed in its windows. Of course it did. It wouldn't just appear in a dirty alley somewhere. She already knew that.

She kicked herself for falling for the trick, but she couldn't hold back despair. The Dark poison still infected her soul. Nothing could take that away—nothing but the real Shard of Hotha.

The Shard would only take her Darkness away if it joined with another person carrying the other Shard.

She dragged herself onto her knees. Grief and despair crushed her when she looked around this devastated world.

Tears sprang to her eyes. She fought them back, but they wouldn't stay down. How could these Dark forces trick her like this? How could they tempt her with the one thing she most wanted in the world?

She wanted that healing more than anything—even more than to marry Anríq and raise children with him. Anything would be better than to live with this Darkness any longer.

Yann crawled over to her, put his arms around her, and rested his head against her temple.

He didn't have to say anything. He must have seen and felt it in the illusion. He felt that she was whole and healed—the way all three friends hoped she would be.

They'd been searching all this time for a way to heal her. He must have been so happy when they thought they actually found it.

His arms around her broke the last straw keeping her anguish contained. She broke down in tears right there on the ground. She couldn't even think about fighting any of the magical demons attacking her right now.

She activated her magic just enough to surround herself and Yann with a ball of protection. She couldn't do more than that.

She just needed a few minutes to sit here and sob over something she never had to begin with. Why did the Shard have to do this? She already wanted to take it. She already felt herself being drawn to it.

She didn't need this temptation to stab her in the guts. She didn't need to see and feel just how wonderful it would be once she took the Shard. She didn't need to see and feel just how awful her life would be without it.

Her life already was that awful. She'd been living with this poison for so long. Maybe she would never heal.

Yann broke that bond first. He pushed her back, gripped both of her shoulders, and moved his face close to hers while he murmured low under his breath.

Tears glistened in his eyes. She didn't let herself feel how bad this was for him.

"Listen to me," he murmured. "We're going to keep going. We're going to find Anríq and then you two will take the Shards together. You'll feel that way with him......"

"I betrayed him!" she wailed and tears flooded from her eyes. "I betrayed him by feeling that way about you!"

"You didn't!" he insisted. "You didn't choose that. You love me as your brother. That's all. He knows that. He would want you to feel that way and be healed even if you can't be together with him—but that's not what's going to happen. You and Anríq will take the Shards. You'll live together forever and love each other like that—and you will be healed. Look at me! It will happen. I promise you. Do you understand?"

She nodded, but she couldn't stop crying. She only wished she could believe him.

Even if he was right, even if she and Anríq took the Shards—then Yann would be left out in the cold alone.

She bit back tears as much for him as for herself. How could she rob Yann of that happiness—the happiness he really deserved?

He was Yimichi Ocuron's grandson—the destined King. He had to take the Shard.

He pulled her to her feet. She choked down despair and ran her sleeve across her face. She had trouble thinking clearly about anything after that sudden shock and letdown.

Her anguish started to turn to fury against whatever force did this to her. She wanted to destroy someone for this.

Yann set off through the jumbled landscape again. Neither of them talked.

The routine of deflecting all these magical attacks became more automatic. The objects, buildings, and shapes around the pair followed more predictable movements.

She didn't have to think about what she was hitting. Driving these things off took no effort at all.

Yann got more used to the process, too. He knocked attacking forces out of the way more easily. Both he and Eliska saw things coming. They could prepare themselves better.

They came to another avenue leading straight to the White Spire. It towered over their heads less than a few miles away.

The apparition of Yann and Eliska taking both Shards got the travelers closer to the spire, but she didn't trust that this would make the coming battle any easier.

She glanced up at the Shard in the window. She let her eye trail downward along the spire's walls. There had to be another way inside.

"I don't see a door," she told Yann. "Once we get near the walls, I'll blow a hole in the wall so you can get inside. That business of climbing up the outside is too dangerous. The spire is bound to have defenses."

"Can you tell what the defenses are?"

"I can't tell from here, but I'm going to go out on a limb and say that barrier that brought us out of our illusion was one of them. It stopped us from going near the spire. Hey, maybe the whole illusion was one of the spire's defenses. Maybe this whole city is one giant defensive barricade designed to stop anyone from getting near the spire."

Yann pursed his lips and narrowed his eyes at the spire. "Can you defeat the defenses?"

"I can defeat them on the outside. I don't know what you might be facing once you get inside."

"I'll just have to deal with it," he muttered.

"I'll try to get inside and help you. If I can, I'll try getting near the...."

She broke off when she saw Anríq in the landscape again.

She caught a glimpse of commotion in the corner of her eye—commotion that didn't follow the same pattern as all the other stuff fighting in this city.

She looked up and saw him, but she immediately looked away. She didn't want to get depressed over another distracting apparition.

She spun back the other way when he yelled out. She knew his voice too well not to recognize it. He was in trouble.

She looked for the first time and saw what she didn't let herself see at first. He fought another mob of two hundred people, but these pursued him, attacked him, and made him stumble away before he took a stand to defend himself.

He yelled over his shoulder, but he was still too far away for Eliska to understand him.

She didn't have to. The wild desperation in his eyes and voice told her loud and clear. This was the real Anríq and he needed help.

The instability transformed the people attacking him. None of them had any faces. Blank, smooth skin covered their faces where their eyes, noses, and mouths should have been.

The attacking people made no sound. They just hacked their weapons at Anríq, knocked him off his feet, and sent him sprawling onto his back before they all rushed in to slaughter him.

He raised his axe, but he couldn't get off the ground fast enough before they all piled in on top of him.

Eliska reacted in a heartbeat, blasted out a wave of magic, and cleared all those people away from him.

She sent them flying backward, slammed them into nearby buildings, and they fell to all the other combatants who attacked without mercy.

Eliska hurled another binding and transporting spell at Anríq, magicked him back to her and Yann, and then transported all of them away.

Chapter 23

Yann stood back out of the way and watched Eliska lunge for Anríq, throw her arms around his neck, and crush him in a huge hug.

She burst out laughing and then kissed him right in front of Yann. "You're all right!" she exclaimed. "I thought I lost you!"

Anríq's features shone with so much happiness that it almost hurt to look at him. He mumbled into her hair, "I thought I'd lost you, too. I was so worried about you."

She let him go and they both beamed into each other's eyes for a minute before they remembered that Yann was there.

He couldn't resent them for sharing that happiness with each other. He cared about both of them and they loved each other too much for him to begrudge them.

Eliska pulled herself together, took a step back, and slipped her hand into Anríq's before she faced Yann. She had to work hard to straighten her expression.

He waited for them to finish and tried to pretend she wasn't that happy to see Anríq again—and that he wasn't so obviously just as thrilled to see her.

Neither of them would be that happy to see Yann if they got separated. Of course it wasn't the same thing, but it made him acutely aware that he didn't have anyone like that anymore.

He didn't have anyone who would throw her arms around him and burst into happy, excited laughter over the prospect of seeing him again after only a few minutes apart.

"We should get going," Eliska announced—as if Yann wasn't the one telling her the same thing just a few minutes ago.

"Did you see anything out there?" Yann asked Anríq. "Did you see anything that could help us get into the spire?"

"I didn't see anything other than what we've already seen. The city kept throwing so many obstacles in my way. It took me this long to get this far."

Yann scanned the area. "The sun will be going down soon. We should try to find a place to take shelter overnight. We can't travel in this mayhem in the dark."

"I know a place," Eliska announced.

Yann's head shot up. "You do?"

She nodded. "I can find my way around this city now. It isn't hard. The problem is all the obstacles—and the mind tricks. We're likely to see a lot more of those as we get closer to the spire."

"So where do you say we should take shelter?"

She led the way into another alley. The walls extended clawed hands and other appendages to grab, tear, and assault the friends.

They had to fight their way through before she ducked into one of the side buildings.

Intact interior walls still sectioned off the ground floor into rooms. All the walls came to life—or they must already have come to life before the friends showed up.

Mountains of trash, broken furniture, and even some reanimated bodies revolved in a whirlwind inside every room.

Yann had to raise his hand in front of his face to protect his eyes. Even then, he had to constantly take his hand down so he could use his glaive to defend himself.

"What are we doing in here?!" he yelled over the noise. "There's just as much crap in here as there is outside!"

Eliska halted in the center of the room, blinked at the walls seething all around the friends, and let out another quick burst of a protective magical ball. It popped to the walls and flattened everything back inside the surface.

The same rippling, churning faces, monsters, and shapes swirled right outside the field, but nothing could penetrate inside.

"Why didn't you do that outside?" Yann asked once the noise died down. "We wouldn't have to fight our way through all that."

"We wouldn't have to fight our way through it, but the ball won't help us get past the spire's defenses." She selected a piece of floor and sat down. "It also won't protect us from any illusions."

Anríq looked up. "Did you see more illusions?"

She looked away and nodded. "We went into an illusion where Yann and I both took the Shards. They transported us toward the spire, but we hit one of the defenses and fell down. The illusion shattered."

He sat down next to her and used one finger to push her hair out of her face. "I kept seeing you in the landscape—but it wasn't you. I tried to get back to you, but you kept disappearing. I realized it wasn't you because you kept evading me."

Her features spasmed when she tried to smile at him. "I kept trying to find you. I would never evade you."

He smiled back, slipped his hand against her cheek, and kissed her again.

Yann looked away, sat down, and then stretched out on the floor. He shut his eyes so he wouldn't see them together.

He would have gone off on his own, but he didn't want to risk getting lost again.

Shutting his eyes didn't help at all. That feeling of overwhelming happiness and contentment—he shouldn't have felt that for Eliska. His connection with her had been totally platonic, but it still left him cold and empty.

He shouldn't have shared that with anyone he didn't plan to spend the rest of his life with. He should only have shared that with someone he planned to marry and build a family with.

Sharing the Shard's magic with her made him love more than anything—but only as a sister. He could never feel any other way about her.

The illusion left him just as drained and hopeless as it left her. He would have given anything to heal her and take her Darkness away, but he didn't want to do it that way.

Anríq and Eliska taking the Shards—that would be the best way for everyone. Then what would Yann do?

He didn't really care. He would probably just wander out into the Coil, find some no-name town, and join the Black Watch.

He would be happy to live the rest of his life defending some wall against Darklings that weren't a danger to anyone anymore.

Then he wouldn't have to worry about finding another woman to replace Marine. He could just spend the rest of his life dreaming about what might have been.

Chapter 24

Eliska glanced over her shoulder at Yann lying on the floor with his eyes closed. He wasn't asleep yet, but he would be soon.

She cast a spell around herself and Anríq so Yann wouldn't be able to hear their conversation. She didn't have to look at him to feel how uncomfortable they made him—especially after she and Yann shared that illusion of taking the Shards.

He didn't feel resentful or jealous of Eliska and Anríq—not at all. Yann was just lonely—and who could blame him?

Anríq got her attention by stroking her face again. She turned around and burst into another grin when she found herself gazing into his eyes.

She didn't have to hide her feelings from him anymore. They both already knew they were together.

She let herself touch his face, finger his hair, and rub his arms. Every part of him felt good. He was here. They were together again.

"What did you see in the illusion of taking the Shard?" he asked.

She looked down so she wouldn't see the way he was looking at her. Lowering her eyes only brought her face to face with the Servant's mark tattooed across his chest.

"We were in congress together—or whatever you call it," she murmured. "It felt amazing—like the most exquisite happiness I've ever felt—and the Shard healed my Darkness."

Anríq's eyes popped. His warm fingers never stopped tracing her cheeks, neck, and rubbing her back. "Really? That's incredible!"

"It wasn't real," she husked. "As soon as the illusion shattered, it all came back as bad as ever. I wish I never felt that good. It made coming back even harder—like it did with Yann when he left the Wishers."

Anríq peered deeper into her eyes. "Are you okay? Did it make you sick?"

She shrugged. She couldn't look at him. "I don't know. Maybe the fact that I feel this bad about it is part of the sickness."

She faltered for a second and then blurted out the rest. She couldn't hide anything from him.

"I thought I might have betrayed you by feeling that way about him....but he said no. He said you and I would take the Shards.....and that we would be together forever....."

He cupped her chin and forced her to look up. "I want that. I want that with you. You know that. It's all I want."

"If we did that.....we wouldn't be wanderers anymore. We would stay there in the Hall of Light." She gulped. "We wouldn't be Servants anymore."

He cocked his head to study her. "That really bothers you, doesn't it?"

"Of course! It's what I love the most about you." She stopped herself again when she realized what she just said.

She already knew he loved her and she loved him. Yann and Anríq talked about it. She overheard their conversation through her magical connection with both of them.

Neither she nor Anríq ever said it to each other before.

She shrugged that off. She didn't care if she said it. She loved him. She would tell him so all day long if she thought he wanted her to.

She took a deep breath and forged ahead. "I don't want anything but for us to be wandering Servant's together. Nothing makes sense if we aren't Servants in the Coil the way we always have been. That's more than I ever dreamed of. I don't want us to be some King and Queen in the White Spire. It doesn't sound like us at all. It sounds....."

He waited for her to finish. "It sounds what?"

"Boring!" she blurted out. "It sounds boring—and stuffy—and....and all regal and everything."

He burst out laughing.

"What?!" she exclaimed. "Come on! You don't really see yourself as King in the White Spire, do you? Admit it. You don't want to be King."

He wouldn't stop grinning at her. "No, I don't. You're right. I don't want anything but to be a wandering Servant. That's all I've ever wanted. I never dreamed I would meet a woman who wanted to do it with me. The thought of taking you with me is a dream come true for me, but we're Servants. If the Coil needs us to take the Shards, then that's what we'll do. What we want is secondary."

She would have liked to drop the subject, but she couldn't tear her eyes away from his. She finally let herself feel just how much he meant to her.

All the trials and troubles they'd been through made him so much more precious to her.

She laid her hands on both sides of his cheeks and leaned and kissed him for a long time. "I love you," she murmured. "I never want to lose you again."

"You won't," he breathed back. "You're going to be stuck with me for a long, long time."

Her heart flipped at those words. She wanted nothing but to be near him.

She would have liked to attack him right here on the floor, but she contented herself with just climbing into his lap and tucking her head against his neck.

She stroked his neck and jaw, fiddled with his hair, and just enjoyed the feeling of his arms around her.

"Do you remember how it was with the children in the forest?" she murmured. "Before all the death and destruction?"

"Yes, I remember," he breathed down into her hair. "That was such a nice time."

"It could be like that again—with us. We could have a family."

He pressed his lips against the top of her head. "I would love that. You were so wonderful with them and they loved you for it. You were a hero to them."

She didn't say the other part. She and Anríq would never have that—not out in the wild Coil the way it was with the children.

The only way she and Anríq could survive this and save the Coil would be for one or both of them to take the Shards.

If she and Yann took the Shards, then she and Anríq would never be together. If she and Anríq took the Shards, they wouldn't go back out into the Coil.

Everything she loved about their time together would come to an end one way or the other—if they survived at all.

Knowing that made this moment more priceless than gold.

He held her on his lap for a while. After another hour, he swiveled her onto the floor and they both stretched out to go to sleep. Yann was already asleep, but she kept the spell around herself and Anríq so they wouldn't disturb Yann.

She turned on her side to cuddle up to Anríq, but he turned on his side to face her. He folded his arm under his head and his other hand kept tracing down her face, raking his fingers through her hair, and rubbing her to keep her warm.

"I thought I was going to lose you when you fought the Voyant," he murmured. "I thought the Darkness would take you."

"He would have killed you—both you and Yann. I couldn't let that happen—even if I turned Dark."

"You'll probably have to use your Darkness to get into the spire, too, won't you?" he breathed. "You'll have to use your Darkness to break the spire's defenses and get the Shards."

"I suppose I will."

He leaned in and kissed her on the forehead. He let his lips linger there. "I love you for doing this. I know it isn't easy for you."

She wrapped her arms around him as tightly as she dared. In the darkness under his hair, she could finally whisper her worst fears into his ear.

"I just wish there was some way we could be together," she choked. "I can't stand the thought of anything happening to you. I don't see how either of us can survive this—and we'll never go out into the Coil together—not the way we want to. Something will happen to stop it—or one of us will die."

He scooped his hand up to the back of her neck and held her there in the safety of his arms. "I have the same fear—but we have to keep doing this whatever the outcome. We have each other, either way. You'll always have me no matter what happens."

She didn't dare to open her eyes. She didn't want this moment to end—not ever. She didn't want to face whatever came after it.

She held onto him until they both eased off and settled down on the floor. She couldn't fall asleep without feeling that he was still there next to her.

When she did fall asleep, she saw herself battling her way across the city toward the White Spire. Anríq and Yann fought by her side.

She used her Dark power to break the spire's defenses one after another until the three friends came to the outer walls.

She levitated into the air fighting countless magical forces ejecting from the spire. They escalated in strength and intensity to attack both her and Anríq.

She had to harness the full depth of her magic to defeat those forces. She bombarded the spire, smashed a hole in the wall near the ground level, and Yann vanished inside.

Nothing happened for a while. Anríq battled the defenses on the ground until he forced his way to the breach. He disappeared inside, too.

Eliska swooped in behind them and caught up with them on a vast internal staircase spiraling all the way to the top tower.

The three friends charged up there and wound up in the little observation room the Voyant used to study his Coil projection.

The Shard of Hotha glimmered and flickered in the window, but it wasn't just the Shard. It was both of them overlaid on top of each other.

Yann stood back while she and Anríq approached the window. Anríq held out his hands to take the first Shard, but it plunged into his chest before he could touch it.

Then the second Shard did the same thing to Eliska.

She experienced again the devastating rush of happiness and relief when she and Anríq faced each other. All her Darkness evaporated.

She was whole—and now she and Anríq could live together forever. They never had to worry about anything ever again.

They faced each other and love throbbed between them from one Shard to the other. Their Shards joined in a perfect union of understanding and heartfelt connection.

He clasped both her hands—and the same outward spreading wave swept all the destruction away. The city rebuilt around them and the Coil stabilized everywhere to create new Islands.

Brilliant white light surrounded the spire, washed it clean, and polished it to blinding white.

The beautiful gardens and prosperous neighborhoods of the surrounding city came back to life. Birds soared around the high tower.

Light, love, and happiness enveloped Eliska and Anríq. She never once thought about what happened to Yann. He wasn't part of their congress.

Nothing existed but Anríq and this unbroken connection between their hearts. Nothing could ever separate them now.

She and Anríq joined hands and turned to look out the window at their domain. He was the King in the White Spire and she was his Queen. This was a dream come true......

The minute she turned to look out, her magic gave her an unbroken view of the whole Coil. She saw everyone and everything in it simultaneously. Her memories of their experiences told her where everyone was and what they were doing to rebuild their lives.

Men of the Black Watch rebuilt their walls and stood guard to protect their towns in case anything went wrong. The Corsairs and Barbarians were still out there marauding and robbing. That would never change.

She even saw a few Servants wandering in the wilderness. The sight of them brought her back to her senses in a split second.

This wasn't real. She wasn't Queen in the White Spire and Anríq wasn't the King.

She rolled over and tried to sit up when she woke up back in the empty room. Darkness blocked out any light from coming through the window. It was still the middle of the night.

She tried to get away in time, but her legs gave out and she slammed down on her knees before she puked into the corner.

Anríq stirred at the noise, but her spell stopped Yann from hearing.

Anríq scooted over to her, rubbed her back, and massaged her neck from behind while she caught her breath. "That hasn't happened in a while," he whispered. "What was it this time?"

"The illusions......" she choked. "They come from the Dark......"

"Did you go into one of the illusions?"

She nodded. She couldn't tell him what it was.

He kissed the back of her head and went back to rubbing her. "The Dark must be catching up with you. You've been using it a lot lately. You'll need to be careful and not overtax yourself before we get to the spire."

She didn't answer. She sat up and wiped her mouth on the corner of her cloak. The sting burned the inside of her mouth, but she just had to spit it out and live with the aftertaste.

She already knew what Anríq meant before he said it. She might turn herself completely to the Dark. She might have to just to get into the spire.

If that happened, she wouldn't be able to take the Shard. She wouldn't trust herself not to use its power for Dark purposes.

Then Yann and Anríq would have to take the Shards while she.....

She would go out into the Dark Layers where she belonged. The rest of the world could rebuild the Coil without her.

The Coil would stabilize with her out there. No one would ever see her again—and maybe that was for the best.

Chapter 25

Yann woke up first, took one look at Anríq and Eliska lying asleep in each other's arms, and got to his feet. He went to look out the window so he wouldn't see them.

Daylight streamed through the window from the morning sky overhead. The area outside looked as chaotic as ever. None of the stuff out there ever seemed to destroy itself no matter how hard everything tried.

Maybe this whole city was one big illusion of chaos to derail anyone from getting to the Shards. He would have believed just about anything at this point.

Anríq and Eliska both woke up in a little while. Yann waited, but it didn't take long for the three friends to leave their sheltered room.

Eliska kept her protective field around their party on the way outside. It held all the random flying debris at bay and stopped most of the monsters and mutant wagons and bathtubs from attacking.

The ball field also had an eerie way of blocking out all the noise. The quite unnerved Yann more than the outright attacks.

She stopped a mile away from the spire. "This is as far as we can go without fighting the defenses. We won't be able to use the ball. We have to go at it and try to break in."

"Can you still not tell us anything about what the defenses are?" Yann asked.

"Based on what I saw last night....." She broke off and cast a terrified glance at him.

He didn't ask what she meant. He knew by now not to ask how she did anything.

She gulped.

"It's all right," he told her. "Just tell me what you saw."

"The defenses aren't anything as specific as we saw from the Voyant. It's just magical blasts and ejections shooting out at anyone who tries to get near the spire."

"So what do we have to do?" he asked.

"Anríq and I will assault the tower like we decided. I'll shoot a hole through the wall—over there. Once you get inside, you'll find a spiral staircase leading up to the top room. Then you'll be able to...."

She trailed off again. She didn't even look at him this time.

He brushed that away, too. "Let's take it one step at a time. If you can break down the defenses enough to get me inside, then we'll go from there."

"In the vision, we all went inside," she blurted out. "You went in first and then we followed you...."

"And then?" he asked. "It sounds like you want to tell me everything that happened."

"Then....Anríq and I took the Shards."

He brightened up. "Great! That's perfect....isn't it? Isn't that what we agreed on?"

She looked away and clamped her mouth shut to stop herself from answering.

He let it go and turned back to the spire. Getting inside would be daunting enough. He would worry about the rest later.

The other two seemed to come to the same conclusion at the same moment. Eliska let her protective ball evaporate and all the chaos of the surrounding city swooped in to attack.

All three friends sprinted forward at top speed. They had to fight their hardest to carve a path to the spire.

The spire launched its defensive attacks right away. It blasted jets of magic from the topmost tower and bombarded the pavement all around the friends.

Some of those shots hit Anríq and Eliska. He clubbed them away or chopped his axe to stop them from wiping him out.

Eliska hacked her staff back and forth to deflect them. Yann fell back and wound up defending both of them from behind as all the flying debris and monsters from the city tried to flank the party from the rear.

He turned his back on his two friends and concentrated everything on making sure none of that stuff hit them.

He slashed his glaive, smashed random projectiles to the ground, stabbed monsters in their faces, and had to destroy objects and even a few larger appliances in the process.

He heard the noise of Anríq and Eliska getting farther away behind him. They must be fighting their way closer to the spire.

He backed up to keep pace with them, but right then, Eliska yelled out, "Come on, Yann! You can get through now!"

He swung around to run after them, but at the same instant, the spire released another colossal jet of magic.

This one hit between the three friends and the shockwave blasted them apart. Yann flew backward, crashed against a wall, landed hard on the ground, and scrambled to get to his feet before some other horror attacked him.

He froze with his glaive raised when he saw that he was completely alone. Anríq and Eliska were both gone.

He glanced left and right. He was the same distance away from the spire, but he was in a completely different part of the city and facing the spire from another direction.

He had to swipe his glaive at some surrounding debris to stop it from attacking him, but he didn't care about that.

Now he was the one isolated. Were Anríq and Eliska together somewhere?

Yann really hoped they were still fighting their way into the spire. In the best scenario, they would take both Shards and the city would transform before he ever had to get involved.

That was too much to hope for, so he measured his position and started working his way back through the streets to where he got separated from his two friends.

He had to fight his way through every painstaking block. The same combination of kitchen utensils, books, furniture, dead animals come back to life, sections of buildings, plants, and mutated people kept coming at him everywhere he turned.

He no longer even paid attention to them. His eyes and arms went through the worn-out routine of fighting everything off. He didn't have to think about them to keep them away from him.

He worked his way back through miles of neighborhoods, but the scene never changed. Whatever obstacle this chaos intended to throw in his way didn't bother him anymore.

The many illusions caused a much bigger problem.

Anríq and Eliska might get into another illusion where they thought they were taking the Shards when they were really still trapped out in the city. Yann might never find them and then the Coil would fall.

He couldn't do anything about that. He didn't have their magic. He wouldn't be able to go near the spire by himself.

He made his way back to the place where he, Anríq, and Eliska first launched their assault on the spire—for whatever that was worth.

He showed up just as Anríq came around the corner from another direction. The two boys eyed each other and then they both looked around.

"Eliska isn't with you?" Anríq demanded.

"I thought she was with you," Yann returned. "You don't know where she is?"

"If I knew where she was, I would be with her." Anríq shut his mouth to stop himself from snapping, but he failed to keep the annoyance out of his voice.

"It's all right," Yann told him. "We'll find her. She'll go after the Shard and we'll find her. She must be around here somewhere."

"Of course she'll go after the Shard," Anríq countered. "She's a Servant. What else would she do? Anyway, we have to go after the Shard in case something happened to her. We can't wait around."

"How can we?" Yann asked. "You don't have the magic to break into the spire on your own."

Anríq pursed his lips and looked away again. He scowled at the spire and the surrounding neighborhoods.

He had to continually bat away objects and projectiles with his club. He hit them a lot harder now than Yann remembered.

"If you don't have a way to get into the spire, maybe we should withdraw," Yann suggested.

Anríq barely looked at him. "I suppose so."

"Let's retreat out of line of the spire's defenses. We might be able to find another sheltered place. We can keep the spire under surveillance in case Eliska comes back. If you're right that she'll assault the spire on her own, then we'll be able to see her when she does."

Yann retreated into the surrounding neighborhoods. Anríq lingered there and squinted at the spire and all the nearby buildings and combatants.

He finally followed Yann away.

Yann headed for a nearby building. He didn't know how he could find a place for him and Anríq to take shelter while they waited for Eliska.

He just had to trust her to either find him or go after the Shard herself.

He turned into a side street to explore the buildings down there when he stopped in his tracks.

The Shard of Hotha hovered in the doorway he'd just been about to enter. The Shard cast a hypnotic aura over him and Anríq.

Anríq halted at his side. Some part of Yann's mind already knew this was another illusion. The Shard wouldn't be down here. It was up there in the spire where it belonged.

Anríq must have known it was an illusion, too, but the Shard entranced both of them.

The spell only lasted for a second—just long enough for the first Shard to whizz toward Yann.

He should stop this, but by the time he shifted his brain into gear enough to think what he should do, the Shard had already buried itself in his chest again and the second Shard entered Anríq.

The same unbelievable relief and contentment took over Yann's being. He turned to smile at his friend—the brother he never had.

Pure love and admiration overflowed Yann's heart for the man standing in front of him. Their connection blocked out everything else.

He didn't notice when the light changed around both of them. It blazed blinding bright and then faded just enough for him to see the two of them standing in the middle of a magnificent garden.

He couldn't tell where it was and he didn't care. He only knew he wanted to stay here with Anríq forever. They didn't belong anywhere except here together.

The two men rushed each other and Yann crushed his friend in a bone-breaking hug. All the barriers between them disintegrated.

The Shards' magic radiated outward from both of them, swept over the city, restored everything to its former glory, and then kept spreading outward to the rest of the Coil.

Nothing mattered to Yann more than spending all his time with Anríq.

They both looked around them at this splendid garden. Gold leaf covered the elaborately carved surface of a high, arched door at the top of a marble terrace not far away.

The doors stood many times higher than a man's head. A fully loaded wagon could have driven under the arch.

The minute he looked up at it, the doors swung open on both sides and eight beautiful women entered the garden.

They lined up on the terrace and smiled down at Yann and Anríq.

Yann's intuition told him who these women were and why they were here. He was the King in the White Spire. His affiliate was a man, so Yann needed a Queen to give him an heir.

He turned away gulping down the urge to be sick. He didn't want anyone else interfering with his connection to Anríq. No one could possibly understand that.

Anríq glared up at the terrace and his lip curled in the same snarl of disgust when he looked at the women up there.

He turned away. His eyes met Yann's—and they both froze as the truth hit.

"This isn't real!" Anríq's gaze darted around the garden. "Eliska... ..she's out there alone."

"Come on. We have to find her." Yann spun on his heel and headed for the terrace. It was the only thing he could see that resembled an exit.

He got halfway there before he realized Anríq wasn't with him. Yann glanced over his shoulder to ask why not.

Yann froze a second time when he saw Anríq. They weren't in the garden anymore.

Anríq stood in the top tower of the White Spire. The Shard of Hotha hovered in front of him—and he was all alone.

He extended his hands to take the Shard. No one else was with him.

Yann lunged for him to knock him away. "NO!!" Yann yelled and slammed Anríq down on the floor.

Anríq fought back to get away. He used all his great strength to hurl Yann off.

Yann flew twenty feet and hit a wall. When he tried to pick himself up, he found himself back on the street where the two boys started.

Anríq came toward him from farther up the block. Anríq frowned down at Yann when he saw him on the ground. "What happened to you?" Anríq took hold of him and picked him up. "You disappeared out of the garden."

"You...you were in the tower.....You were going to take the Shard—by yourself. You were going to become the new Voyant."

Anríq scowled even more darkly. "I was? That's not like me."

"I attacked you...." Yann looked away. "I'm sorry. We got into a fight....."

"Good," Anríq returned. "Attack me again if it happens like that in real life."

Yann blinked at him. "Really? You mean it?"

Anríq dipped his chin once. "Of course. Don't let me become the Voyant. That would be a disaster."

Chapter 26

E liska spun around trying to figure out where she was. That last blast from the White Spire transported her to a remote part of the city.

She was nowhere near where she and the boys had been just a few minutes ago.

She activated her magic and located both boys close to the spire. She really hoped they both had the good sense not to try to break into it by themselves.

She detected Anríq using his magic, but he might just be defending himself against all the surrounding chaos. He would have to do that to protect himself and Yann.

She considered magicking herself back to their location, but right then, a dozen massive Darklings came out of a nearby building.

They roared at her and hurtled in to attack her with all their teeth bared and their tentacles hissing and snapping in the air.

She spun around to confront them, but all her alarm died as soon as she saw them.

These were just ordinary Darklings. They weren't apparitions cooked up by the White Spire to confuse the three friends.

She hadn't seen Darklings in this Island before, but the sight of them actually relieved her. She understood these Darklings.

The spire or the Coil or whatever it was that she should consider her enemy now—none of those things sent these Darklings to attack her.

These Darklings weren't part of the spire's defenses. Instability brought these Darklings to this Island.

She extended her Dark power toward them and let it invade them. She could control them here as easily as she controlled them in the Dark Layers.

She turned the Darklings in different directions and controlled their movements. Her power merged with theirs.

She started to drift into the eternal memory of all the destruction they wreaked on the Coil.

She went through all the eons of Islands destroyed, populations annihilated, and civilizations brought crumbling to the ground.

Her memories included all the collective experiences of all the people who died in those disasters.

She couldn't let it happen again—not when she came this close to taking the Shard of Hotha for herself.

She turned the Darklings on each other and watched from a detached reserve while they ripped each other to shreds. They eviscerated each other until they fell to the ground—utterly destroyed.

She turned away. She didn't care about them. She didn't have to.

She was on a mission here. These Darklings would interfere with that mission if she let them live. If they didn't interfere with her mission now, they would threaten someone else later on down the road.

She walked off into the landscape heading back toward the spire, but just then, she saw another crowd of people fleeing through the destroyed landscape.

She reacted before she thought about it, raced over there, and fired her protective field over them to shield them from all the flying shrapnel and debris.

The Island reacted to her just as fast. The area collapsed worse than before. Deep rumbling earthquakes shook the ground and exploded the remaining buildings.

Blocks, boulders, and whole wall sections smashed down on her field and shattered it. The fleeing civilians screamed, threw their arms over their heads to protect themselves, and tried to run anywhere to save themselves.

They would have scattered and run straight into the path of more falling debris.

She reacted instantaneously, took hold of the whole slab of pavement under the crowd, broke it off, and magicked the whole thing twenty miles outside the city.

The upheaval died as soon as she set the slab on the ground. The civilians took their arms down and looked around blinking in wonder at the countryside.

She realized the minute she got there that none of these people could possibly have survived in that city for so long.

The instant she thought that, the people vanished and so did the slab of pavement she used to bring them here. None of it was real.

She let out a shaky sigh. This city knew exactly how to distract the three friends.

She located the two boys and transported herself to within one block of their location, but when she got there, she didn't see them anywhere.

She glanced up at the spire—just once. The Shard of Hotha exerted its magnetic attraction on her.

It haunted her mind with irresistible power. Her Dark poison wanted to harness the Shard for Dark purposes.

If she took the Shard right now—by herself—she would become the next Voyant.

She would be able to use the Shard to destroy whole words. She could bring the whole Coil crashing down.

She could level civilizations, make them crumble into ruin and destruction, and leave the Islands deserted for new civilizations to rise.

She experienced all the eternal shades of memory from her visions. She tasted blood, heard the clash of weapons, and saw the bodies fall under the churning hillsides as they rearranged themselves.

She forced herself to look away. She turned her back on the spire and strode off into the city streets on a straight line to intercept the boys.

Chapter 27

Yann and Anríq made their way through the streets. Anríq defended Yann while he tried to find a place for them to shelter.

Yann tried not to notice that he and Anríq were getting farther away from the White Spire. If they didn't find Eliska soon, they would have to withdraw from the city.

Yann had no idea what the boys would do after that. Their whole mission might be dead without Eliska.

He came to another building and glanced inside. Anríq turned his back on Yann, raised his club, and used it to stop a million flying particles, splinters, and timbers from attacking him.

Yann didn't go into the building. The same tornado of whirling mayhem filled the rooms. "We can't go in here," he announced over his shoulder. "This place would be a death trap."

Anríq was too busy to answer. Yann heard Anríq still outside.

Yann started to turn away when an almighty blast tore the building apart right in front of him.

The walls detonated outward and ripped both boys off their feet. Yann barely had time to raise his glaive before another hurricane of revolving forces assaulted him from all sides.

He struggled to see in the mayhem before he hit something solid. It felt like a wall, but he only stumbled into it. He didn't fall down.

He turned around and squinted into the confusion just long enough to see Eliska battling her way out of the storm.

He pushed off the wall to try to get near her, but at that moment, a dead horse cartwheeled in front of him and vanished into the dust clouds to his right.

He looked around a second time, but he didn't see Eliska anywhere now. He didn't see Anríq, either.

Yann couldn't stay here, so he blundered back the other way, stumbled into another avenue, and spotted a solid brick wall across the street.

He charged it, flattened himself behind it, and gasped for breath while he assessed his situation.

The wall blocked the worst wind. Whatever destroyed that building created a vortex of fast-moving air right on the spot where the building just stood.

All the splintered wood, dust, hardware, bodies, and other trash left over from the building spun, tumbled, and rotated in the funnel.

The cyclone obliterated a dozen blocks. Yann couldn't see if Anríq and Eliska were still over there or not. He couldn't go back in there to find out.

The upheaval attacking the rest of the city was still the distorting, morphing, transforming kind. He had to pay attention when the wall behind him came to life and extended hands and arms to grab him and hold him there.

He fought his way out of their grasp, wheeled around, and stabbed and hacked his glaive at the hands to free himself.

He inched away, but he made sure not to go inside the hurricane again.

He circled it searching for any sign of Anríq and Eliska. Nothing.

He wouldn't be able to find them unless they found him first, so he headed back toward the White Spire.

That last explosion threw him farther away from the spire than it should have. The blast must have been another one of the spire's defenses. He had to trek at least a mile to get back to the same place he started.

He kept repeating the same mantra in his mind. Anríq and Eliska would go back to the spire. They both had magic. They would try to get to the Shard. He could find them there. He wouldn't be able to find them anywhere else.

He made it ten blocks before he passed another building. The other frame structure looked sturdy enough with most of its exterior walls blown out.

The interior looked much calmer than the other buildings he'd seen.

He considered going in there and resting for a while. He wasn't likely to find another sheltered place like this.

He took a few steps toward it and froze when he saw several hundred people fleeing through the city streets on the other side of the same building.

He froze in his tracks trying to understand how so many people could have gotten trapped in this city—and how they could have survived the chaos all this time.

Right then, a host of shapes, forces, objects, and skeletons attacked the crowd from both sides. The crowd streamed up one of the avenues trying to get out of town.

The attackers closed from both sides, tore children away from their families, and pounced on defenseless civilians to devour them.

Yann burst into a run and raised his glaive to defend the refugees. He sprinted through the building from one side to the other, burst into the avenue, and skidded to a halt when all those people disappeared.

The magical attackers didn't disappear. They went after each other, and as soon as Yann got there, they turned on him, too.

He fought his way back to the same building, but two skeletons followed him. They backed him against another wall that tried to grab him and hold him still so the skeletons could maul him.

He slashed his glaive at the skeletons, shattered both of them, and then took off running into a different part of the city.

The streets here suffered the same kind of collapse he'd been seeing everywhere else. He didn't see anything to make him think this was another illusion—or maybe all of it was an illusion.

He set off toward the White Spire again. He couldn't let anything else distract him from finding Anríq and Eliska.

He passed another eight blocks down one of the central avenues. All this chaos slowed him down.

He was just making up his mind to run there when he turned a corner and stopped in his tracks again when he saw the exact same crowd. He even recognized all the same people.

Now he knew this was an illusion. He glanced sideways to gauge his direction to the spire.

He saw it in the distance. He could follow this street straight toward it, but a ground-shaking bellow made him spin back the other way.

His stomach dropped when the people he just tried to help reared off the ground and changed into Darklings right in front of his eyes. Hundreds of them erupted out of their skins, sprouted tentacles and fangs, and charged him in murderous fury.

He raised his glaive and immediately changed his mind when he saw how many of them there were.

He turned away and ran for it. He didn't even take the time to check that he was running toward the spire. He just had to get as far away from those Darklings as possible.

He made it three more blocks sideways before he let himself believe that they weren't coming after him. He could finally turn down another thoroughfare and start the long, slow, painstaking process of battling his way back to the spire.

He only made it another half mile before exhaustion brought him to a standstill.

He didn't waste time trying to find a building to shelter in. He kept an eye on the surroundings, spotted a pile of rubble right in the middle of the road, and circled it until he found a slab of marble angled against another.

They formed a tiny hollow underneath—just big enough for him to crawl inside. He honestly didn't give a flying crap anymore how comfortable it was. He didn't need comfort.

He wedged himself inside along with his glaive, collapsed in exhaustion, and shut his eyes inhaling a shaky breath.

The same sounds of shrieks, rumbles, and shattering crashes came from outside. He listened to them with half an ear to make sure they couldn't get to him.

He didn't open his eyes while he concentrated on calming down his heartbeat just a little bit. All the stuff out there was too busy attacking itself and everything else. None of it came after him. He was safe in here for now.

He stayed awake longer than he should have. He couldn't calm his nerves enough to relax.

He sent up a silent prayer to Eliska to find him. She didn't need to see him to locate him in this disaster zone.

He might as well stay in here for the rest of forever if she didn't find him. At least he would be alive in here—until he starved to death.

That wouldn't happen because he wouldn't stay here. He wouldn't die like a rat in a hole.

He came here to get the Shard of Hotha. If he was going to die, he would die fighting even if he had to fight an unwinnable battle against an invincible magical force.

He couldn't do it now. Nervous exhaustion dragged him into the dirt underneath him. He couldn't move and he didn't want to.

He kept his eyes shut and drifted off to the sounds of battle coming from outside. He kept startling awake whenever something struck the mound too close to him or crashed into the dirt just beyond his feet.

His own fatigue eventually forced him to fall asleep. He drifted into another hazy dreamworld like the one he'd seen in the Royal Palace in the Verdant Gorges.

He found himself standing on a dais that looked remarkably similar to the phantom gathering hall in the palace.

The courtiers wore the same style of clothes, but this throne was made of carved white marble instead of black stone.

The massive carved stone crown didn't hang over the throne and the throne itself stood much taller than the one in the palace.

The throne room itself towered much taller with light streaming from every inch of the walls and ceiling. The room glowed with blinding light.

Yann stood in front of the throne wearing a full-length white robe and a gold crown on his head. It wasn't the same crown. This one lacked the multi-colored gemstones.

A ring of massive diamonds studded the circle of plain gold around his head. That was all. The crown didn't need any other decoration.

A beautiful queen stood at his side while all the courtiers cheered and bowed to the King and Queen.

His Queen wore a plain white robe, too, and a smaller, more feminine crown resting on top of her long, luxurious dark hair.

His heart stopped when he recognized her. He turned all the way around to stare down into her eyes. It was Marine—the real Marine this time—not some distant relative put in her place.

She smiled up at him with the same warmth and affection he remembered from her saner moments.

His eyes stung with tears. She really was back. She was with him—and she was sane. She looked at him the way he always secretly hoped and dreamed he would see her looking at him again.

A hush fell over the crowd when he took a step toward her. He almost didn't dare to touch her. Was this real?

The minute he thought that, she exploded out of her skin and turned into a Darkling. He stumbled backward to get away in time, bumped into another broken wall somewhere in the devastated city, and raised his glaive to defend himself.

He thought for one split second that he would have to stab Marine to kill this Darkling—and then he jolted awake in his hollow under the rubble mound.

He stared up at the slabs just inches above his face. He gasped for air and fought his racing heart back under control. Sweat drenched his face, hair, and clothes.

He clenched his fingers around his glaive handle forcing himself to think. It wasn't real.

That wasn't Marine. She didn't turn into a Darkling. She wasn't here. She was miles away in the Coil if she was even still alive at all.

Chapter 28

Eliska dove for Anríq and shoved him out of the tornado. They broke out of the whirlwind—and back into the ordinary kind of instability turning this city into a war zone.

She pushed him out of danger just long enough to check that he was all right. "Are you okay?!" she yelled over the noise. "Are you hurt anywhere?"

She clamped her hands on his shoulders and stared deep into his eyes. She could already feel that he wasn't hurt anywhere, but he shook his head anyway.

"I'm okay!" he panted. "We lost you! We gotta find Yann...."

"We can't!" she countered. "The blast magicked him too far away. Come on! We have to go to the spire now! This Island is becoming even more unstable. I don't know if we'll have another chance."

She took hold of his wrist and pulled him into the next avenue.

They weren't that far from the spire, but the escalating chaos made it seem a thousand miles away.

All the same confusion of morphing objects turned the streets into a battleground. Everything attacked everything else in a confused tide of voices, crashes, and smashes.

More and more Darklings appeared out of the woodwork and got involved in the fighting.

They lumbered through the streets, hurtled through the air, attacked each other and random stuff wherever they found it, and all the other whirling combatants ganged up on the Darklings to tear them limb from limb.

Eliska did her best not to get mixed up in all that madness, but she had to when the combatants came too close.

The Darklings posed the biggest danger. They rushed her baring their fangs and roaring. She had to let go of Anríq, launched herself at the Darklings, and bounded from one to the next.

She unloaded her Dark power into each one and dissolved them the way she did in the maze under the Keepers of the Dawn's monastery.

She landed on the ground, ran alongside four Darklings, dragged her fingertips down their sides before they stopped fighting each other long enough to notice her, and infected them with her Darkness to destroy them.

She cleared forty of them from this thoroughfare alone, but more came from all directions. The whole city seemed to be sprouting Darklings from every corner.

Anríq followed her all the way. She swerved down another street and came out closer to the spire before she noticed some of the combatant objects changing into Darklings, too.

Anríq didn't get a chance to fight them before she got to them first. She could destroy them so much faster.

She even sent her Dark poison into Darklings she couldn't touch. She took control of them and turned them against each other. She made them rotate away from her and Anríq to clear a path through the middle of the street.

Her actions caused everything else in the landscape to react with an equally murderous counterattack.

All the spinning shrapnel, splinters, objects, monsters, and projectiles caught in the mayhem hurtled inward to target her.

She erected her protective ball around herself and Anríq, but the Darklings could protect her better.

She made them rear up on either side of her path. All those missiles hit the Darklings—or most of the missiles did.

The smaller fragments and needle arrows whizzed around the Darklings, avoided their thrashing tentacles, and bombarded her field instead.

She channeled more power into it to make it stronger. She didn't have to tap the full depth of her power to counter these attacks.

Anríq stayed with her all the way down the thoroughfare to its other end.

The bombardment kept building to a brutal din. Darklings dropped everywhere she went. She barely had to touch them to bring them down.

She poured her Darkness into them, too. Their own tentacles transferred her Darkness to every other Darkling. Her destructive power spread outward from her in a widening circle of destruction. Darklings collapsed for blocks in all directions.

She sprinted in sight of the spire and pulled Anríq into a sheltered corner. She leveled enough Darklings to buy herself a few seconds' reprieve before they came after her again.

Her protective ball held the chaos at bay just long enough for her to face Anríq.

She had to gasp out their plan in a few words before they both charged back out into what might be the last fight of their lives.

The words stopped in her throat when she saw his shocked, horrified expression. He stared down at her in stunned disbelief.

She read it all in his eyes. He didn't see her in the monastery. He only heard about it from her afterward—and she skipped most of the gory details—precisely because she didn't want him to react like this.

This was the first time he saw her use her Darkness firsthand. She didn't reduce the Voyant to jelly like this. That fight turned out to be relatively tame compared to this.

She looked away. "Sorry," she mumbled. "I understand if you don't want to...you know...."

He snapped out of his trace, grabbed her arm, pulled her around fast, and kissed her hard—harder than he'd ever kissed her before.

"I want you to," he blurted out. "Let it all out! Don't think about me. Do whatever you have to do. Get as Dark as you need to get."

She blinked at him. "Really?"

He nodded. "Let go. Let go completely. Use your Darkness to its limit."

Now it was her turn to stare at him in stunned horror. She didn't even know what letting go completely looked like. She wasn't even sure if she could.

He rallied first, pushed himself back into the open, and shot a flinty glare toward the spire. "We're going out there, aren't we?"

She nodded. She already knew what she needed to do.

He cast one last critical glance behind him and to both sides. It was a casual, meaningless glance intended to steel his resolve before the final act of their assault.

He went very still and stopped breathing when he happened to look up one of the nearby alleys. "My God!" he whispered. "It's them!"

Eliska had to shift her position to see what he was looking at. She and Anríq both stared at a group of Barbarians marching through the city streets.

They looked so out of place that it had to be an illusion. It was the perfect illusion to distract Anríq from the task in front of him.

All the Barbarians wore full war regalia, hair spikes, elaborate jewelry and decorations, eye paint, and carried their weapons.

They passed a part of the alley where Anríq and Eliska got an eyeful of Taitus, Hoch, Baoco, and all Anríq's relatives and friends from his tribe.

Eliska even recognized plenty of people from the Dinu band that took the refugees in after their home Layer collapsed. The whole tribe was here.

Anríq's family passed another building and filed out of sight. He immediately started forward to intercept them.

Eliska rushed him to tell him this was only an illusion, but she hesitated to bring him back to reality so fast.

She followed him just to give him one last look at his family before they evaporated out of his life again. He must have been longing for the day he found them alive somewhere in the Coil.

The two travelers came to the end of the alley and looked out at another avenue where all the Barbarians filed past. They headed north out of the city to the countryside where they would be safe.

Anríq stopped there to stare at them all—and that was the moment when they all turned into Darklings and attacked.

Dozens of them rushed Anríq and Eliska. The rest of the column fell on each other slashing, dismembering, and cutting each other to ribbons with their tentacles.

Anríq sprang forward, yanked down his axe, and bellowed, "NO!!" but the Barbarians were already bursting out of their skins too fast for anything to stop them.

Eliska didn't even try to stop him from going out there. She wouldn't have been able to overcome his strength—not without seriously turning her magic against him.

She magicked herself in front of him and unleashed a torrential wave of her own Darkness on the attacking Darklings.

She reduced those closest to her to steaming puddles of goo. Her Darkness infected the others in another outward-radiating domino effect of death and destruction.

Anríq stood stock still with his axe raised for a second. Then he buckled onto his knees gasping and whimpering in despair.

"No!!" he choked. "No!"

She didn't turn around to face him. She couldn't be the one to rob him of this one last glimpse of his family—the only family he had left.

"They can't all be dead!" he whimpered. "They can't be! They have to still be there!"

She gulped down a lump in her throat, but she still didn't let herself turn around, not even to comfort him.

She faced the Darklings that weren't here anymore. Her Darkness leveled them all. It would keep spreading through the city and kill Darklings she couldn't see.

It wouldn't stop more Darklings from appearing. Any feature of the landscape could turn into a Darkling anytime.

The Coil's disintegration would continue to manifest as Darkness here and everywhere else. She had to act.

Anríq recovered first. She heard him stand up, sniff, and then he turned away.

By the time she followed him, he was already storming down the alley heading back to the thoroughfare where they'd just seen the spire.

She caught up with him at the same spot. He didn't seem to notice when she surrounded both of them with another protective ball to hold off all the particles and attackers zooming around in the breeze.

"We're doing this," he snarled through gritted teeth. "We're going to break into the spire and take both Shards."

"Right," she replied.

He barely glanced at her. She didn't interrupt his grief. She couldn't do that to him.

He dealt with it in his own way. He must already know that his family was all dead.

They weren't there anymore. They weren't waiting for him in the Sojourner's Sanctum the way he wanted them to be. He would never be able to go back there and visit them when this was all over.

This was another heartless trick to show him something he could never have. It was cruel and his despair turned to fury just like Yann's and Eliska's did.

He gave her one last hard look. "You get that Shard no matter what," he snapped. "Understand? Don't hold back for anything."

She nodded. She didn't plan to hold back. She couldn't let whatever this force was hurt anyone else she cared about.

She and Anríq faced the spire. This was it. This was the moment the three travelers had been working toward all this time.

She and Anríq started forward at the same moment. They didn't discuss it first before they both burst into a run.

They broke across the last street and all the spire's defenses unleashed on both of them.

Chapter 29

E liska launched herself into the air to draw the bulk of the spire's
assault away from Anríq.

Right at that moment, she saw Yann running toward them from a
side street.

She couldn't help either of the boys except by getting away from
them. She shot high over the street and released a devastating thump
of power on the spire.

She concentrated everything on the topmost window. The bombardment came from there, but the window held.

Some part of her still held back. She didn't want to destroy the
Shard.

She also wanted to make sure Yann, Anríq, or both of them got
inside the spire so two of their party would make it to the top at the
same time.

She didn't want to risk one of them taking one Shard and leaving
the other. Another Voyant was the last thing any of them needed right
now.

She took another hellish barrage from the spire, but she deflected it
easily and turned it back on the window. She paused her counterattack
for one second—just long enough to fire down at the lower walls the
way she did in her vision.

She blasted a breach in the wall, but Yann couldn't get near it.

He and Anríq got trapped in different places at a distance from the spire. Neither of the boys could get any closer.

Yann fought Darklings that came out of nowhere to stop him. He couldn't kill them with just his glaive.

Eliska had to divert power away from the spire to hit those Darklings. She couldn't concentrate well enough to eliminate them all.

When she eliminated any of them, Yann sprinted forward. He covered only a few blocks at a time getting closer to the spire before more Darklings brought him to a halt again.

The spire unleashed its magical torrents on Anríq. He fought his way closer to the spire from the ground, but he slowed down to keep pace with Yann.

Anríq kept darting out of position to attack Darklings and draw them away from Yann.

Anríq lured the Darklings into line between himself and the spire. The spire's bombardment hit the Darklings and killed them faster than Anríq could kill them himself.

He had to constantly defend himself with his axe and club against the spire's volleys.

He only advanced a few steps at a time before he had to stand his ground, pinwheel his weapons in wild flurries, and deflect those shots before they hit him.

Something was bound to come to a head. He missed one of his parries and a jet of magic from the spire hit him in the knee.

His leg gave out underneath him and then a catastrophic impact released from the spire.

Eliska didn't see it coming even though she'd been looking straight at the spire when it happened.

The shockwave hit her, smacked her backward with epic force, and she hit the ground.

She must have passed out for a second because she woke up—and looked all around her.

She had to blink the stars out of her eyes when she saw Anríq standing not far away—but this wasn't the Anríq she knew.

He seemed to have gotten bigger—or maybe the tall hair spikes sticking out of his shaved scalp made him look that way.

He wore full Barbarian war gear, black paint around his eyes, and dozens of trinkets tied to different parts of his clothes.

He wore a black leather chest harness studded in spikes instead of his plain old vest. Spikes and studs covered his shiny black leather pants.

He didn't carry any weapons. He actually looked more intimidating without them.

He didn't see her lying on a pile of cushions in a tent. It was a Barbarian tent like the ones she and Anríq stayed in when they visited the Dinu Tribe's camp.

He stood to one side talking in a low murmur to his brother Hoch. Anríq's other brother Baoco stood next to them listening to their conversation.

"I told you to take care of Sarvin a week ago," Anríq snarled. "Now I have to do it. Do you realize how bad this looks—when my own warriors don't carry out my orders?"

"I told you he escaped," Hoch murmured back. "Someone must have tipped him off about your order in time for him to make a run for it. He's been hiding in the hills all this time. I sent out our men to scour the countryside. They just found him a few hours ago."

"Who betrayed us?" Anríq demanded. "Who told him what we planned to do?"

Hoch lowered his voice to a whisper. "It was Andor. He left the camp early that morning and didn't rejoin us until later. He was gone the whole time we were traveling out there. He had plenty of time to double back, tell Sarvin all his secrets, and rejoin us like nothing happened."

"Bring them both up here," Anríq ordered. "This has gone on long enough."

Eliska froze to her cushions. Anríq couldn't see her with his back to her, but she didn't dare to move.

This must be the Anríq that might have been if he'd taken over as Chieftain in his father's place. He was the one in charge of his brothers and all the other Barbarian warriors of their tribe.

She held her breath watching him storm outside with his brothers. Hoch and Baoco split away.

Anríq planted himself in front of the tent flap where she could see and hear everything he said and did. Did she really want to see this?

He wasn't a Servant anymore. He didn't care about healing and serving humanity. He only cared about holding onto his power and enforcing his authority—just like a real Barbarian warlord.

Hoch and Boaco came back with a different warrior tied hand and foot with ropes. Someone had stuffed a rag into his mouth and bound it in place with another length of rope tied tightly around his head.

More warriors dragged a second man into the center of the camp. The second captive came kicking, screaming, and protesting his innocence.

Anríq watched with his arms crossed while the other warriors threw the second man on the ground and kicked him a dozen times to make him lie still.

Anríq glared down at both prisoners. "How is it possible that Sarvin is still alive, Andor, when our men set out to kill him a week ago?"

The second man craned his head to look up at Anríq, but Andor didn't dare to get off the ground. "I don't know anything about this, Anríq! I swear it!"

"Did you know I gave orders for our men to execute Sarvin—and don't lie, Andor," Anríq fired back. "I already know you told him about the order in time for him to escape. He would be dead right now if you hadn't told him."

"I didn't......" Andor babbled.

"Then who did?" Anríq waved at the camp. "Are you really that much of a coward that you would pin the blame on one of your fellow warriors—just to save your own worthless hide? Be a man for once in your life and admit what you did. We all know you're guilty. Then you and Sarvin can die together—which is more than either of you deserves."

Andor choked, his lips started quivering, and he cast his eyes to the ground. He couldn't control his mouth well enough to answer. He didn't have to.

Anríq swiped his forefinger at his men. "Take them."

All the warriors rushed in, raised their weapons, and started hacking at the two captives. Andor screamed out once and then fell silent under the rain of blows.

Chapter 30

Anríq turned away from the Barbarian warriors attacking the two prisoners, strode back into the tent—and saw Eliska watching the whole episode.

He burst into a smile—but it wasn't his usual boyish smile she knew so well. There was nothing boyish or innocent or even appealing about this man.

His eyes had gone hard and cruel. His smile had a toothy, predatory quality that made his eyes harden with sadistic intent.

"Hello!" he murmured. "You should have told me you were awake. You didn't have to see that."

He pulled down the tent flap to block her view of all the warriors bending over what was left of Sarvin and Andor.

She didn't tell Anríq that she'd already seen enough. She could see enough just by looking into his eyes.

She couldn't tell from here if he really had grown bigger, more muscular, and more powerful or if he just looked that way from her perspective.

He strode over to her cushions and sat down next to her. He didn't seem to notice that she wasn't wearing Barbarian clothing nor did she cut her hair.

She still wore the same patched rags, black cloak, and long hair she had on when she first met him.

She read the whole scene in a heartbeat. This must be his other illusion—the illusion of becoming the chieftain his father wanted him to be. She was his wife in this version of his past and future.

They would have been living like this if he'd accepted his father's offer. Anríq and Eliska would have stayed with the Tribe and ruled it in Taitus's place.

Anríq bent over and kissed her much more forcefully than he ever had before. He didn't wait for her to respond. He gripped the back of her head and steered her mouth into his as deeply as he wanted to.

He didn't seem to notice whether she responded or not. He straightened up and smiled down at her with that same hawkish, toothy, murderous grin.

She stared up at him in.....she couldn't even call it surprise. She actually really believed in that moment that she was looking at a completely different person.

The man she loved didn't live here anymore—and then she realized.

Tattoos covered his chest, arms, neck, and even his back and stomach—but he didn't have the Servant's mark anymore.

He had it when he visited his family with her. He would have still had it if he'd accepted his father's offer then.

This Anríq never became a Servant. He never left his home Tribe. He became his father's heir when he was younger—so how did she meet him?

That didn't matter because none of this was real.

He didn't notice her reaction—or lack thereof. He only grinned and lowered his voice while his hands traveled up and down her arms, over her face, and through her hair.

"You'll find the Shard of Hotha for me like we talked about, okay?" he murmured. "You'll bring it to me. I'll be able to harness its magic and become the greatest Barbarian chieftain in the Coil. The Shard will help me conquer the other Tribes—but I can't get it without you. I'm counting on you. Do you understand? We'll rule together."

His eyes smoldered with suggestive fire, but nothing he said or did meant a thing to her.

This wasn't Anríq—not the Anríq she cared about.

The man she loved just told her to use her Darkness to take the Shard for the good of the whole Coil. The man she loved didn't give a hoot about conquering anyone or harnessing the Shard's power for his own gain.

Maybe this fake version of Anríq mistook her silence for enthralled worship. How should she know?

She raised her hands, touched his face once, and then planted both her palms on his chest—right where the Servant's mark should have been.

She unloaded a colossal thump of Dark power into him and shattered the illusion. She would have hit him a lot harder, but she knew exactly how much magic to use to knock him out of this.

His body ripped backward off the cushions and he went flying. The same concussion blasted her out of the tent, sent her cartwheeling in the opposite direction, and she landed hard on the pavement.

She landed right where she would have landed if the spire's last shot hadn't sent her and Anríq into that illusion.

She scrambled to her feet and saw him lying crumpled on the ground against a nearby building.

He didn't move, but she saw from here that this was the real Anríq. He wore his old plain vest, beaten pants, and his hair hung in long blonde dreadlocks down his back.

She rushed over to him and immediately took another crushing bombardment from the spire.

He wasn't a threat to the spire anymore and neither was Yann. She was the only combatant left on the field.

She flung a protective ball in front of her to guard her from the spire's assault. She kept her magical shield in place around both herself and Anríq while she turned him over.

She checked him everywhere and felt countless broken bones, damaged internal organs, and internal bleeding all over his body. Did she do that? Did she hurt him that badly by bringing him back from the illusion?

She didn't care because she had him back. The Servant's mark darkened his torso under his vest. His face returned to its old boyish look, especially when he was sleeping or unconscious.

She flooded him with her magic and healed all his injuries. They were so severe that he didn't regain consciousness right away.

A deep rumble and a crash caught her attention from behind. She glanced over her shoulder in time to see Yann bolting for the breach in the spire wall.

She didn't see how he got away from the Darklings. The spire must have turned all its attention on her when Anríq went down.

Yann darted inside the spire. He made it that far. Now he needed her help.

She left Anríq lying where he was. He was sound asleep. The spire would leave him alone now that he wasn't trying to break into it.

She launched herself off the ground and all the spire's magical fire followed her upward into the sky. The spire didn't shoot at Anríq again.

She vaulted as high as the Shard's window and unloaded her magic on the whole structure. The walls rumbled and groaned.

She escalated her assault and so did the spire. She built to an almighty barrage to draw every ounce of the spire's power to herself. She had to hit the spire hard enough that it wouldn't see an imp as a threat.

The spire pounded her with countless shots. It built in strength to match her as she emptied more and more of her Darkness into it.

Deep impacts thumped against her protective ball. It shattered, but the spire's bombardment still didn't damage her.

She felt herself projecting a glowing magical halo around herself. It resembled the Voyant's except that this halo was pure Darkness. The full assault deflected off her halo so none of the spire's magic penetrated.

She hammered the spire back and concentrated especially on the upper window, but she couldn't damage that, either.

The Shard hovered there in plain sight. Could she rush in and take it right now?

She could have, but she held herself back. She didn't want anyone to take it until two of the friends got near enough to take both Shards at the same time.

Movement caught her eye just then. She glanced down to see Anríq stirring. He started to get to his feet.

The spire reacted instantaneously and unloaded on him just as hard as it just had been unloading on her. He couldn't survive an assault like that.

She plunged between him and the spire, took the impact on her halo, and right at that moment, Yann leapt out of the spiral staircase into the top tower room.

He halted right there in front of the Shard—close enough to touch it.

The instant he entered the room, the Shard started to fade. Its light dimmed and the facets of its carved surfaces started to disappear.

Eliska launched herself up there to get there before the Shard vanished entirely. She couldn't get there in time, but right before the stone disappeared from view, Yann lunged for it, dove on top of it, and they both went down behind the windowsill.

A catastrophic boom blasted across the landscape, stripped Eliska away, and she really did black out this time.

Chapter 31

E liska dragged herself off the ground.....and had to stop for a minute when she realized she was touching grass. She wasn't in the destroyed city anymore.

The long, dry grass smelled pungent and clean in her nose. She wavered there and winced when pain stabbed her in the head.

She must have gotten injured when she....

Her head shot up when she remembered how she got here.

She only had to lift her head above the grass to see exactly what was going on.

She lay sprawled on the same distant hilltop where the Voyant transported the three friends to this Island.

She hauled herself to her feet just as Anríq stood up out of the grass a few yards away. He made eye contact with her and then cast his gaze out to the city in the distance.

He and Eliska straightened up, moved closer together, and fell silent. The city churned with just as much chaos and upheaval as before—maybe even more so.

The whole landscape heaved and seethed. Buildings shuddered, quaked, collapsed, and reformed into different shapes.

The White Spire stood up tall and dark against the farthest horizon. The Shard of Hotha glistened and flashed in its upper windows.

A different light shone over the landscape now. The dark figure of a person hovered high in the air near the tower. A brilliant halo of golden light surrounded the dark outline in the center.

Eliska couldn't see any other distinguishing feature of the person from this distance, but she already knew who it was.

"It's Yann," she murmured. "He took the first Shard. He's the new Voyant."

"He isn't the one causing this," Anríq pointed out. "He isn't trying to attack us. The Shard is making the landscape unstable. The Shard is searching for an affiliate. The only way to stop him is to take the second Shard." He turned to face her. "You have to take it."

"What?! No!" she exclaimed. "This isn't what we agreed! We said you and I would take both Shards. If I take it, you and I can never be together! We'll probably never see each other again!"

"If no one takes the second Shard, millions of people will die," he insisted. "If no one takes the second Shard, Yann will die. If we try to remove the Shard from him to give it to one of us, he'll die. You have to take the second Shard. You're the only one with the power to get near it. I'll help you all I can, but it has to be you."

"No!" Her voice spiked out of control. "I can't!"

"If you don't take it, I'll have no choice but to take it and then you'll walk out of here alone while I stay with him."

"No, no, Anríq!" she moaned. "You can't do this to me...."

"I have no choice. If someone doesn't take the second Shard, the Coil will kill more people and all those deaths would be on my head."

She looked around wildly in all directions for some way out of this. Not even her vision of herself and Yann as affiliates truly prepared her for this. Nothing could prepare her to lose Anríq forever.

The words tore out of her along with all the choked sobs she never let out. They would all come pouring out as soon as she let herself fully believe she had to do this.

"I love you," she husked. "I only want to be with you."

He pulled her in and crushed her head against his heart.

"I want that, too," he murmured into her hair. "I want it more than anything, but I'm a Servant. My only purpose is to serve and heal. My magic would destroy me if I threw that away to become a selfish mercenary with no care for the needs of others. I would be useless to you and to myself and to the world. I would be worse than dead."

She clamped her eyes shut against those words. Why did she have to see him as that just a few minutes ago?

Did that vision come to her right at that moment to seal what he was telling her right now?

"You wouldn't love me as that," he went on in the same broken undertone. "You would hate me. You would regret turning your back on Yann and the Shard and all the good you could have done with it. You would yearn to come back and take the Shard so you could serve and heal, but by then, it would be too late."

"I can't lose you!" Her tears broke the last barrier. She couldn't hold them back anymore. This was really happening. She was about to walk away from him forever.

He pushed her back, cupped her cheeks in both hands, and gazed deep into her face.

This was the man she really loved with all her heart. His eyebrows twitched with all the pain and concern he cherished for her.

"You won't lose me if you take the Shard," he murmured. "You'll gain yourself. You'll gain Yann and you'll gain the whole world."

"There has to be a way!" She lost the fight and broke down in sobs. "There has to be a way we can be together."

"There isn't—not without killing Yann and all these other people. Neither of us will let that happen. I know you won't let that happen. You're a Servant as much as I am if not more. You'll do the right thing for all humankind—and that means stabilizing the Coil."

"But...." She floundered for any excuse not to go through with this. "What if I use the Shard for Dark purposes? What if it turns me completely Dark?"

Tears sprang to his eyes and his features spasmed out of control. He never stopped looking into her eyes. She couldn't look away as long as he held her there.

"The Shard will heal your Darkness. You'll live in the Hall of Light and be happy."

"I don't want to be happy with Yann!" she shrieked. "I want you!"

He folded her against his heart again. She even heard it pounding through his sternum. She just healed that heart a few minutes ago.

He stood here right now as strong and kind as ever because of her. She healed him so he could leave her and she could leave him.

"I would give anything to heal you, even if it means giving you up," he rasped. "I don't want to lose you, but I would do it for you. That's more important than what I want."

She couldn't argue anymore. This wasn't happening—but it was.

He held her for a long time before he let her go. She clamped her eyes shut in the darkness of his arms and poured out all her tears.

She always knew she and Anríq would never get to be together—not the way they both really wanted to.

She just never thought it would end this way. She never thought she would be the one to walk away from him.

She couldn't. She wouldn't. She refused to—but she already knew she would.

She gave herself to the Servant's path because of him. She never wanted anything but to be worthy of him.

She could only do that by becoming a Servant—a real Servant. She had to follow the Servant's path for its own sake no matter what happened between them.

She was a Servant. That undeniable fact stamped itself into her being long before she ever thought she could get together with him.

If anything happened to him, she would continue to be a Servant on her own. She would have continued to be a Servant on her own if he never came to find her when she took charge of the children.

She would have wandered the Coil healing, protecting, and helping anyone who needed it.

He kissed her forehead one more time and she straightened up. She couldn't look at him.

The Shard magnetized her gaze to the spire on the horizon. She was a Servant with one task in life.

Yann would make it a thousand times harder for anyone to get near the second Shard. Anríq was right that she was the only person with the power to get it.

The instant she looked at the Shard, she knew what she had to do and how to do it. All doubt evaporated out of her mind.

She and the Shard belonged together. Anríq completely vanished from her consideration the minute she looked at the Shard.

She would have set off for the city then and there, but she couldn't do that to him. She turned to face him for the last time.

He read the truth in her eyes. She was already gone. It was over between them. They could never be together again in this life.

He cupped her cheeks one last time, kissed her, and straightened up. "Bye," he whispered.

"Bye," she murmured back. "I love you. I always will."

His lip twitched in a broken attempt at a smile. "I know. I love you, too. I love you more than anything."

He lowered his hands and turned away blinking back tears. Neither of them looked at each other again when they started down the hill heading back to the city.

They walked side by side for twenty feet before they both burst into a run.

Chapter 32

Crashes and booms echoed out of the city ahead as Eliska and Anríq got closer. Anríq raised his weapon and Eliska raised her staff, but neither of them attacked—not yet.

"Something's wrong!" she yelled over the noise.

"Take us to the spire!" Anríq told her. "Get us as close to the walls as you can!"

She hesitated and probed the city ahead with her magic. "I can't! The landscape is changing!"

She didn't have to explain it. The pair ran closer to the city's outer edge. Anríq could see how much different the city looked now.

None of the shapes, mutated people and animals, and random objects battled through the streets anymore. Eliska couldn't really see the streets or any shapes at all now.

A solid mass of spinning chaos obliterated all the space between the last remaining hulks of buildings. They loomed out of the murk while clouds of dust, debris, and whizzing shards of random junk hurtled everywhere between them.

Anríq and Eliska slowed at the city's outermost neighborhoods and eventually came to a stop there. The two travelers stared into an impenetrable sea of confusion with no end in sight.

Eliska's magic gave her an instant of clarity. The whole Coil would be like this. The whole thing was collapsing and falling into chaos. This Island was nothing out of the ordinary.

She couldn't see the White Spire or the Shard of Hotha's characteristic purple-pink glow. She couldn't see anything but the wall of mayhem in front of her.

"This is it," she called over to Anríq. "This is the quest. We have to go through this and deal with it."

"And Yann will be waiting for us on the other side, won't he?" Anríq's features hardened and he tightened his grip on his weapons. "We better get to it, then."

He and Eliska stepped forward at the same time. She didn't tell him the truth.

Yann wouldn't wait for them on the other side. He wouldn't hang around the spire waiting for Anríq and Eliska to show up and make a play for the second Shard.

Yann would come out to meet them. He would find them in this confused landscape of shadows and danger. Then his presence would make the landscape even deadlier if that was possible.

Eliska's resolve took root in her soul. She set out to do this even if it cost her life.

She'd already lost Anríq forever. Now only the Shard mattered.

The Dark poison taking over her life craved the Shard. She had to have it. Insatiable hunger for the Shard wiped out everything else that might distract her from her goal.

She and Anríq stepped forward into the confusion. The tornado of whistling shrapnel, broken glass, splintered wood, and rock chips stung their faces and peppered their bodies.

Eliska burst into a run again and Anríq followed her, but they couldn't navigate through the city without the spire to orient them.

Eliska tried to use her magic to measure the city's layout, but that didn't work anymore, either. In a few minutes, she got lost in the confusion.

Only Anríq seemed real. He kept adjusting his position and veering one way or the other to keep running by her side.

They collided with each other and had to find each other when one of them ran around a corner while the other kept going straight.

They bumped into each other for the tenth time. Eliska grabbed his arm and steered him toward one of the few intact buildings.

She pushed him against it. "We can't keep doing this!" she yelled over the noise.

"Raise your protective ball!" he told her. "At least give us a few minutes to catch our breath."

She did it. Why didn't she think to do that before?

The ball held all the crap away from the two of them. The noise died so she and Anríq could catch their breath and hear each other.

"So you can't find your way through this?" he asked.

She shook her head and surveyed the area outside the ball. "I can't even see anything. I don't see any figures or Darklings.....or anything."

"Then there's no point in going anywhere. We could be running away from the spire."

"What should I do, then?" she asked.

He looked up and gave her a sharp glare. She winced and looked away.

She was the one who had the power to take the Shard. She should have been the one to decide what to do.

She didn't seem to be able to decide anything. The confusion of this city seemed to take over her mind.

"Can you take this ball to somewhere high over the landscape?" he asked. "Can you find the spire and navigate a course to take us to it?"

She only had to think about it to know the answer. The view of this city from the far hilltop flashed into her mind. "I can't see the spire from outside this cloud. We're stuck in here."

"There has to be a way," he insisted. "We'll just have to keep going and see if we can find anything. We might find some of those big streets we recognize from last time."

She couldn't be so sure. All her magic probing of this city told her one thing.

This cloud of confusion covered the city all the way to the spire itself. She didn't see how they would ever be able to navigate anywhere.

She didn't argue when Anríq pushed away from the building and set off through the mayhem.

She kept the ball around both of them, but in a little while, the deeper the two of them went, the more intense the bombardment became.

She and Anríq started out by migrating slowly between the buildings. The tempest of pounding debris scoured the ball and made a constant drumming sound in Eliska's ears.

The noise was really starting to get on her nerves, but it kept building the farther the two travelers went.

She found what once must have been one of the broad thoroughfares bisecting the city. She couldn't see the outer sidewalks or the central garden strip at all.

The tall buildings on either side offered the only guide that she was moving in the right direction—or what she hoped was the right direction.

She and Anríq kept going. Countless projectiles blasted against the ball in a hurricane of tiny attacking bullets. They converged on the ball so fast that they blocked visibility, too.

Pretty soon, the two travelers couldn't see anything outside the ball.

"We must be getting closer!" Anríq yelled over the noise. "It's getting stronger. It must be trying to stop us."

Eliska couldn't be sure of that, either. She couldn't be sure of anything.

For some reason, everything about this city bothered her now. It annoyed and agitated her far beyond what it should have.

The noise of random particles striking her ball shouldn't have gotten under her skin like this.

She looked around everywhere at the chaos outside the ball. She couldn't see anything nor could she sense anything with her magic.

This little ball of existence was the only thing left in a world of Darkness. The constant impact of tiny, unseen objects striking the ball pressed in on her awareness.

She spun one way and then the other trying to see everything that wasn't there to be seen. All this stuff crushed her under its weight. It would implode on her any second now.

Her anxiety escalated with the attack. Every instinct told her to run for it and break out of this world of cloud and confusion.

She kept turning to look all around her. She couldn't tell which direction she and Anríq had come from to get here or which direction to go to get out of this city even if she did run.

She panicked, but she couldn't even decide what to do about it.

The attack didn't affect Anríq at all. He just kept walking along and watching it impassively. He didn't notice her agitation or the panic taking over her mind.

The noise striking the ball kept getting louder, deadlier, and more insistent. She couldn't hear herself think.

That feeling blasted out of her and she screamed. Her hands flew to her ears to block out the noise, and right then, a brutal crash slammed into the ball from somewhere.

The ball imploded and hurled her and Anríq out into the wild mayhem with no protection.

They both sprawled on the pavement with dozens of strikes attacking from out of the haze. Blows rained on Eliska from all sides.

She screamed again and floundered over to Anríq just as he blundered toward her from a different direction.

She tried again and again to raise some protection around both of them, but nothing worked. She couldn't concentrate well enough to do anything.

He grabbed her and pulled her through the fog. She had no idea where they were going or even why they were going there. This confusion obliterated her mind.

He yelled something directly into her face, but she couldn't understand the words. He kept tugging and shoving her forward.

She tripped over things and unseen objects battered her beyond sight. She kept trying to cover her head to protect herself, but Anríq wouldn't let her. He refused to let go of her hand no matter what.

Chapter 33

Anríq forged ahead into the cloud. It got so thick and dense that it blacked out the area.

A constant rain of particles, gravel, splinters, and even larger projectiles bombarded the two travelers. That attack kept intensifying the deeper into the city they traveled. Some of those projectiles felt like nails, tree branches, or even large rocks.

She screamed again and again and even fought to break out of Anríq's grip. She would have run into the murk in panic and gotten lost, but he wouldn't let her go.

He crushed her hand in a painful grip and eventually shoved her around another corner into the alcove of some building somewhere.

The noise and bombardment died enough for her to hear him, but the panic, confusion, and disorientation didn't lift.

Anríq moved his face in front of hers. "Look at me, Eliska!"

She struggled to focus on him. Her eyes kept darting around everywhere while she scrambled to think straight. She couldn't concentrate on anything or get her thoughts into any kind of order.

"This is the quest," he insisted. "You said it yourself. This is the trial and the journey you have to go through to get the Shard. Don't you understand?"

She didn't understand—not really. She frowned at him.

He compressed his lips in annoyance and looked away for a second before he came back to glare at her. "Listen to me. This city—it's going to throw obstacles in your path the same way it did before—but they'll be worse this time. They're mental obstacles. The physical fights and battles will just be a part of it. The quest is in your mind. Can you hear me? Can you understand me at all? Nod if you understand me."

She frowned at him trying to get her brain to function.

Her response only seemed to annoy him more. She couldn't tell just by looking at him if he was suffering from the same reaction to the landscape.

She'd always been able to read and understand every shade of his facial expressions before.

Just a few short minutes changed all that. That one decision to end their relationship cut the connection. She couldn't understand him anymore—not the way she used to.

"The hurricane seems to diminish beyond this point," he told her. "We can get out of it if we just keep going. We're moving toward the center of the city. The spire is there. We can find it. Come on. I'll help you as much as I can."

She wouldn't have been able to respond. She wouldn't have been able to decide to leave this alcove. She wouldn't have been able to do much of anything.

He took her hand again and dragged her into the open. Did he really plan to drag her all the way to the spire and up its internal spiral staircase? Did he plan to force her to take the Shard?

He would have to if she stayed like this. She couldn't think clearly enough even to do that.

She stumbled after him and they stepped out into the same street full of revolving debris caught in tempest winds.

He turned out to be right, though. The assault slackened after a few more blocks. It didn't hammer the two of them so much, but it didn't stop entirely.

The confusion didn't lift from her mind, either. Would it ever stop? Would she ever come out of this?

The bigger, stronger, harder, more direct attacks only got worse as the smaller bombardment faded.

These new attacks didn't come from any surface nor did they belong to any definite shape. The Darkness itself delivered blows that sent Anríq and Eliska staggering before these forces retreated just as fast.

Some of them hit Eliska in the head and face. The blows stunned her and left her dizzy and more disoriented. Her eyes lost focus and she almost fell over before more strikes pushed her in a different direction.

She collided with Anríq and then bumped into unseen obstacles in her path. She lost contact with him more than once. He kept yelling out in the chaos, but he always found her eventually.

He ran into her, strapped his arms around her, yelled at her to keep going, and forced her in one particular direction or another.

Were they even still going in the same direction? He might have gotten turned around in the struggle. He could be steering her back and forth across the same few city blocks. She never would have known the difference.

The escalating assault drove her into another panic. Her magic gave her a fraction of an instant's warning before each blow landed on her. She raised her hand and fought her brain into gear just enough to defend herself.

She blocked half the blows coming at her and missed the other half, but anything was better than nothing.

That one instant of victory helped her come out of it at least a little bit. She could think just well enough to know where to direct her magic to deflect these attacks before they landed on her.

Anríq didn't fare so well. He couldn't predict them quickly enough to raise his weapons in time.

The impenetrable shade of so many projectiles spinning around made it impossible to see anything before a curling mass of some Dark object rocketed out of the shadows to strike him.

He kept yelling out, grunting in pain, and roaring when he tried to defend himself and missed. She stumbled over to him, and this time, she was the one who grabbed onto him.

The minute she made contact with him, she sensed more strikes coming from out of sight. She blasted out her magic just enough to catch them a few feet away from her. It wasn't much, but it gave her and Anríq just enough space to keep going.

She kept going in the same direction. She just had to trust him to know where they were going.

She protected him enough for him to straighten up and get his bearings. She was just hoping he would be able to tell her where to go when another strike came out of the mayhem to her left.

She raised her magic in front of the incoming attack. Her magic would have intercepted it and blasted it apart at a distance from her and Anríq where it wouldn't damage either of them.

She didn't think about it. She was too busy trying to understand what was happening to her. She only paid enough attention to anticipate the next attack.

At the last second before the two forces met, the assault changed and took shape. She didn't see it in time before it changed into a massive Darkling, smashed straight through her magical defenses, and collided with her and Anríq.

The Darkling reared, widened its huge mouth, and dove downward to devour both travelers. Anríq raised his axe, but not fast enough to save him and Eliska.

Her magic reacted on pure instinct. She should have magicked herself and Anríq out of danger, but she didn't think of it soon enough.

She had been shooting off these bursts to defend them against these murky assaults. Her addled brain did the same thing now and blasted out a starburst of magic between her and the Darkling.

She lost control of herself for a second and exploded the Darkling to a cloud of bloody goo, but all the strikes that had been hammering her and Anríq—they all changed into Darklings just as fast.

They started out as vaporous, unformed forces in the sea of confusion. They took shape a dozen yards from the travelers, became Darklings, and converged by the dozen—or maybe by the hundred.

Eliska unloaded her magic in all directions, but she couldn't think well enough to mount an effective defense.

She could have leveled all of these Darklings in a matter of minutes, but for the life of her she forgot how to do it.

She fired off one blast after another. Anríq staggered upright and raised his weapons. He knew how to fight Darklings.

They never stopped coming. Their numbers gathered from all sides. Did every single whizzing shard of broken gravel turn into a Darkling?

She got so consumed with fighting them that she didn't think of anything else—not even continuing her journey.

She raised her hands and fired countless blasts of magic toward the spire. Curtains of Darklings erupted out of the shadows to bomb in on her. She exploded them all as fast as she could blink and still they kept coming.

Anríq grabbed her from behind and yanked her away. "Come on!" he roared. "Keep going!"

She didn't want to turn away. She didn't want to stop shooting at the Darklings.

She had to turn her back on them to walk farther down the street.

More of them came from the other side where Anríq had just been fighting them.

The Darklings rushed in on the pair as soon as Anríq and Eliska stopped defending themselves.

Anríq held onto her with one arm, swung his axe with his other hand, and pounded the Darklings with deep booms of magic, but they kept closing tighter on that side.

Eliska could hold them off better on her side. She floundered back to some form of sanity enough to let off those blasts in a complete circle around her and Anríq.

She defended both of them until he yanked her around another corner into a different street.

She still couldn't see anything through the dust, debris, and whirl-wind bombardment.

She didn't have to see anything other than a glowing halo of light. It hung suspended at the end of the street. The halo cast the only light in the shadowy confusion.

Anríq and Eliska stopped in their tracks when they recognized the tall figure inside the halo.

A man glared out at them with an expression of pure, murderous hatred. He bared his teeth in a vicious snarl and all that hate poured out at the world through the brilliant rim of his halo.

He wore a full-length white robe embroidered with gold. His face seemed to have aged beyond his youth just in the few minutes since Anríq and Eliska had seen him.

His hair had grown since he left Middleborough. It no longer surrounded his head in curls. His hair hung down longer than it should have, but Anríq and Eliska both recognized him instantly.

It was Yann Dilnao—the new Voyant Mendicat.

Chapter 34

Eliska stopped breathing when she saw Yann as the new Voyant. For just a second, her hazy mind refused to believe that he could really attack her.

He had always treated her so kindly. He would never glare at her like this.

Somewhere deep in her gut, she already knew the truth. He didn't have to attack her. The Coil created all this chaos.

Yann wouldn't attack her any more than Noleron Kupero attacked her. The Voyant wasn't malicious.

The mayhem and instability of the solo Shard caused these attacks. It caused the Dark to break out of the Layers and take over the Coil.

No Voyant could stop this. Yann couldn't stop it. He probably couldn't even decide where he was or what he was doing. From the way he glared at his own friends, he might not even be aware of them.

Maybe he was glaring in pain or resentment over his own situation. Maybe the Shard already ate away at his insides. It might already be killing him. In fact, she knew it was.

The instant she and Anríq laid eyes on Yann, the surrounding Darklings rushed him instead. They plunged into his halo and it became blurry and indistinct, too.

The view of him inside the halo faded in a sheet of light. The Darklings kept streaking out of the shadows, diving into the halo, disappearing, and diffusing the light more and more.

The halo evaporated in a blinding flash of brilliant white, but just as fast, the halo exploded outward. The original deadly forces that became Darklings—they all blasted outward to the points of the compass.

The halo reestablished itself, turned back into the crisp image of Yann, and hurled the Darklings away. They disintegrated, turned back into their original shadowy vapors, and disappeared into the confused tornado of particles.

The concussion hit Anríq and Eliska. Anríq dove in front of Eliska to tackle her out of the way. He raised his axe between him and the Voyant.

The explosion hit his axe just enough to save both Anríq's and Eliska's lives, but not enough to defend them against Yann's assault.

The impact hurled Anríq and Eliska a dozen yards backward and they both hit the ground.

Eliska jumped up and turned on the Voyant. All thought went out of her head that she was fighting her brother.

She registered a split-second's awareness that Anríq was lying injured on the ground. He didn't get up.

She didn't have time to check him before the Voyant hammered her with his strongest volley yet.

The first strike nailed her to the building wall behind her. He held her there while dozens of blows hit her all over.

She rallied her Darkness to counterattack, but everything she tried only bounced off his unbreakable halo.

He stood over there at the end of the street as tall and terrible as Noleron ever was.

He pounded her with a devastating barrage. She couldn't get off the wall. She just had to hang here and wait for him to pulverize her to death.

Just enough of his shots flashed sideways after they hit her. She caught a glimpse of his face twisted in sadistic fury.

This wasn't her brother. This wasn't the considerate young Watchmen who took such good care of here all these weeks.

This really was the Voyant Mendicat—her old enemy.

He didn't let up his relentless hammering assault. She tasted blood and felt her bones breaking. Her consciousness slipped and he still kept it up.

She unleashed her magic to the limit, but she couldn't free herself. She panicked again and jerked hard from side to side. Her mind exploded trying in every way to get out of this.

He hit her so hard that he smashed the wall behind her. He forced her broken body through it, into the ruined building behind her, and delivered one last punishing smash that sent her flying.

She cartwheeled through the air flying backward, crashed down on the ground, and the Voyant exploded another building on top of her.

Mountains of rubble pounded down to bury her and crushed what little was left of her already destroyed body.

She came to her senses in the dark. Brutal pain racked every pore. She fought to breathe, faded out of consciousness, and swam back into a world of agony.

She really wished she could just die and get it over with, but right at that moment, she became aware of Anríq out there in the devastated landscape.

He lay where he'd fallen when the Voyant threw Anríq away.

Eliska couldn't even think of that thing as Yann anymore. Whatever Yann might have been during his life, he wasn't that anymore.

He was as vicious and destructive as the Voyant ever had been or maybe even worse.

Noleron never attacked like this. He never singled out one person to beat them to death and destroy a building to fall on top of them.

She tried to get up, but something held her down—something other than all her broken bones. Her expanded magical awareness showed her where she was in the city with tons of rock and concrete slabs piled on top of her.

The Voyant returned to the same place hovering over the White Spire. He would probably stay there standing guard over the spire from now on.

He would only leave to attack anyone who went near the Shard of Hotha. He would keep attacking until he killed Anríq and Eliska—if he hadn't succeeded already.

Anríq's vital signs flickered. He would die if she didn't help him.

She couldn't fight the Voyant, so she would just have to take Anríq and retreat. She had no other option.

She sent a flow of magic through her own body and healed her own injuries. It took a long time to fuse all the bones, stop all the bleeding, repair all the damage, and reduce all the swelling.

She would have passed out from exhaustion, but the sight of Anríq failing forced her to rally. She couldn't let him die.

She lacked the strength to get herself out from under this rubble, so she sent a flow of magic to Anríq from a distance. She didn't know until right now that she could even do that.

She healed his injuries and he really did pass out. She envied him that.

She wilted under the pile and let her eyes sink closed. She didn't want to go out there and face the chaos. She didn't want to face the Voyant. She didn't want to face any of this.

All the crippling fear of her first encounters with the Voyant came back to haunt her. She hadn't been able to defeat him then and she couldn't defeat him now.

She just wanted to lie here in the silence and forget everything—especially the part about separating from Anríq.

Every step she took toward the Shard took her another step away from him. Every ounce of effort she put toward getting the Shard drove the wedge deeper between them. It pushed him farther out of her life.

As soon as she took the Shard, he would disappear out of her life completely. She probably wouldn't even remember him or all the amazing influences he had on her life.

He made her wasted life worth living. He was the only thing that gave her pathetic existence any meaning.

He was the only person she'd ever met who gave her something to live for—and not because they loved each other.

She gulped down despair. She would have liked to block him out of her awareness entirely, but he still lay exposed on the pavement out there.

The whirlwind of spinning gravel, broken glass, and splintered timbers revolved all around him. He could get just as injured just from lying there asleep.

She pushed herself to gather her strength and sent her magic into the rubble pile on top of her.

She started with the topmost boulders, lifted them off, and unburied herself.

She stepped out into the same turbulent hurricane of debris, but she had no trouble erecting a ball of protection around herself.

She stood there wavering on the sidewalk while she thought about her situation. She still found it difficult to think clearly—about anything.

Anríq. She didn't have to think about anything. She just had to help him.

She stumbled through a dozen streets until she found him. Her magic showed her the way through the city in ways she hadn't been able to decipher before.

She found him sprawled on the ground where she left him, surrounded him in her protection, rolled him over, and went over his body one inch at a time.

She poured a ton of magic into him to make sure she healed him the rest of the way.

He didn't wake up. She didn't know how long he would need to sleep, but she couldn't stay out here in the open.

She used her magic to survey the area and found another tumbled-down building with a few broken walls angled together. They formed an alcove underneath them.

She took Anríq by both hands and transported him there without waking him up. She laid him out on the ground, placed her protective field over the opening, and finally let herself collapse on the floor next to him.

How could she possibly get the Shard if the Voyant defeated her so easily in their very first battle? She couldn't overcome his power.

How could he be so much more powerful now than Noleron ever had been? She defeated him easily once she actually let herself use the full depth of her magic.

Something must have happened when Yann took the first Shard. Maybe the fact that someone actually got close enough to take the second Shard activated his power to make him stronger.

She didn't understand any of this. She couldn't even keep her eyes open.

She let the exhaustion of her own injuries overtake her and she fell into a deep sleep.

Chapter 35

E liska woke up to see Anríq sitting next to her. He must have gone
outside because a small fire crackled at the end of the alcove—far
enough away for the smoke to escape through the gaps between the
slabs.

He cocked his head to look down and study her. "You've been
asleep for a long time. You must have gotten badly hurt."

She put her head back down and stared at the wall. "I can't defeat
him. He's too strong."

"You'll find a way. You defeated him before."

"He's much more powerful now. The second Shard must give him
more destructive energy."

He bent over the flames and added a few scraps of wood to the coals.
He must have gathered that wood from the landscape outside.

"We're closer to the spire now than we were when we started," he
remarked. "We can see more of where we are. We should keep working
our way deeper into the city. We'll get back there eventually."

"The city will get more destructive the closer we get to the spire,"
she pointed out. "If he knocked us down this badly during the very
first battle, what hope do we have of getting near the spire?"

He looked up at her. "What's the alternative—give up and go
home? You wouldn't do that."

She looked away again. "I don't think I can defeat him."

"You don't have to defeat him. You just have to take the second Shard. Ignore him as much as possible and concentrate on getting near the spire."

"I won't be able to ignore him. He'll attack us. You didn't see him. He attacked us in ways Noleron never did."

"Then you'll have to fight him, but only so you can get to the spire."

He rummaged in his bags, shifted closer to her, and handed her something. "Eat this. You need your strength."

He handed her a package of some kind of sticky paste that tasted rich and sweet. She ate it in silence. He must have found this in the landscape, too. She was too grateful to refuse it.

She tried to take the time to think about defeating the Voyant, but her mind always wound up coming back to the sensation of his magic pounding her body, breaking her bones, and then bringing that building down on top of her.

Every instinct told her not to reengage with him—not if he could inflict that much damage on her.

She didn't come up with any answers. This moment of clarity allowed her just enough use of her magic to probe the Voyant's halo while she engaged with him.

She couldn't penetrate it. She couldn't damage it. She couldn't even touch it.

He would attack again the minute she went near the spire. The simple fact that someone in this Island wanted to get the Shard caused him to attack.

She and Anríq hadn't been near the spire when he attacked just now. Neither she nor Anríq had been in any position to get the Shard.

Their desire alone set off the Voyant. The intention to take the Shard magnetized him to them the same way the Shard magnetized them to it.

This whole situation was a powder keg ready to blow the minute Anríq and Eliska set foot outside.

He took out some food for himself and an ominous brooding weight hung over both of them while they ate.

She couldn't connect to him and read his thoughts and reactions the way she used to, but he must be coming to grips with the reality of the situation the same way she was.

He couldn't defeat the Voyant, either. Anríq wouldn't be able to take the Shard or even help her take the Shard. Their whole mission could come to an end right now.

He didn't interrupt her thoughts nor did he encourage her to leave the alcove sooner. He just waited.

Part of her wished he would leave. She didn't want him here if she couldn't have him.

All the connection between them died when they entered this city.

She was too grateful for his help and support to say anything. She wouldn't want to face this alone, but she didn't know how to talk to him anymore.

She found it hard even to look at him. He might as well have been a stranger to her and yet he meant more to her than anyone else in the world.

His presence alone pushed her to sit up, pull herself together, and decide to leave the alcove. She couldn't keep sitting here alone in the quiet with him.

All the times they spent together—all the times they could have spent together—they all came together to make this one of the most agonizing parts of this whole experience.

They left the alcove together. She created her ball of protection around both of them and they returned to the nearest thoroughfare.

It wasn't the same one the three friends used to get to the spire the first time.

This thoroughfare ended at the spire, too. She could have followed it to the end, but that wouldn't happen.

The chaos of this disintegrating city stood between her and the spire. The Voyant's looming presence haunted every corner and alley all the way to the city's outer edge.

He ruled this domain with an iron fist. His total awareness gave him a clear view of everything happening in this city. No one could hide from him.

He even knew the secret intentions of her heart. He knew she wanted the Shard. She would only travel in one direction—toward the spire.

Her magic made her turn left down the sidewalk, and automatically, he materialized over the street right in front of her.

The Voyant attacked in a split second and his magic pulverized her and Anríq just as hard. He swatted both of them back and they both went down.

The whole exercise of Eliska healing them both and then her and Anríq spending that time resting in the alcove—it might as well never have happened.

Anríq landed hard, but he scrambled to his feet just as fast as she did. She helped him up—and glanced over her shoulder at the Voyant hovering right in front of them.

Her magic gave one split second of recognition before the same sinking realization hit her. She couldn't face him.

His power terrified her to her core exactly the way it did when she first encountered him in the Coil. She grabbed Anríq and ran for it through the surrounding hurricane.

Her own fear seemed to set off the whole Island. Clouds of splinters, needles, and bullets zinged through the air to plaster her and Anríq. Her protective field saved their lives, but the Voyant came after them no matter where she ran.

She darted from one street to another, around corners, transported herself and Anríq miles through the city, and clambered over fallen obstacles trying to get away from the Voyant.

He always rematerialized in whatever street she happened to enter next. His power followed her everywhere. He blinked from one location to another the instant she tried to escape from him.

Her heart strained to the breaking point from pounding so hard. She couldn't breathe. She barely kept hold of Anríq while she kept magicking him to one place after another, but the Voyant always kept up with her.

He unleashed barrage after barrage, smashed buildings mere seconds before she vanished, destroyed obstacles while she was still trying to climb over them, and ruptured the pavement under her feet.

He smashed her protective ball again and again. She had to keep reestablishing it every few seconds.

She finally turned in the only direction left and took off running for her life for the outer edge of town. She would just have to keep on running until she made it back to the hilltop outside of town. To hell with the Shard of Hotha.

Anríq didn't try to stop her. He must have realized how hopeless this was. He ran right alongside her and he could definitely see where they were going.

The Voyant didn't follow. Maybe he actually planned to let them go once they stopped trying to get the Shard.

She only thought that for a second before he let off another explosion. He waited just long enough for the pair to run behind another building.

They lost sight of him before he bombarded the building with a catastrophic blast that brought the building down again.

It didn't crash on top of Anríq and Eliska this time. She magicked both of them out of the way just in time, but not before the shockwave hit them both.

She lost contact with Anríq and the impact tore him away from her. She landed in a heap across the street, and when she stood up to look around, Anríq was gone.

Chapter 36

Eliska groaned when she dragged her sad, sorry brain back to consciousness. She couldn't keep doing this.

She didn't hear any sounds of explosions or commotion. She squinted at the surroundings. For some reason known only to the Voyant himself, the chaos didn't seem to be tearing the city apart the way it did before.

The area sounded unnaturally quiet without all that noise. She pushed herself up to sit on the sidewalk, but she didn't trust herself to stand yet.

She cradled her pounding head just long enough to heal all her own injuries. She felt old and worn out after so many punishing insults. When would it end?

That last fight against the Voyant—it wasn't even a fight. He showed up and flattened her the minute she turned toward the spire.

He didn't let up when she ran away. How could anyone fight an enemy like this?

She no longer wanted the Shard. Screw it. Nothing was worth this. He could keep it if it meant that much to him to drive everyone away.

She jumped when she heard a sound nearby. She held her breath and listened to her own pulse pounding in her ears before she realized what the noise was.

Some stones pattered in a ruined building next to her. The sound echoed in the silence. Then everything went deathly still.

She didn't dare to breathe. How long would the Voyant wait before he attacked her again? He might follow her to other Layers. He might hunt her down and kill her.

He could have killed her already, so why didn't he?

She already knew why Noleron didn't kill her or his friends. She couldn't say the same about Yann. He certainly seemed to be trying a lot harder.

She hauled herself to her feet and stumbled up the block to a different building. Did she dare to hope he wouldn't come after her at all as long as she didn't want to get the Shard?

She measured her position in the city and froze when she realized she really was quite a bit farther into the city than she thought. Anríq was right about that.

The two of them had somehow penetrated halfway through the city. She stood on a spot exactly halfway between the spire and the city's outer edge.

Just for one second, she thought she could get to the spire just as easily as she could leave this city. One direction was as good as another.

Right then, almost as if the thought threw a switch in her mind, she became aware of Anríq. He had penetrated even deeper into the city toward the spire. He was still going after the Shard—of course.

The Voyant attacked him with brutal force and pinned Anríq between two fallen buildings.

The Voyant unloaded a deafening torrent of unstoppable power on the walls. Anríq hid behind them, planted his axe against the wall in front of him, and channeled all his magic into it to stop the wall from disintegrating.

The tough walls saved his life, but he couldn't get out.

Seeing him in danger caused an equally automatic reaction in Eliska's magic. She magicked herself deeper into the city—to a location between the Voyant and the spire.

She didn't give a rip about the Shard right now. She just wanted to save Anríq.

Her maneuver worked better than she hoped. The Voyant instantly broke off his assault and came after her instead.

He blinked across the landscape to her location, but she transported herself away again and again to keep ahead of him.

They whizzed all over the city. She even led him back to the spire itself, but she couldn't stay in one place for very long.

He unloaded on her every time only for her to disappear from in front of him.

His magic gave him some uncanny insight into her movements. He anticipated her and appeared in each place at the same instant she did. He didn't have to wait for her to arrive before he transported himself there, too.

In her last desperate act, she magicked herself to Anríq, grabbed him, and then magicked both of them to the hilltop outside of town.

They both buckled onto the grass panting hard. She sprawled onto her back and shut her eyes. She actually heard birds chirping in the air and the wind rustling in the grass.

Anríq fell over rasping for breath. He didn't get up nor did he tell her to get up.

She rolled onto her side and made up her mind to stay here forever if she had to. No way could she go back in there.

She only used her magic to make sure Anríq wasn't injured. She didn't know where she would take both of them after this, but she had to go somewhere.

A different kind of rustling in the grass made her bolt upright. The wind didn't cause this sound.

She shot onto her knees and looked around everywhere for the Voyant, but she only saw a mouse scuttling between the long grass stems.

She wilted in shaky relief, but the little creature only reinforced what she already knew.

Her eyes drifted back to the city. It seethed with instability, but the same chaotic mixture of noise no longer rumbled out of the place.

Her fear of the Voyant didn't lessen, but maybe she shouldn't let that stop her. The Voyant was just another mouse scuttling through the grass.

He wasn't even the Voyant. It was Yann—her brother.

Her eyes snapped to the spire. The hazy revolving dust and sand scattered in the wind obscured the Shard's purple glow, but she could see it.

The Shard cast its old hypnotic effect on her mind—and on her magic. She wanted it. Her Darkness wanted to harness the Shard's power and turn it on the Coil.

If someone was going to use the Shard to destroy Islands, civilizations, and whole populations, then she should be the one to do it.

She was Dark enough—and she was Dark enough to take the Shard away from the Voyant. He didn't deserve it.

He was a good person caught in the Shard's power. He didn't do any of this deliberately.

She could destroy him and take both Shards. Then she could rule the Coil alone. No one would be able to stop her.

She shook that thought away, but she still had to get the Shard. Her magic wouldn't let her turn her back on it. It offered too great a temptation.

She got to her feet and went over to Anríq. He lay sprawled on his back with his eyes closed. He didn't release his fingers from his axe handle.

He opened his eyes when she pried the weapon out of his hand, clasped his hand once, and tried to smile at him. "I'm going back in. You don't have to come....."

He scrambled to sit up. "Don't even say that. I'm coming with you."

She didn't say anything else. She waited for him to stand up.

They both faced the city and the same certainty settled in her guts. She couldn't defeat the Voyant. She would just keep throwing herself against the spire until he killed her and Anríq.

Anríq wouldn't quit, not even after she fell. He would try to get to the Shard and the Voyant would take him down, too.

She didn't give herself a chance to think about that. She put the Voyant out of her mind. Only the Shard mattered.

Anríq picked up his axe in his left hand, so she took his right hand and magicked both of them as far into the city as she dared.

She already knew her arrival would set off the Voyant, so she chose a location a little distant from the spire itself.

She didn't want to deal with the Voyant's assault and the spire's defenses at the same time.

She appeared on a sidewalk three blocks from the spire, let go of Anríq's hand, and immediately magicked herself five blocks away to draw the Voyant away from Anríq.

She didn't trust the Voyant not to go after him anyway, so she launched herself into the air to meet the Voyant there instead.

She shot forward and discharged a blistering volley of her Dark poison at him before he had a chance to strike her first.

She caught the first barrage from his halo, dumped it back on him, and forced him to retreat back toward the spire.

She pursued him and attacked his halo the way she defeated the first Voyant. She ripped his power away from him to reveal the man inside.

He was an imp. He possessed no magic except what the Shard gave him.

As soon as she broke his power, she would bring him to the ground and crush him the way she crushed Noleron.

She penetrated his halo and unleashed the full depth of her Darkness on him, but as soon as she hit the man himself, his halo ricocheted back at her and blasted her away.

He bombarded her with a cruel series of hits and sent her wheeling through the air.

She tried to rally, but he kept it up, smacked her again and again, and drove her back across the city.

She retaliated and defended herself as well as she could, but his halo reestablished itself instantly. She couldn't penetrate it a second time.

She would have flown back across the countryside, back to the hilltop. She had come to think of that hilltop as some kind of sanctuary where she would at least be safe enough to regroup and catch her breath.

He didn't give her a chance even to do that. He pummeled her as far as the outermost neighborhoods, caught her in a powerful vortex of rotating blows, and held her there while he went to work on her with all his cruel ferocity.

He didn't hold her against a wall because there was no wall here hundreds of feet above the ground.

He didn't need a wall. His magic formed a solid surface behind her. All the blows in the world wouldn't knock her through it.

She crumpled under the beating. Her body and her magic couldn't sustain this kind of damage, but he didn't let up even for a second.

She bellowed in desperation and struggled her hardest, but she found herself trapped again. The confinement of his grip made her panic—and she realized. Her fear made him stronger—or it made her weaker—one or the other or maybe both.

He reacted to her thoughts, delivered one last brutal concussion, and smacked her down full force on the ground.

Chapter 37

Eliska didn't groan in agony or tremble in fear or jump at mice. She used her magic to heal herself and pulled herself to her feet.

The Voyant drove her almost all the way out of the city this time—almost all the way.

She stood up in a residential neighborhood full of wrecked houses, torn-up yards, bodies, conveyances, and ruined vegetation scattered everywhere.

The chaotic hurricane of flying shrapnel didn't strike this part of town, either. Maybe the Voyant was getting tired of that kind of collapse.

Nothing moved in this neighborhood. None of the chaotic winds or shrieking madness clouded the skies deeper into the city. The White Spire and the Shard of Hotha dominated the horizon right where she could see them.

All the murderous Darkness in her soul flared to life the instant she saw the Voyant hovering back in his old place next to the spire.

She was all done being afraid of him. She hated him. She wanted him dead.

She really hoped she could find a way to defeat him. She would kill him, take his Shard, and then she and Anríq could finally be together the way they both wanted to be.

Yann Dilnao would die. Good riddance. Then she never had to worry about him again.

She hated him for doing this to her. He was the one who robbed her of Anríq's love.

Yann went through a big song and dance about Anríq and Eliska getting together. Now he was the one who destroyed any hope that they could ever be happy together.

She had been working so hard lately to release her Darkness—first on Noleron, then on the spire, and now on him.

Her Darkness took over exactly the way she feared it would, but she didn't try to stop it. She hated him. She hated the world. She hated everything.

Pure, unbridled, rotten lust for power drove her to get the Shard. She deserved it. She would turn it Dark and become unstoppable. Yann couldn't do that.

Every object and dead body she laid eyes on burned her insides with pure Dark fury. She hated this whole world and everything in it.

Everyone left alive in the Coil could die for all she cared. She would make sure they did as soon as she took the Shard for herself.

She stormed off toward the center of the city. Her intention to take the Shard would bring the Voyant to attack her again. Good.

She marched over piles of rubble and stepped over bodies and a few faint traces of living things in the wider landscape.

She only noticed them enough to know there were still people and a few animals still alive in this Island.

Most of them were small animals like that mouse. They could conceal themselves and find sheltered places from the mayhem.

A few people did the same thing, but they didn't concern her. She turned all her attention to the Voyant.

He stayed in the air above the spire. He didn't attack even when she walked straight toward it.

She wanted the Shard more now than she ever did before. She finally found a way that she and Anríq could be together. She should have thought of this before.

She just had to stop being a Servant. How stupid she was to limit herself with those concerns.

She couldn't let anything stop her, especially not some misguided notion of helping people who didn't deserve it.

She channeled her magic toward the Shard so the Voyant would be certain she was going after it. He still didn't attack. He stayed the same distance and the same altitude in his usual guarding posture over the Shard's window.

She passed through a few different neighborhoods. When he still didn't react, she decided to provoke him by magicking herself closer to the spire.

She reappeared on the same spot where she put Anríq down last time. The spire towered directly in front of her. The Shard gleamed so close she could practically touch it.

She didn't let herself second-guess. She launched herself upward, slowed in front of the Voyant, and engaged with him.

She started to unload her magic on his halo, but this time, she harnessed the depth of her hatred to let loose in new ways.

She discarded all thought of him as a man or even someone she knew and once cared about. She turned her old care against him. She hated him for making her care about him.

She hated him for seeing her at her weakest. She hated him for ever making her think he or anyone else could ever care about her. He obviously didn't if he could do this to her.

She let her thoughts and feelings turn their Darkest—Darker than she ever let herself go before.

She surrounded his halo in Dark vapor. Wisps of Darkness ate into its outer glowing edge and chewed the halo apart. She reveled in the sadistic horror of tearing him to pieces right in front of her eyes.

She wouldn't stop once she penetrated his halo. She tasted blood. She would watch her own Darkness devour him, reduce him to a defenseless broken imp lying bleeding on the ground, and she would give him the long, slow, painful death he deserved.

Thinking this way increased her power and weakened his. Did he still care about her? How pathetic.

She let the rush of cruel pleasure break out of its box. She really did have more power than she knew.

She could tap the Darkness of the entire Coil, not just the poison she took from all the useless people she saved.

Her poison gave her access to an unlimited well of hate, greed, corruption, and fury. God, it felt good to finally let herself feel all of that.

She unloaded it all on the Voyant's halo. It started to weaken, but before it could destroy him, he vanished.

She stared at the spot where he'd just been hovering next to the spire. He couldn't be gone. He couldn't be so cowardly that he would just run out in the middle of a fight just because she started winning.

He left the spire undefended—except for the spire's own defenses, of course.

The instant he disappeared, all the Darkness she dumped on him rushed back into her where it belonged. Its power overwhelmed her and she crashed down hard on the ground.

She didn't injure herself, but the Darkness overcame her ability to control it. She floundered to contain it. She had to somehow reintegrate it into herself before it destroyed her, too.

She never really released it before—not like this—not even during all the times she used it to overcome obstacles, heal people, and rescue her friends from danger.

She used it more and more lately, but never like this. She always believed Yann and Anríq when they told her she could use it for good.

She wasn't using it for good now. She felt herself going over to the Dark.

She should have pulled herself back from that. She should withdraw.

Her eyes drifted up to the spire's top window. The Shard hovered right in front of her. She could fly up there and take the Shard right now.

All this Darkness counteracted with itself somehow. She didn't understand how that was possible. She wanted the Shard and her Darkness wanted the Shard. What was so complicated about that?

She glanced around the city and choked down another disgusting wave of hatred. She hated everything, including the Shard, the spire, this wretched city, the Voyant—everything.

She even hated herself for going Dark. This was all wrong. She understood that in the marrow of her bones.

She violated everything that mattered to her by doing this, but she couldn't stop it now.

This must have been coming for a long time—ever since she fell into that Dark river.

Everything that happened to her since then added to her Darkness and made it worse. She was always going to end up going over to the

Dark. It was inevitable. The only question was when it would happen and how.

She tried every trick under the sun to stop it from happening. She worked her tail off to be a good person, but the Dark took over in the end.

Now it defeated her. It took her over. It controlled her. It made decisions for her. It ruined her relationships.

She hated herself for that. She never should have let Yann and Anríq convince her to use her Darkness. She should have done absolutely anything to stop this from happening.

Now it was happening and she couldn't take it back. Too much of her wanted to keep going. This felt too good.

She curled her lip in disgust at everything around her. She hated everyone she'd ever known. They all let her down.

She set off stomping back through the city, but she didn't approach the spire. She didn't walk away from it, either.

She hated the Shard and the spire too much to go near them even though she did still plan to take the Shard.

The Voyant wouldn't be able to stop her from taking it. She could take it whenever she wished. It was already hers. She could wait until the right time.

She didn't know where to go next, so she circled the spire and made her way through the surrounding neighborhoods. She always kept the same distance away from the spire to keep it in sight.

She scanned her magic over the outlying areas to make sure the ongoing instability didn't threaten her. She hated all of this—the destruction, the unpredictability, the mess, and all the meaningless loss of life.

She hated herself for wanting to cause more of it, but she also thirsted for the day when she could cause more of it.

She wanted to make herself as Dark as possible. Then she wouldn't even think there was anything wrong with what she was doing.

She barely looked up when she heard footsteps coming toward her. Anríq strode around the corner and hustled up to her. "You did it!" he exclaimed. "You defeated him! I knew you could do it."

She swiped her hand at him to stop him from touching her. "Don't touch me!" she snapped.

He jolted back in surprise and she experienced another mind-blowing wave of hatred both for him and herself for letting this happen.

She snorted at him and then grimaced at the surroundings. This whole city was such a dump. Everything looked ugly.

She couldn't deal with Anríq or his encouragement or the way he was looking at her right now.

She walked away and continued on her route to circle the spire. She hated him for coming with her. She didn't want him anywhere near her.

Just then, she heard another rain of falling gravel in one of the nearby buildings. The stillness amplified every other sound.

An interior wall collapsed inside the building. It didn't put her in danger. It just infuriated her.

She spun around, roared out all her vicious spite at the building, and exploded a brutal eruption of magic that demolished it to smithereens. It imploded and fell down in a pile of rubble.

She stood there fuming in burning hatred for everyone and everything. She wanted to destroy and keep on destroying forever.

Anríq stood right behind her watching. She couldn't stand the feeling that he knew exactly what was happening to her.

She lashed out by jerking the other way, bellowing at the next building in line, and bringing that one down, too.

Her Darkness spiraled out of control. She sprang from one building to the next pulverizing them with all her power. She couldn't destroy the world fast enough to satisfy this gnawing ravenous need to wreck everything.

She came to the end of the street. Mountains of debris blocked her path and she unloaded on them, too.

Once she started, she didn't want to stop. She raged through the streets detonating everything in sight.

She didn't have to turn around to sense Anríq following her. He didn't try to stop her until she came to one of the few intact garden strips in the middle of the city's main thoroughfare.

A few twisted trees, bushes, and flowerbeds still survived in that strip. She stormed up to one of the trees and inhaled a deep breath to bellow out all her hate at that, too.

Anríq darted in front of her exactly the way she knew he would. She only expected him to do it sooner.

He started to say, "This isn't you, Eliska....."

She struck him much harder than she realized, smashed him with a ruthless outburst of magic, flung him across the street, and pinned him to the wall.

She glared at him in outright hatred. How dare he intervene in anything she did? How dare he even speak to her after he threw her away like this?

He choked trying to catch his breath while she stalked across the street coming closer to him. Her mind twisted on all the excruciating ways she could make him pay for ever entering her life.

"Eliska....." he croaked. "You care......you hate everything because you care.....you wouldn't be doing any of this if you didn't care......"

She hated him for saying it, but she hated herself even more because it was true.

She hated everything about this, especially how Dark she was getting. The Dark consumed her in horrible ways.

She never wanted to hurt people before. She never wanted to destroy the people she most cared about. She always tried to protect them from her Darkness.

She spun away, released him, and didn't turn around when he crumpled to the ground.

She barged down the street and bellowed at five more buildings to destroy them just to spite him. He couldn't stop her. She would kill him if he tried.

Chapter 38

E liska stormed through the streets not thinking or caring where she was going, but right then, the Voyant flashed into view right in front of her.

She grinned in wicked hatred for him. She could unleash as much of her Darkness on him as she wanted to. She didn't have to wonder if hurting him was right or wrong. Hurting him was always right.

She blasted her Darkness at him and started eating her way through his halo again. That worked last time, so she did it again.

She poured more and more of her Darkness into the vapors attacking his halo.

He withstood it better this time. His halo even seemed to burn more brightly the harder she attacked it.

He returned fire and his shots actually hit her this time. He made her stagger under the impact.

The two of them traded bombardments for a while. She couldn't make any more headway through his halo nor could she damage it. None of her other tactics worked. He remained as intact as always and he didn't run away this time.

Frustration and resentment drove her out of control. She couldn't attack him, so she turned her Darkness on the spire instead.

She launched off the ground, fired a volley at the Voyant to hold him off, and picked up speed heading for the top window.

The Shard hovered right in front of her eyes, but the spire retaliated with all its defensive power and smashed her away.

Her Darkness held for a minute and she unloaded on the tower even more furiously than she unloaded on the Voyant.

The Shard was hers. Why would the spire or the Voyant try to stop her from taking what she justly deserved? No one else was using the Shard.

She summoned as much Darkness as she could muster, but the spire only seemed to bounce all her efforts back at her.

The harder she hit the spire, the harder the spire returned her assault. She drew from the deepest pit of her hate and fury, spat a devastating torrent of brutal magic on the spire, and the spire stung back at her with such force that it sent her flying.

She somersaulted to another neighborhood miles away. She touched down on the ground, scoffed at the surroundings, and took off marching back the way she came.

That rotten spire couldn't stop her. Nothing could stop her from taking what rightfully belonged to her.

She was the one who defeated the previous Voyant. The Shard belonged to her. No one else deserved it.

She didn't care what they did. She would best them in the end. It was only a matter of time.

They couldn't stop her from going completely over to the Dark. That was the only reason she didn't get the Shard yet. She hadn't gone Dark enough.

She'd been trying for too long to be some Pollyanna goody-too-shoes pretend version of a Servant. She had been trying to be Anríq. How stupid was that?

She should have gone Dark long ago. She should have gone Dark in the monastery. She would have the power to take the Shard now if she only listened to the monks then.

It didn't matter because she would march right back to the spire and take it now. She didn't have to think. She just had to defeat these ridiculous defenses. Even the Voyant was nothing but a molehill in her path.

She hated her situation enough to destroy every rotten building she passed, but she didn't want to stop. She passed ten blocks before she spotted Anríq coming toward her from the direction of the spire. What the hell did he want from her now?

She would have liked to unload on him, too. She could have killed him right now just for having the nerve to show his face to her. God, she hated him!

She hated him for loving her and she hated herself for loving him back. She hated everything about him and she hated herself for admiring him.

She barged straight past him without looking at him. He swiveled in next to her just like the chump that he was and started walking fast to keep pace with her.

"Are you okay? Did you get hurt? Did the spire injure you?" he jabbered in her ear.

She would have liked to tell him to go straight to hell and leave her the hell alone and to crawl back into a hole in the Coil where he belonged.

She found it impossible to say any of those things to him. She didn't understand why because she really wanted to say them. She meant them, but she only mumbled, "No. I'm fine," instead.

"Are you going back there? Are you planning another assault? How will you defeat him if you haven't been able to do it yet?"

"How the hell should I know?" she snarled.

He checked himself before he said anything else. She really hoped he never said anything else to her again for the rest of eternity.

At that moment, a section of the pavement peeled up on his other side. The landscape had been so quiet until right this minute.

The paving stones reared off the ground with no warning, formed some kind of jointed monster, and opened a gaping mouth to attack Anríq.

He raised his club, but Eliska shot out her hand and blasted the thing to powder right then and there. She could hate Anríq all she wanted. No one and nothing else was allowed to threaten him.

His eyes widened at the pile of dust on the ground and then his gaze shot to her face.

She hated that expression and she hated him for making it. She whirled away and took off back toward the spire.

More features of the surrounding landscape came to life the way they did before. Walls broke away from buildings. Overturned furniture put itself into bizarre shapes so they could start moving around.

He kept raising his club and then lowering it each time she darted in front of him and destroyed each thing as it moved in to attack.

He followed her in silence through the whole incident. He waited a full half an hour before he murmured, "Thank you."

"Just don't start being nice to me," she barked over her shoulder. "I swear I'll kill you if you do."

"I wasn't planning to be nice to you," he countered. "You're lost to me already, so give yourself to the Darkness. It's the only way we can end this."

She bit back the urge to spit a bunch of insults at him. She wished she could. She didn't understand why she held back just because it was him.

The fact that she cared about him made her hate him all the more, but she hated herself worse for acting like this.

She should have been able to handle this better. She shouldn't be out here storming around the streets flying out of control just because she heard a noise.

She turned her back on him. She couldn't stand to look at him or have him look at her.

Maybe now he finally realized the stupidity of encouraging her to use her Darkness in this war.

She'd always known it would turn her completely to the Dark. He couldn't complain now that it was actually happening.

He stayed behind her, thank the stars. She could pretend he wasn't there even though her magical awareness never let her forget it.

She could let her Darkness out by blasting away at every living object, monster, and creature that tried to attack her. She saw herself protecting Anríq, too, but she pretended she wasn't.

She actually enjoyed barging down the thoroughfare and leveling everything in sight. Wreaking destruction on the world gave her the only relief from this torturous hatred toward absolutely everything in existence.

The thoroughfare ended at a side street where another avenue crossed the rest of the way to the spire. She had to turn a corner, and when she did, she came face to face with another crowd of imaginary people.

She didn't even have to check to find out if they were imaginary. They wouldn't be here if they were real.

She unloaded on them, too, bellowed in fury, and poured out a catastrophic wave of destruction on thousands of people.

She let herself pretend they were real. She savored the feeling of killing them, tearing them apart, and burying them under the wreckage of their own civilizations.

She shifted back into old memories of Corsairs razing whole towns and putting the survivors to the sword—only this time, she experienced the sadistic thrill of being one of the attackers.

Killing felt insatiably good. She could have left here and gone rampaging through the Coil killing everyone in her path. That's what she really wanted to do.

Her Darkness gave her the power to do it, but the Shard would give her the vehicle to do it on a mass scale.

Yann and Noleron could have been doing it themselves if they weren't such pathetic do-gooders.

Chapter 39

Eliska whirled away so she wouldn't see Anríq's reaction to her killing spree. Those people being apparitions didn't change who and what she was on the inside.

She didn't want him following her around thinking whatever he was thinking, so she shot into the air to get away from him.

She covered the miles back to the spire, but the Voyant didn't wait for her to show up.

He rocketed across the city and met her in a devastating mid-air collision of opposing powers.

She picked up speed to rush him. She wanted to hurt him. She wanted to hurt him real bad and make him suffer. She wanted to tear him limb from limb for even thinking about trying to keep the Shard from her.

She released her Darkness again and it flared out of all bounds when she actually deliberately tried to hurt him.

She swooped in to get right up next to his halo. She lunged for him to grab his halo with her bare hands and sink her claws into him. She wanted to feel herself ripping him apart and know that she was the one who caused his death.

Only when she got that close did she notice him grinning at her. She knew that grin. This wasn't Noleron. It was Yann—the same young man who smiled at her like that during their travels in the Coil.

The sight of him brought back so many memories that she actually stopped for a second. She slackened her assault, but not enough to let his counterattack put her in danger.

His smile slipped. It wasn't Yann's kind, understanding, fun-loving smile he used out in the Coil.

He grinned at her in devilish, murderous glee. He wanted to hurt her, too—and now he had to magic to do it.

He detonated another almighty barrage on her. She had no choice but to respond in kind, but he just kept escalating. Her assault didn't damage him. It only seemed to make him stronger.

She made the connection in a split second and retreated away from the spire to clear her head. Her Darkness made him stronger. If that was true, how did her Darkness defeat Noleron?

Was it because he'd been living alone with the Shard for so long? Did it weaken him so much that her Darkness actually worked on him?

Yann was young and much stronger. Then again, she hadn't attacked Noleron right outside the spire's walls, either.

She didn't see what difference that made, but she couldn't defeat the new Voyant using her Darkness. She didn't know what weapon could defeat him, but it wasn't that.

She watched and waited for a second before she satisfied herself that he didn't plan to come after her. He stayed in his usual place next to the spire and let her retreat with her dignity intact—this time.

She finally turned her back on him and magicked herself away into the farthest city neighborhoods.

She wanted to think about this, but in the end, she wound up magicking herself back to where she left Anríq.

She didn't want to see him or even talk to him, but she had no one else to consult.

God only knew why she wanted to consult with him in the first place. He wouldn't be able to advise her on how to use her Darkness. The guy didn't have a Dark bone in his body.

Too many unanswered questions crowded in her head. She couldn't decipher them on her own.

She magicked herself a few blocks away from him. He saw her when she showed up. She still took a long time before she made up her mind to go over there and talk to him.

She hated herself for needing him and she hated him for being the one she needed.

She didn't want to need anyone and she didn't want him around passing judgment on everything she did and everything she thought while she did it.

He cocked his head when she stopped in front of him. She couldn't look at him. She wound up looking everywhere else.

"What's going on over there?" he asked. "Are you making any headway against him?"

She shrugged at nothing. "He's feeding off my Darkness," she mumbled under her breath. "It only makes him stronger."

"That's no good." He studied her for a second, but he didn't say out loud what they both already knew.

She was acting like this because of her Darkness. She did what he and Yann told her to by letting this power out. Now it was turning her Dark.

"Why don't we go back to the spire together this time?" he suggested. "We can try to avoid him....."

"I can't avoid him," she snapped. "He always attacks me."

"And you attack him back, don't you? You always try to fight him. What if you don't? We can concentrate our efforts on getting into the spire instead. That's what we really want. He's just a distraction."

"This Darkness is the only power strong enough to defeat him or the spire," she countered. "I have no other option. I have to use it."

"Let's try it this way. If it doesn't work, we won't lose anything by trying. We'll try to do what we did before. I'll try to get to the walls and use my club to break in. Once I get inside, I'll run up the stairs to the Shard. You deal with the spire's defenses, and once you see me go inside, you follow me."

"Then what?"

Now it was his turn to shrug. "Then you'll take the second Shard and you'll be healed of your Darkness. Only one of us might make it that far, in which case the question will answer itself."

She looked away again. "I guess so."

"You had plenty of magic before you started using this Darkness. We'll find a way to deal with him, but just remember that the only way to defeat him is to take the Shard. He won't be dangerous to anyone, not even you, once one of us takes the second Shard."

She couldn't think of anything civil to say, so she just turned around and walked away. He followed her, the bastard.

She hated that he had to be so sensible and always see the best in her. She really wished he would start seeing how rotten and evil she really was. Then he would leave her the hell alone.

They headed back toward the spire, but at the next intersection, she spotted more movement to one side.

She barely glanced at it expecting it to be more apparitions of people fleeing the chaotic city.

It was, but she stopped in her tracks when she saw her mother over there.

Eliska had only ever seen Alexiane LaFauve in a photograph. She looked completely different in real life—but she couldn't be here in real life. Alexiane was dead—or as good as.

Even if by some miraculous twist of fate she was alive, she wouldn't look as young as she did in that picture. She would have aged the way Yvan did.

Alexiane looked barely over twenty-five and she sure moved around like she was alive.

She got cornered by an enormous giant misshapen monster that must have grown out of some kind of forge bellows. It lumbered toward Alexiane to trample her while a monstrous kitchen stove attacked her from the other side.

She jabbed a broom handle at both attackers and fired magical jets of crackling energy from the end.

She used the broom handle the same way Eliska used her staff—the way Eliska sometimes used broom or mop handles as staffs when she couldn't lay her hands on any other weapon.

Eliska blinked at the scene in stunned disbelief. Alexiane couldn't be here. This wasn't possible.

Eliska only took an instant before her brain switched back on. This *wasn't* possible and that wasn't Alexiane LaFauve. It couldn't be.

Alexiane LaFauve was an imp. She came from a whole family of imps. That's why she ran away from the Shard in the first place.

The dawning realization turned Eliska's shock to fury. This rotten illusion cooked up another phantom from Eliska's path to distract her. This was the same nonsense she and her friends had been seeing since they entered this stupid Island.

Her hatred turned against her mother—or whatever the hell this thing was that pretended to be her mother.

The apparition held her own against the stove and the bellows. Alexiane had to continually rotate from one direction to another to blast them away from her.

Eliska really hoped they pulverized Alexiane. Eliska's hatred toward everything took over every other consideration. She even forgot to go after the Shard in her fascination with this scene.

She wanted to watch these Dark forces destroy the apparition. She only hoped the apparition could feel enough pain to give Eliska some satisfaction.

The apparition didn't go down so easily. Eliska's sadistic fury didn't want to wait any longer. She fired a single jet of magic across the street and shattered the broom handle.

It exploded in Alexiane's hands and the two attackers pounced before she could do anything to defend herself.

The forge bellows hefted one huge iron foot off the ground and brought it down on top of her with bone-breaking power.

It caught her shoulder, flipped her sideways, and the stove jumped in to help. It leapt on top of her and bounced up and down to flatten her to a pulp.

Eliska chuckled under her breath at the sight, but right then, more movement caught her attention from behind.

She turned away before the stove and the bellows finished with Alexiane.

She stopped again when she saw Yvan and the other Watchmen fighting off a whole mob of deformed people that had been mangled by the Dark.

The attackers surrounded the Watchmen. They all tried to defend themselves with the same combination of weapons they used in real life.

Barsali, Niyazi, Rien, Vidal, Omer, and Niels were all here—but they weren't here.

Eliska didn't even have to guess why she was seeing them. She strode down the street and looked in at each scene as it unfolded.

Wesh fought a magical battle against a bunch of trees from the gardens.

Marine backed into another corner trying to drive off against a bunch of skeletal mummified corpses of farm animals.

Aja fought ten pieces of furniture that moved in to surround her. She whirled her fighting sticks in all directions and blasted two couches, an armchair, a kitchen table, and a bunch of chairs that bounced along the ground trying to keep up with her speed.

Eliska didn't plan to stop to watch any of these people fight what might be their last battles. They would die in this city—except that they wouldn't die because they were all already dead.

Aja and Marine might as well be dead, too. Eliska hoped they were. She wouldn't wish this chaos on her worst enemy.

She hated all of these things for making her see her friends, family, and loved ones one last time.

Someone created these images to weaken her. These people certainly didn't show up here to strengthen her.

Yann better not have done this—but she already knew he didn't. She and the two boys started seeing these apparitions from the past before Yann took the Shard. He saw them, too, and they bothered him just as much.

She turned away from them to continue her hike back to the spire. Everything standing between her and her destination was just another delay.

Chapter 40

E liska stopped again when she looked down the final alley and saw
the monks from the Keepers of the Dawn fighting a whole host
of creatures down there, including dozens of Darklings.

The monks had to be apparitions, too, but she still hesitated to
leave.

What if they were real? What if they showed up here to make a bid
for the Shard of Hotha?

She destroyed their monastery and killed everyone inside it, but
anything was possible. Some of their members might have survived in
other parts of the Coil. They could have carried on their mission to
come here and take the Shards' power for themselves.

If they really were here.....if they really were alive and fighting
Darklings over there....

A sick thrill electrified her blood when she saw the Darklings overcome the monks, slash them to pieces, and bring them to the ground.

She let her power invade the Darklings. She felt their bloodlust and
the pure Dark rage and satisfaction of killing these people.

She wilted when the bodies vanished. The monks were only apparitions, too. What a pity.

She turned away for the final time and put the apparitions out of her mind. She glanced around for Anríq....and came face to face with Yvan Dilnao.

The other Watchmen were nowhere in sight. He was all alone.

His features twisted when he looked down into her eyes. "I'm sorry...." he croaked.

"Go to hell!" she spat. "I don't want your worthless apologies! You ruined my life, you bastard!"

His eyes misted over, but that only made her angrier.

"I never meant to hurt you!" he half-whispered. "I never knew you were alone! I would have done anything to be there for you!"

"Well, you weren't! You should have stayed here and taken the Shard the way you were supposed to! Then none of this would have happened. None of it would have happened to *me!* You were both weak—you and Mother! You were weak and selfish and *I'm* the one who suffered because you thought being in love was more important than saving the whole damn Coil! How could you do this to your own children?!"

He clamped his lips shut trying to control himself. She shouldn't have vented on him like this.

Part of her knew perfectly well that this was an apparition, too. Yvan Dilnao was dead. He died never knowing she was his daughter.

Facing him again—seeing him alive—talking to him as her father—the moment intoxicated her out of all rationality.

His face spasmed under her onslaught. She wanted to say a lot more. She wanted to hurt him where it counted. Then maybe he would feel some of the pain she'd been living with all these years.

"You abandoned me!" she blurted out. "You could have gotten a magic-user to find out where Mother and I were. You could have done a million things to get back to the Layer where you got separated from us. You could have at least tried, but you didn't do any of that, did you? You didn't even try. You buried yourself in the Black Watch. You gave all your time and attention to raising Yann and you put me and Mother as far out of your mind as you could. Admit it! Come on! I'm your daughter! You owe me the truth! You turned your back on me to take care of yourself exactly the same way you took care of yourself when you ran away from the Shard."

He barely made a sound when he answered, but at least he had the spine to keep looking into her eyes when he said it. "You're right. I could have tried harder. I felt sorry for myself because I had to take care of Yann alone. I could have looked for you, but I took care of myself instead. I'm so sorry, young one. I let you down. I love you! I always have. I loved you as a daughter even when I thought you were a stranger."

"You got a hell of a way of showing it," she snapped. "You threw me in jail the very first night we met."

He opened his mouth to say something else, but she didn't stick around to hear it. This conversation brought up too many buried resentments and long-forgotten grief.

She never had to grieve for Yvan because she never met him. She never had that conversation with him while he was alive......and she never got to tell him that she loved him.

She never got to tell him how much she needed him and missed him—how much his protection and guidance would have meant to her if things had only played out differently.

She couldn't start thinking about that now or she really would lose it.

She walked away without looking back. She put him as far out of her mind as she possibly could the same way she did when she was younger. She couldn't function otherwise.

She only made it twenty feet before she ran into the apparition of Wesh. Did she really have to go through the whole damn squad and relive all the torture of emotions left over from their time together in life?

"What do you want?" she snarled.

His features went through the same combination of wretched, tortured anguish. "I want to help you, my dear. Let me help you the way I should have done when I was alive."

"Why didn't you help me then?" she fired back. "You could have. You could have done more for me."

"I tried....but you wouldn't let me. You wouldn't let anyone close to you."

She rolled her eyes to Heaven and smacked her lips in annoyance. "That's crap, Wesh, and we both know it. You never tried. You would have been very happy to let me wander off on my own and let me be someone else's problem. You would have made no effort to stay with me at all if we hadn't gotten stuck together the way we did. You traveled with me for less than two days. We would have parted when we got to Middleborough and you never would have thought about me again."

He opened his mouth to say something else, but she didn't listen to that, either. She just wanted this whole ordeal to be over.

She sidestepped around him, and like some kind of nightmare, she came face to face with Alexiane.

Her mother blocked her from getting out into the open street where Eliska would have been able to get away from these stupid apparitions.

Alexiane's countenance went through the same spasms of guilt, grief, and longing. Eliska was getting sick and tired of the same passion play from all of them.

"Don't say it," Eliska snarled. "Don't you dare even say it."

"Darling...." her mother choked.

"Shut up!" Eliska roared. "All of you shut the hell up and LEAVE ME ALONE!! I was better off without all of you!"

She barged past Alexiane and turned a deaf ear to her mother's footsteps following her toward the street.

Eliska just hoped and prayed the apparitions would be confined to these alleys. They would have no choice but to stay behind as soon as she got out into the open.

She approached the mouth of the alley and started looking around for Anríq. He didn't just vanish. Did she pass into some enchanted illusion world again?

At that moment, a mass of Darklings swooped down the avenue outside. She froze in place waiting for them to pass by, but they didn't.

They turned into the alley and rushed straight at her.

She sprang back to get away from them and bumped into Alexiane. Alexiane gasped in alarm and that sound brought Eliska out of her Dark haze.

She spread her arms to herd Alexiane backward into the alley. One thought consumed Eliska's mind. Everyone she cared about was in this alley. Alexiane. Yvan. Wesh. Marine. The Watchmen.

The Darklings charged her. She stood alone between the Darklings and all her loved ones.

Some distant possibility still remained that some of these people might be real. Alexiane and Marine might really be alive.

Wesh could have survived that fire before the rest of the Watch fell through into another Layer.

Yvan.....

Eliska didn't give herself a chance to think about how Yvan might be alive. She saw him die. She helped bury him, but that didn't matter.

No Darkling was going to attack these people. Her sadistic resentment toward them vanished in a breath of wind.

She unleashed her Dark poison on the Darklings and brought down dozens of them, but more flooded into the alley from the street beyond. She couldn't kill them fast enough, not even by infecting them with her Darkness to make them disintegrate before her eyes.

Yells echoed backward up the alley behind her. The resentment she just harbored against these people caused her to lash out in protective fury.

Someone else was trying to hurt them. If anyone was going to hurt them, she would be the one. She was the one who earned the right to hurt them as much as they hurt her.

Her resentment, hatred, and burning rage unleashed in a Dark torrent. She carved a wider and wider space between the Darklings and the people behind her.

The noise behind her escalated just as fast. She didn't find out why until she broke through into the next street—the street where she'd just seen her friends and loved ones fighting for their lives.

They still fought for their lives, but instead of fighting all the forces of mayhem and disaster in this city, the apparitions turned on each other.

The Watchmen fought Wesh and Marine on one side of the street. A bunch of the Tenby defenders and even people Eliska saved in Symphorian moved in to attack Alexiane and Yvan the minute they came out of the alley.

Eliska spun backward yelling out, but she couldn't think who to stop first. She couldn't stop them all—not without fighting her own loved ones.

All the protective fury she vented on the Darklings turned to the very people she was trying to protect. She wanted to destroy them for threatening people she cared about—but they *were* people she cared about.

All that Darkness, confusion, pain, and longing blasted out of her. It built to an overpowering surge of emotion that translated into magic.

She yelled out one last time and an avalanche of magic detonated outward from her beyond her ability to control it.

She knew these people were all apparitions. They were nothing but cruel shadows sent to mess with her head.

She still suffered unspeakable tortures when she swept her Darkness across the street and evaporated all of those apparitions out of existence.

Her heart wrenched when they vanished before her eyes. She would never get to tell each and every one of them how much they meant to her—how much she missed them every day—how much poorer her life was without them.

She turned away fighting down despair. It twisted into fury and cruelty toward everyone and everything, especially herself.

She must be truly Dark if she could destroy her own people—the people she fought so hard to save.

She would give anything to have them here—and then they were here. They said all the things she most ached for them to say—and she destroyed them. She was the one who delivered the final blow to make them leave her alone.

She must deserve this. She must deserve to walk alone with no one. Not even Anríq was here anymore. She was completely alone—the way she should have been all along.

She never should have let herself think she deserved anything else. She never should have let herself believe she might have a place in their lives. She obviously didn't if she could do something like this.

Chapter 41

E liska stumbled through the alley fighting back tears, but they were tears of anger at herself for even feeling this.

She brought this on herself the very instant she let herself start caring about these people.

She never would have found out who her parents were if she just left Middleborough when she first got there.

She never would have known she had a brother. She never would have found out anything about this whole ridiculous Shard disaster.

Everything would have been so much better if she just left the Watchmen alone with Wesh and gone her own way the way she originally planned to.

This was all her fault. All this pain was her own doing. It was a natural result of her own stupidity and weakness. Now she was reaping the rewards because she was just too gullible to learn from her mistakes.

She blundered out of the alley into the other thoroughfare—the one she'd been walking down when she first let these apparitions distract her. That was another stupid mistake—letting the Coil distract her by tugging at her heartstrings.

She stopped dead in the middle of the thoroughfare when she saw the Voyant's halo in the distance.

Her Darkness turned to fury against the one available target. He was the one who did this to her.

Yann was the one who initially got her to care about the Watchmen enough to stay with them. None of this would have happened if he just left her alone the way she told him to.

She launched herself at him. She didn't waste time walking there. She magicked herself to within forty feet of the spire and fifty feet up. She materialized right in front of him and charged him with all her might.

She came within a dozen feet of him and let all that pain and Darkness loose on him. She attacked him a thousand times harder than she ever did before.

She wanted to kill him. She didn't give a damn about the Shard. She wanted revenge. She wanted to make him suffer the way she had been suffering all these years.

He retaliated, but he couldn't swat her away like a pesky bug anymore. He could only hold his ground and return her bombardment.

She gritted her teeth and willed herself to find the power to destroy him once and for all. The world would be a better place with anyone else as the Voyant.

They pushed each other back and forth. She anchored her Dark vapors into his halo and wrenched it out of shape. It started to fade only to flare back to a blinding light.

That light infiltrated her Darkness and started to drive it out of her. She couldn't let that happen.

Of course he went after her Darkness. Of course he wanted to rid her of the one power she could use to defeat him.

She slashed Dark vapors at the weakest spots on his halo and actually succeeded in breaking through it.

She delivered a few telling strikes to his face and body. She could actually attack the man inside now. Her Darkness must be working.

He doubled over from the blows and tried to return them even as his own magic healed his wounds.

His light stabbed through her Darkness and she screamed in pain when those shafts impaled her.

Her Darkness healed her just as fast, but right at that moment, at the climax of their battle, a devastating smash hit the White Spire behind them.

They both looked toward the sound and saw Anríq standing at the base of the spire. He hauled back his club with one hand, pounded it into the walls, and fought off the spire's defensive barrages with his axe in his other hand.

He shattered the stone, but it still took him another four strikes before he smashed a breach in the walls.

The spire's defenses escalated beyond what he could cope with. The spire doubled down and forced him to use both weapons to defend himself. He couldn't take even a split second to dive through the breach.

The Voyant broke away from Eliska and turned on Anríq, too. She rushed the Voyant to hold him here, but right then, another blast of magical energy torched up from the ground and punched through the Voyant's halo.

All three combatants spun around. Eliska forgot to fight back when Alexiane, Marine, Yvan, The Watchmen, and Wesh rushed out of a nearby street. Wesh, Marine, and Alexiane fired magical bursts at the Voyant and the spire.

The spire and the Voyant turned their firepower on the newcomers. That left Anríq free to dive for the breach.

The sight of both the spire and the Voyant about to shoot down her loved ones skyrocketed Eliska's Darkness out of control again. She unloaded on the Voyant and sent him tumbling backward.

He slammed into the spire wall. Her Darkness actually hurt him. He pulled himself up snarling in menacing fury, compressed his lips, clenched his jaw, and a colossal shockwave split from the spire.

It hurled Eliska and Anríq far away into the city. The same blast completely obliterated all trace of the apparitions that came out of the Coil to help her.

She and Anríq crashed hard in some forgotten neighborhood. She couldn't even drag herself off the ground this time.

She rolled onto her seat, buried her face in her hands, and succumbed to all the sobs she didn't let herself cry when she saw those people before.

"They're all gone!" she wailed. "They're gone and I'll never see them again! Now I'm all alone."

Anríq crawled over to sit down next to her. "You aren't alone. I'm still here."

She couldn't even look at him. Darkness didn't make her crash like this. This anguish—this heart-wrenching loneliness—it was all real.

She stopped herself from feeling it for as long as she could remember, but it had always been there. It had been the one truth of her whole life.

She was alone. She always had been alone. She always would be alone.

Isolation had been stamped into her being when she was just a baby. It was the foundation stone of everything she was.

Everyone she ever cared about—everyone who ever cared about her—they all either left her or they died or she pushed them away first.

They always passed out of her life one way or the other. No one ever stayed because she wasn't made for that.

She would always walk alone. It was her destiny and her nature. She couldn't undo it.

She barely felt Anríq putting his arm around her and hugging her. He couldn't fill this void. He didn't even really exist.

He was just passing through her life before he disappeared, too. He *would* disappear as soon as she took the Shard—or one of them died—or he took the Shard and she disappeared.

Whatever they felt for each other had been too good to last. She never should have let herself feel that way about anyone. She could have spared herself this pain if she only protected herself sooner.

She ran her hand across her face and looked around. She searched every yard, street, and corner for the people she'd already lost.

He was one of them. She searched for him, too, but he wasn't here anymore.

She stumbled to her feet and wandered through the city searching for any sign of those people.

If she could just find them again, she could tell them how much she loved them—how much she needed them. She never wanted to be away from them again.

She had to find them. She had to keep them with her—but they weren't here anymore, either. She lost them all a long time ago.

She didn't keep track of where she was going until she turned a corner and saw the Voyant's halo in the distance. He never left the spire.

"Yann!" she breathed. "He's there! I have to go to him...."

Anríq caught her and held her back. "Eliska! You can't go near him! He's the Voyant. He'll attack you."

"He's all I have left! I have to go!"

She turned down the avenue heading toward the spire. Nothing mattered but being with the one person still alive in this hellscape.

He saw her coming from miles away. She only made it a few blocks before he blinked across the city, came to a stop hovering over the street, and hammered his magic down on her again.

She got so obsessed with seeing her brother that his assault took her completely by surprise. She just wanted to talk to him and see that he still cared about her.

His first barrage slammed her against a building. Anríq jumped out of the way in time to avoid getting hit himself.

She vaulted into the air to get to Yann's level, but he just kept pounding her again and again. He glared at her out of his halo with the same scowl of murderous determination to kill her.

She took his strikes one after the other. He had to hurl her against another building before she fully accepted that he really was attacking her.

She soared away from the building and took a position fifty yards away. She could see him from here, but he didn't attack again.

He would if she went any closer. He scowled at her just as ferociously. His eyes flashed with dangerous fire and he set his face in a mask of pure fury.

She blinked at him in sinking horror. He wasn't her brother anymore. He really was the Voyant. The one person she had left—her only living relative—he was gone, too.

Chapter 42

Eliska drifted to the ground and all the fight went out of her when she stared up at Yann floating above her. His hard, cruel eyes registered not a flicker of recognition when he glared at her. Did he even know who she was?

She turned her back on him. She didn't care anymore if he attacked her, but something told her he wouldn't.

She returned over the same distance she traveled to get here, passed through the city's outer neighborhoods, wandered into the surrounding countryside, and somehow made her way back into the city.

She didn't care where she went. The same instability and upheaval took over the landscape both inside and outside it.

Chaos transformed creatures, objects, plants, trees, houses, buildings, and the tiniest pebbles into whizzing monsters and attacking horrors.

None of them interested her enough to hold her attention. She meandered aimlessly anywhere and everywhere. She just didn't care about anything anymore. She didn't even care that she was in this city.

She occasionally noticed Anríq wandering along at her side. She didn't care enough to notice if he stayed there or if he went off on his own.

Maybe he didn't stay with her at all. Maybe he just happened to be in the same place and going in the same direction.

He barely looked at her. They didn't talk.

She paused every now and then when she saw people from her past caught in the mayhem. She watched them fighting, suffering, dying, and moving away from her.

None of their troubles touched her. She only distantly considered if those people might be real. She didn't care enough whether they were or they weren't.

She turned her back on them, too. She didn't usually even stick around long enough to see the outcomes of their fights. It never crossed her mind to intervene.

She turned a few corners and spotted Anríq watching his father and brothers battling for survival in the unstable landscape.

Sometimes, during those times when he traveled with her, he would stop and watch these distant memories. He never intervened, either.

She stopped and watched with him. She recognized some of those people from her visit to Anríq's home tribe. Some were strangers to her, but obviously not to him. He wouldn't stop if he didn't know them.

Neither he nor Eliska talked or even looked at each other when they stopped or if one of them moved on without mentioning it to the other.

She found it impossible to connect with him. She didn't consider him at all. He wasn't even here.

She wouldn't have considered if any of those other apparition people followed her around the city, either. He was no more real than they were. Why was he even here?

He must have been thinking the same thing about her. He never said anything or even noticed if she got up and walked away without a word or a backward glance.

She didn't care if she never saw him again. She didn't care about anything that happened in this city or in the rest of the Coil.

She and Anríq wandered close to the White Spire a few times. Neither of them wasted time attacking it or trying to get to the Shard. What difference did it make either way?

Once, they passed a few blocks away and noticed a different group of a dozen people attacking the spire and the Voyant.

Eliska's magic told her these people weren't apparitions. These people were far too real.

They were all powerful magic users who fought with all kinds of weapons. Each person used a different weapon.

One man used a sword and shield and wore armor like a knight. Another man wore a monk's habit and carried an orb glowing with dark, shadowy light. Brilliant jets of magic fired from the orb and landed punishing hits on the Voyant.

A woman in a long grey cloak fought with a staff. Another younger woman wore a glittering silver gown like something the friends might have seen in the Hallowed Vales.

This woman wore a golden gem-encrusted crown around her wavy blonde hair. Her magic fired from the gemstones and blocked the spire's defensive strikes from hitting her companions.

Eliska stopped where she was to study this strange collection of magic-users. None of them wore the same outfit or used the same weapons as anyone else, but they all worked together remarkably well.

They made a much more effective assault against the spire than Eliska and Anríq had been making lately.

These strangers used the same strategy. Some of their members occupied the Voyant. Others countered the spire's defenses while three individuals darted forward and tried to break into the spire.

The spire had magically repaired the breach Anríq smashed in the walls. These strangers had to start from scratch, but they came much better prepared.

The monk, a big muscular guy with a giant mace, and the older woman planted themselves next to the wall while their friends defended them from the spire's bombardment.

The guy with the mace raised his weapon and swung it into the wall with a shuddering boom.

The monk held his orb near the point of impact. Light beams shot from the orb and nailed the surface to weak it for the mace's next strike.

The others surrounded the Voyant landing blow after blow on his halo. Eliska couldn't tell from here if they got inside it to damage him.

The princess stood back shooting countless colored beams from her crown. They rained around the trio at the walls, caught the spire's strikes, and exploded them into harmless curtains of colored sparks.

She surrounded her friends with a film of protection and she wasn't the only one person protecting them.

The guy with the mace raised his weapon for his third hit when the Voyant whirled in a circle and fired down at the princess.

She wasn't even looking at him when he knocked her flat onto her back. His second shot skewered her to the ground and a massive splat of hot, wet blood stained the front of her dress.

Her protection evaporated and the spire plastered the trio by the walls. The first volley took out the big guy and the monk.

The older woman stood her ground one second longer before a blistering eruption burst out of the same hole the three friends had been trying to break in the spire wall.

The rest of the party tried one more time to attack the Voyant. He completely ignored them and went after anyone who had been defending the ground team.

They saw their friends go down, spun around to defend themselves, and the spire finished them off while their backs were turned.

Once the killing started, it didn't end until the Voyant and the spire brought down every single member of the party.

The Voyant and the spire mowed down all of them until they covered the ground. They fell with blood pouring from their wounds, their necks broken, and their weapons scattered.

Eliska turned away as soon as the battle ended. She couldn't even care enough about these people to ask the obvious question.

The Voyant and the spire killed them, but the Voyant and the spire didn't kill Anríq and Eliska.

Did Yann do that? Did he keep them alive for a reason? Was he trying to get one of them as his affiliate?

It didn't matter because neither she nor Anríq were trying to get the Shard anymore. They wandered off somewhere else and she put the fight out of her mind.

She and Anríq could go near the spire whenever they wanted now. The Voyant never attacked them. He must sense that they no longer posed a threat to him or the Shard.

Anríq and Eliska made it back to the thoroughfares leading out of town. She and Anríq had made it a habit to return to the countryside to camp each night.

They could have found more resources in the city, but the countryside was quieter. She could still hear the commotion from that distance, but it didn't keep her or Anríq awake at night.

Halfway down the thoroughfare, a different figure appeared in an alley to her right. She'd been seeing so many of these apparitions lately that she almost ignored it.

The instant she saw it, she knew this wasn't an apparition, either.

She stopped and turned to stare into the alley. Yann knelt there on the dirty pavement. It really was him. He wore the same white robe he always wore in his halo.

He didn't have his halo around him now, but he did wear his hair longer the way he'd been wearing it since he became the Voyant.

His whole body spasmed, contorted, and he kept wrenching over in pain. "Eliska...." he husked. "Help me..... you have to help me....."

She stared at him and felt...nothing.

This really was Yann. He clawed at his chest as if something tormented him there, tried to straighten up, and slammed down on his hands and knees.

He barely managed to drag his head up enough to make eye contact with her. "Eliska....." he croaked. "Please.....don't let me die like this.....you have to help me....."

She watched him for another minute. Then she turned her back on him and walked away. The sun would be going down soon. She didn't want to stay in the city after dark.

Anríq followed her out of town. They returned to the hilltop where they could look down at the city from above.

The instability didn't extend this far out of town. Both of them sat down the way they usually did. She didn't notice when he walked away a few minutes later.

He came back with an armload of firewood. She would have been content to sit on the ground in the dark, but he went through the old routine of building a fire.

They sat next to it in silence. Every evening passed this way.

He finally broke the silence that neither of them had disturbed for days. "This quest is taking us to some strange places."

She looked up at him. She could understand everything much better from this distance.

All the shades of emotion she'd been going through since Yann took the first Shard—all these different dimensions of experience must be the stages of the quest.

"Are you going through them, too?" she asked.

He nodded down at the flames. "I guess we both have to go through them. The Shard doesn't know or care who will take it. I suppose everyone who goes after it has to go through the same process."

She looked away toward the city. The Shard kept shining in the darkness and casting its eerie light over the countryside.

"I wish I could care enough to go after the Shard again," she murmured. "I actually kind of hoped one of those other people would take it. They deserved it more than I do."

"This is part of it, don't you see? This apathy or whatever you call it—this must be part of the quest, too. It's one of the stages—which means the rest of the quest is on the other side of this."

"Are we supposed to get out of it somehow?" She sighed. "I don't care enough to do anything to fight my way out of this. I don't care about anything anymore."

"Neither do I. Maybe that's part of the quest, too. Maybe the quest is designed to stop anyone who doesn't care enough."

"I guess we could go back into town tomorrow and fight the Voyant again," she suggested. "I don't care if I fight him or not. I guess he'll defend himself if I attack first. He won't attack me if I don't care about getting the Shard."

"I don't care about it, either" he murmured. "I never thought it would come to this, but I really just don't care about anything."

She looked up and studied him. It really wasn't like him not to care. He always cared about everyone and everything, even his enemies.

She couldn't see him as anything but a Servant, but she didn't care enough about how this affected him. She didn't even care how it affected her.

"Then I guess we'll go fight him," she finished. "We have nothing else to do."

He nodded and they fell back into silence. That was the most they'd talked in days.

Chapter 43

Anríq and Eliska got to their feet the next morning. He stepped on the dead coals to make sure they wouldn't come to life again.

The two travelers set off for the city. Eliska felt a small uplifting sensation that she and Anríq actually had somewhere to go and something to do today—something other than just wandering around doing nothing.

She didn't care about fighting the Voyant. She didn't even care about seeing Yann again. She didn't care if carrying the Shard of Hotha alone caused him pain or even if it was killing him the way it killed Noleron Kupero.

She and Anríq didn't talk all the way to the spire. They didn't stop to watch apparitions or battles between disembodied wall sections or pieces of pavement that came to life along the way.

None of those things offered any interest today if they ever offered any interest at all.

Eliska didn't know what to expect when she got to the spire. It looked exactly the same.

The bodies of those strangers had all disappeared. She couldn't fathom where they went.

Maybe the spire magicked all its unfortunate attackers into some underground crypt. Maybe a massive, unmarked grave full of thousands of skeletons lay rotting under the White Spire. She wouldn't have been surprised.

She and Anríq halted in view of the spire. It didn't erect any defenses to stop the pair from approaching it. Either she or Anríq could have walked right up to the walls.

He didn't take down his weapons and she didn't think about assaulting the spire. The Shard in the topmost window held no interest for her at all.

She eyed the Voyant hovering in his halo next to the tower. He looked down at her and Anríq, but none of the three attacked each other.

She and Anríq could walk away right now. The Voyant would have let them leave without a shot fired on either side.

Was she really going to attack him—for what—just to prove a point that she could?

She didn't care enough about the Shard to continue with this quest—if this apathy was a part of the quest.

She actually felt better like this. She remembered feeling a whole lot worse many times in her life.

She would have given a lot during her dark times if she could only have found a way to stop caring about everything.

She carried too many Dark memories of her own. She wished like anything she could stop caring about all of them.

Now she had that. This apathy as Anríq called it—it gave her a huge sense of relief.

She could finally let it all go and just be here. She didn't have to prove anything to anyone—least of all herself.

She didn't have to prove anything by attacking the Voyant, either. Why was she even here today?

She had nothing else to do. That was the only reason she came here. If she came or went, if she attacked him or didn't attack him—none of it really mattered in the end.

She was already here—and he was here—and Anríq was here.

Anríq didn't seem to care enough, either. He didn't care enough to take down his weapons.

Maybe he was considering right now if he should walk away after all. Maybe not caring about everyone gave him a huge sense of relief, too.

He always cared about everyone. He carried the responsibility of their lives and wellbeing on his shoulders. What sane person wouldn't want to get out of that?

She glanced around for no particular reason. Leaving meant trekking all the way back across town the way she and Anríq just came to get here.

She took a step back like she really did plan to walk away. At the last second, she launched herself up and piled in to assault the Voyant.

She didn't catch him by surprise. Maybe he expected this. Maybe everyone who came against the spire to get the Shard went through this apathy. Maybe they all wound up standing here deciding whether to waste the effort to go through with it.

She unloaded her Darkness on him. All these days of walking around in an indifferent cloud only deepened her Darkness and made it stronger.

She channeled it toward the Voyant, imploded his halo, and started to erode the light. Was she finally doing it—now that she didn't care anymore about doing it?

Her Darkness enveloped him and swallowed his halo—but the Darkness also enveloped and swallowed her.

It transformed her into a Darkling with long, dripping fangs and whipping tentacles.

Her Darkness weakened the halo enough for her tentacles to penetrate it. She slashed his face and body. Blood soaked through his robes before he reacted by reflecting that Darkness back at her.

His halo somehow harnessed her own Darkness, gathered it into clusters, and reformed them into Darklings that rushed her to tear her apart.

She wouldn't be able to defend herself against so many Darklings, but she'd already gone so far over into the Dark that it didn't matter anymore.

Her tentacles touched their skin, infected them with her Darkness, and she took control of them. She turned them back on the Voyant and directed them to attack his halo again.

They plunged through it, dove on top of him, and ripped him limb from limb with their teeth. Their magic sparked and exploded off him when they torched him with blasts. Their tentacles hissed and snaked every which way to whip him to death.

He crumpled inside his halo. Could Eliska kill him right now?

Right then, the halo exploded in a blinding supernova—and vanished again. The Voyant escaped and left all those Darklings empty-handed.

She withdrew them back into herself. They vaporized through her skin and shrank into the pit of Dark poison she'd been carrying around for what felt like years.

She lost awareness of it, but her interest in all of this evaporated along with the battle. The Voyant was gone. That battle accomplished nothing except to increase her Darkness.

She floated down to the ground. Anríq stood halfway between their starting point and the spire walls. Did he even try to get inside? Had he been standing here watching her the whole time?

They both turned around and walked away into the city. This battle changed nothing.

They might just keep on walking and leave this Layer altogether. She really didn't see what difference anything they did made.

They made it all the way to the other end of the thoroughfare before they met another group of people entering the city from out in the countryside.

Eliska wouldn't have paid any attention to these people except that they were going in the wrong direction.

All the apparitions tried to flee the city. These new people marched straight up the main thoroughfare on a beeline for the White Spire.

She stiffened when she recognized their cassocks. "You're monks of the Keepers of the Dawn, aren't you?" she asked the first ones she met.

A tall Rector with straight, shoulder-length brown hair like Miloji's nodded back at her. "We're on our way to assault the White Spire, steal the Shard of Hotha from the Sacred Shrine, kill the Voyant Mendicat, and take his power."

Eliska stepped aside to let them pass. "Good luck with that. I hope you brought plenty of magical power."

The same Rector cocked his head at her. "Who are you? How do you know about our order?"

"I had something to do with them in the past. I trained with the Keepers of the Dawn for a while."

The guy brightened up. He didn't even bother to introduce himself. "You could come with us. You could help us break into the spire."

She shrugged. "I've already tried. You seem like you have a lot of monks here. You'll probably have better success."

The guy frowned and then his eyes popped open to stare at her. "You tried....and you're walking away?! You're just giving up?"

She waved behind her toward the spire on the horizon. "If you want the Shard of Hotha, go ahead and take it. I don't care about it anymore. You can have it. Anyone can take it."

He kept gaping at her like she was speaking another language.

She found herself studying the monks just as closely. She had a completely different reaction to their arrival even though her past experience with them had been so painful.

If Anríq was right, then no one could get the Shard without going through the same psychological quest that Anríq and Eliska were going through right now.

The Keepers of the Dawn brought more than a hundred monks for this assault. Half of those were Rectors.

They just walked into town from out in the countryside. They just set foot in this city for the first time a few minutes ago.

They hadn't even started the quest. They wouldn't be able to get the Shard—if the quest was even real. Maybe it wasn't and Anríq and Eliska were the chumps for wasting days of their lives with this nonsense.

The Rector in front of her scrutinized her extra closely. "You have powerful magic, young one—Dark magic. You could come with us. We could get the Shard by working together."

She glanced over at Anríq. He only shrugged.

"I'll come with you," she replied, "but I don't think you'll make much headway."

Chapter 44

The Keepers of the Dawn continued their journey toward the White Spire. Eliska went with them for some reason. Maybe she just wanted to see what would happen.

"What can you tell us about the defenses around the spire?" the same monk asked her. "If you've tried before, you know more about it than we do."

"The defenses are nothing special. The spire shoots magic at you to drive people away from the walls. The Voyant attacks from the air." She pointed up at the spire's top turret. "You can see from here."

"Why do you think you haven't been able to get in yet?" the guy asked.

Eliska thought it over. "Maybe I'm just not strong enough."

"I find that hard to believe." The guy glanced down at her feet and scanned back up to her face. "Your Darkness is as strong as any of our Rectors."

She didn't answer. One Rector wouldn't be able to defeat the Voyant. The Keepers of the Dawn wouldn't have brought so many if they believed that.

She didn't tell him the other part of the equation.

Whatever happened between her and Noleron meant nothing in the long-range scheme of things. Killing Noleron didn't bring her any closer to getting the Shard for herself.

Maybe that's why neither she nor any of her friends had been able to get it when she did defeat Noleron. None of them had even been looking for the Shard then.

None of them had gone on or even started this quest—not really. She and Anríq had to go through this whole painful ordeal before she could even land a blow on the Voyant.

She only accomplished that by increasing her Darkness beyond what it was before.

The confusion, hatred, fury, resentment, and apathy—each phase made her Darkness more powerful—powerful enough to break the spire's defenses.

She might have to kill Yann after all. That might be the only way she and Anríq could both approach the two Shards at the same time.

She had to go through all of this to get to a point where she could actually mentally envision herself doing that.

She wouldn't have before. She would have balked at actually killing her own brother.

She wouldn't have unloaded enough Darkness on him. She would have cared about him too much—and she would have cared about herself too much.

She would have cared too much about what it said about her as a person. She cared too much about being a Servant.

She didn't give a toss about any of that now. She would kill Yann just as soon as she could. She didn't even really care if the Keepers of the Dawn took the Shards and ruled the Coil for their own selfish power.

She walked along next to them on the way back through the city. Anríq went with them. She heard him talking to the other monks about the spire and all his and Eliska's efforts to take the Shard.

She didn't hear him telling the monks about the quest. He never mentioned it as a requirement for taking the Shards.

She knew too much about what he was going through to think he might be deliberately deceiving them to stop them from getting the Shard. He didn't care enough about that.

He didn't care if all these monks lost their lives at the base of the White Spire. They didn't matter much if they didn't go through the quest.

Eliska accompanied them back to the spire, but she didn't hold out much hope for their success.

The Voyant didn't attack when the monks circled the spire's base and searched the whole area. They didn't launch their attack right away.

The first Rector came back over to talk to Eliska. He still didn't introduce himself to her, but she didn't ask nor did she volunteer her own name or Anríq's.

These people would pass out of her life in a few minutes. They would become nothing. She felt no need to get attached to them.

They knew about the Shard, the White Spire, the Voyant Mendicat, and the Sacred Shrine, but they didn't know about the quest. They were in for a rude shock.

"What have you tried before?" the guy asked. "How did you do it?"

"My friend and I engaged the Voyant and the spire's defenses up there." She pointed up at the Voyant. "Then another friend of ours rushed the wall over there, breached it, ran up the stairs inside, and took the Shard from its place in the window."

The guy stared at her again. "Your friend....took the Shard......?"

"He became the new Voyant after the old Voyant died. He took the first Shard alone—so the second one is still up there."

The guy looked away and didn't comment any further. The story meant nothing to him.

"Come stand in congress with us, young one," he told her. "We'll combine our magic to overcome the Voyant's defense."

She followed him to a group of ten Rectors standing together on one side of the spire. The other Rectors divided themselves into matching groups of ten each.

She and Anríq never thought to combine their magic—much less combine it with so many other much more powerful magic-users. This might actually work.

The Rectors formed a circle the way they did in their monastery. Eliska took her place with them.

They extended their hands toward each other on both sides. She copied them.

The monks created their colored crystals that hovered between everyone's hands. Everyone in the circle channeled their magic into the crystals and Eliska did the same thing.

The power started to build as all those crystals vibrated together.

The Rectors closed their eyes for this part. She copied them, but only for a few seconds. Shutting her eyes felt too strange.

She opened them and found herself in a beautiful library somewhere. It looked like the Tenth Library in the monastery where she used to meet the Rectors for her sessions, but this was a different place.

The windows along one side of the room gave a view across an expansive rugged, mountainous country covered in steep cliffs and deep, tall forests.

This definitely wasn't the same monastery. This looked like somewhere in the Hallowed Vales.

The same Rectors occupied the circle around her, but she didn't see the spire or the Voyant anymore. She wasn't in the same Island as the ruined city.

She didn't understand it until the Rectors poured so much magic into their crystals that the vibration gathered into a pounding throb.

Magic pulsed between the crystals and formed a hazy, wavering field in the center of their circle.

Eliska added more and more of her Darkness to the crystals under her hands. The other Rectors used Dark magic, too, and all their power joined into a seamless whole.

It flowed around the circle and connected all the participants with each other. It felt unbelievably good. She couldn't remember any pleasure like this.

That pleasure brought out her power like nothing else. The more magic she added to those crystals, the better it felt to keep adding more.

The Rectors kept their eyes closed. She couldn't tell if they intended to bring themselves back to their library.

They only created this circle for a few minutes before the Voyant appeared right in the center of the Rectors' wavering magical field.

He turned one way and then the other glaring at them all. He didn't glare particularly at Eliska. She couldn't be sure he even realized she was part of this assault.

The instant he appeared, the Rectors' magic took living form. Darkling tentacles whipped out of thin air around the circle. These tentacles weren't attached to any Darkling. The magic itself brought them into existence.

They cracked back and forth, discharged magical bursts against the Voyant's halo, and Dark vapors tore breaches in it. The tentacles penetrated the breaches and unloaded magical explosions straight into his body.

He twisted and thrashed inside his halo trying to defend himself. His halo ruptured magical shots of his own to attack the Rectors. Some of those outbursts struck at the tentacles, some at the crystals, and some hit the Rectors themselves.

A few shots hit Eliska, but none of them could get through her magic. The combined Darkness of all the Rectors working together protected everyone from the worst of it.

The attack escalated as the tentacles' discharges increased in power. The vapors inflicted more damage on the Voyant's halo.

He retaliated with more outbursts from his halo. They matched the Rectors' power and landed more telling blows on everyone in the circle.

The magic inside the circle beat louder, faster, and stronger to crush and tear him under the pressure of all the Rectors working together. He couldn't stand this much longer.

Without warning, he blasted out a devastating shockwave that detonated across the circle. It hit a yellow crystal on Eliska's left and exploded it on impact.

That one crystal weakened the whole chain and the Voyant let loose as never before. He sprayed brutal shots far and wide, took down two Rectors, and even hit the library.

Eliska ducked to protect herself. The circle shattered and the Voyant destroyed another two crystals. Every hit weakened the monks' power. They couldn't hold him.

As soon as their congress dissolved, he released the full torrent of his destructive magic on them.

He blasted the library to smithereens and then went after the Rectors with venomous fury.

He shot three more of them. Some of the youngest men tried to dive for the big oaken doors to get out of the library in time.

The Voyant fired a cruel barrage at the door, imploded it to block their path, and then annihilated the monks down to the last man. Eliska huddled on the floor waiting for the strike that finally ended her long nightmare, but it never came.

The Voyant kept spouting magical eruptions in all directions to explode the library to pieces. He unloaded on the walls, windows, and ceiling until the room caved in and everything fell down on top of her.

Chapter 45

Eliska straightened up and looked around. She found herself back on the sidewalk next to the White Spire. The Keepers of the Dawn were all gone, even the monks who hadn't taken part in the assault against the Voyant.

She didn't see Anríq anywhere, either. So much for that brilliant idea.

She walked off into the city the way she always did, but it didn't feel the same without Anríq.

She returned to the hilltop and sat down by herself. It was still mid-morning. She'd been gone for less than two hours.

She never noticed before if Anríq came or went. She would have sat here all day alone and continued sitting here alone all night. She could wander the city all day or camp somewhere in a ruined building for the night.

His absence took something away from this experience. She couldn't identify what it was because she didn't really care if he was there or not. He didn't talk. Last night's conversation had been unusual and not necessarily in a good way.

It felt strange to feel this way about anyone or anything, but she didn't want to stay here without him. She didn't really want to go back into the city without him, either.

She got up and hiked all the way back into town. She located him with her magic, but she didn't transport herself to his location.

She didn't even really want to see him. Why should his presence or absence make any difference to her? She didn't want to care about someone that much.

She couldn't decide if she should travel with him or not. His presence didn't make a difference because he would only leave or die or do something else soon.

Caring about him weakened her. Abandoning him to his own journey would be the smart thing to do, especially if she was already starting to care about him.

Caring about people got her into trouble in the past. She had to make sure it didn't happen again.

She passed down the thoroughfares on autopilot. She lost her motivation to find him even though she knew where he was.

She stopped keeping track of his whereabouts and her own. She wandered aimlessly for a while, came out in a different avenue, and found him when she wasn't looking for him.

He stood at a different intersection watching some other people through a side street.

He barely noticed when she walked over to him. He stayed where he was and didn't turn away from watching this other group.

They looked like poor village people from somewhere in the Coil. None of them wore fancy clothes or any kind of uniform. Most of them wore working clothes from farms or workshops.

They carried a strange collection of hand tools, farm implements, or household objects to use as weapons.

They brought thirty people, both men and women—all magic-users. They walked toward the White Spire, but they seemed to be caught in the same cycle of dull indifference.

They kept getting distracted by apparitions of different people before the magic-users wandered off somewhere else.

They had to continually remind each other to keep going, but no one seemed to be in charge of this group.

They only made it a few blocks at a time before some of them got distracted by something else, wandered off in a different direction, and occasionally forgot what they were doing.

This other group didn't interest Eliska enough to watch them. Anríq didn't notice or care if she was here or not.

His indifference toward her left her empty. She stared at the side of his head for a long time. He didn't care enough to come with her or even look at her. Why did she come here to find someone like this?

She walked away, and for some reason, he followed her. He turned his back on those other people and fell in next to her the way he did before.

She couldn't decide if him coming with her was anything she should be happy about. She didn't feel happy about anything.

They made their usual migration through the city and observed apparitions and battles between different features of the landscape transforming and attacking each other.

Some of those features tried to attack her and Anríq, but they worked together to deflect the attacks easily. Neither she nor Anríq had to stop walking or move out of position to demolish whatever stood in their way.

They found their way back to the White Spire by the late afternoon. Eliska didn't think much about it. The spire blended into the background landscape along with everything else.

She planned to just walk away from all of this, but without warning, the Voyant rushed her and attacked. He'd never done that before.

He never attacked her or Anríq unless they specifically attacked him first or if they came toward the spire intending to take the Shard.

She had already turned her back to walk away from the spire, the Shard, and the Voyant. She didn't see the point of getting involved in any of this anymore.

His first blast hit her in the back and made her stumble. He could have slaughtered her then and there the way he slaughtered so many others.

That first volley got her attention enough to make her spin around and defend herself. She unloaded back at him, but she didn't have any more Darkness now than she did during their last confrontation. She harmed him then, but she didn't defeat him.

He fought back and their conflict escalated. Anríq battled the spire's defenses down on the ground.

He fought his way closer to the walls like he planned to break through them again. Was he going after the Shard after all?

If he took it, he would stay here as Yann's affiliate. That would leave Eliska free to leave on her own. She wouldn't have to waste her time with any of this anymore.

She plunged into the attack to help Anríq get there. Leaving by herself and never seeing either of them again sounded like the best outcome she could hope for.

She poured out her Darkness on the Voyant, surrounded his halo in deadly vapors, and her Darkness took control of her.

It turned her into a Darkling again. She snapped her tentacles at him, invaded his halo, and landed dozens of strikes on his body.

He went through the same routine, turned her Darkness back on her, morphed her power into Darklings, and sent them after her.

She seized control of them, but at that moment, the other group of village magic-users blundered around a corner. They entered the street across from the White Spire.

She redirected the Darklings toward them instead. They had to gather together and form ranks to defend themselves.

Anríq burst out laughing when the Darklings fell on these strangers, brought down some of them, and mauled them to death.

That sound set Eliska's teeth on edge. How long had it been since she heard him laugh—at anything?

Now he was laughing at the suffering of defenseless people. The sound of his laughter snapped her out of her stupor.

He was a Servant. He never would have laughed at them. He should have tried to protect those people.

A surge of hatred for him wiped out all her indifference. She despised him for what he'd become, but she despised herself even more for letting him become it.

She was the one who led him into this Darkness. She led him to become everything he hated about himself and the world.

This wasn't the man she loved. She committed everything to the Servant's path because of him. He showed her the way to make her life count for something.

She wouldn't even be here trying to get the Shard if not for his constant encouragement and example.

Now that man was gone—replaced by this heartless, lifeless waste of flesh. She hated him for that, but she hated herself even more because she let herself become the same thing.

Her life meant nothing like this. She really would be better off dead than this mindless, careless, worthless lump of nothing.

Those people down there would still be alive if she wasn't here. Her death might actually cause some good in the world. She certainly couldn't.

She turned her Darklings away from them and instantly suffered another crushing wave of contempt for them when they retreated for safety to the city streets.

Those people were weak—too weak to defeat the Voyant and the spire. Those pathetic excuses for magic-users didn't deserve the Shard if they just ran away like this.

No one who needed her to protect them from the Darklings would stand a chance against the Voyant.

The Voyant kept bombarding her with more powerful magic. He knocked her back again and again.

She turned back to meet his assault. She could inflict more damage on his halo by using multiple Darklings to attack him, but some part of her hesitated to send her Darklings after him.

She didn't deserve the Shard, either. She definitely wasn't good enough to rule the Coil. She didn't even want to. She just wanted to protect it. Wasn't that why she came here in the first place?

She must be just as weak as those village magic-users if she turned her back on such power for the sake of total strangers.

A million warring thoughts and emotions collided in her mind. She forgot who to fight and how to fight them.

She hovered in the air taking barrage after barrage from the Voyant's halo, but she still couldn't bring herself to return his attack—with the Darklings or with her magic.

Why should she attack him? She was as bad as he was—maybe even worse.

The contempt she just felt for Anríq and those other magic-users turned against herself. She hated herself for everything she had become—everything she had ever done—every mistake and weakness.

She didn't think about it first before she turned her Darklings on herself and unleashed all her power to destroy herself. Vidal did it to stop himself from turning to the Dark. She could do it, too.

Chapter 46

The Darklings lunged for Eliska. Their magic exploded all over her. Their fangs stabbed into her body and started to tear her apart.

She bellowed and struggled against tormenting pain. She just wanted them to hurry up and finish her off. They should have been able to do it easily, but her own Darkness was too damn strong.

The pain blasted her out of her mind. Bizarre visions floated in front of her eyes—and the visions transported her to a Dark Layer between this world and some other illusion of her own making.

She saw Yann in an open magical battle against Marine. They both tried to kill each other and then Eliska saw him kissing another woman with bright red hair.

Eliska didn't recognize this stranger, but a second later, the woman pulled out of his arms and hacked at him with a giant battle axe way too big for her to hold.

He buckled under the strike and the vision changed to Anríq kissing another woman—a Barbarian woman with blonde hair. It wasn't Lanara. It was someone Eliska had never seen before.

Her hatred for herself and everyone else exploded in a fit of jealousy. She rushed him, knocked the woman away from him, and unleashed a jet of magic to annihilate the woman.

Anríq turned on her snarling in matched fury. "How dare you?!"

"You bastard!" She shoved him once and released a powerful burst of magic from her hands into his chest.

She sent him flying, but he came charging back just as fast. "You traitorous witch!" he roared. "You betrayed me with another man!"

He tackled her with all his weight, slammed her down on some solid surface neither of them could see, and snapped her back into the battle against the Voyant and the Darklings.

The Darklings kept ripping her body to pieces. Another cruel grin twisted the Voyant's lips upward as he watched from his place in the air near the spire.

Her hatred and jealousy blasted toward him instead. He took the Shard of Hotha. It should have been hers. His power should have been hers.

Her Darklings tore away from her at the speed of thought. She healed herself in a split second and her Darklings surrounded him.

She gathered all her Darkness to steal the Shard back from him, but the minute she got the upper hand, her feelings turned against herself again.

She hated herself more than she hated him. She hated her whole life.

She bowed under the tragedy of it all. No amount of healing could ever fix what had been broken and destroyed in this nightmare.

She was the biggest problem of all and now she was turning her Darkness on the one person who still mattered to her.

She wavered between pulling her Darklings back and just continuing. Why shouldn't she continue if she was this Dark? She would never redeem herself. She was beyond redemption.

The Voyant fought back against the Darklings, landed countless magical hits on them, flung them away from his halo, and stabbed their bodies to ribbons.

He turned their magic back on them, but he couldn't take control of them away from Eliska. He couldn't make the Darklings attack her instead. Only she could do that.

She watched from a distance and directed her Darklings and her vapors where and how to attack him.

Her magic picked out the weakest spots in his halo where the Darklings could get through and injure him.

Every hit she landed on him hurt her worse. Her own hits stabbed her in the heart, tore her apart with excruciating pain, and made her want to die.

He writhed under the Darklings' brutality, and in the midst of the attack, he looked up and caught her eye.

She could never be sure before if he knew who he was fighting or if he just fought whoever happened to be in front of him at the moment.

He definitely recognized her this time. His face spasmed with the pain and inner torment she saw when he begged her for help.

"I can heal you, Eliska!" he called out. "I can heal you of this Darkness.....just join me......."

The Shard pulsed in the center of his chest. Its radiant glow touched her across the gap and flooded her heart with its magic.

Pure pleasure poured into her and spread outward to her limbs and senses......and then she felt it. The Shard invaded her with Dark magic—the same Dark power the Keepers of the Dawn used to try to defeat the Voyant in the first place.

All her self-loathing turned to deadly hatred for the person who did this to her. She narrowed her eyes at the Voyant in bloody revenge. She would kill him. She would eviscerate him for doing this to her.

She charged him and bellowed out all her fury—for him, for her-self—for everyone who ever hurt her.

She consumed all the Darklings back into herself and channeled their power into the worst Darkness she could summon.

She got within a few feet of the Voyant's halo when she became aware of Anríq down on the ground. He charged the spire walls under cover of her battle against the Voyant.

Anríq raised his club to strike the wall, and at that moment, both the Voyant and the spire released matching jets of magic to strike him down.

The Voyant did it so easily. He hit Anríq from a distance without ever taking his attention away from his fight against Eliska.

She didn't have time to stop it. The whole thing happened in one instant. The Voyant must have been so much more powerful than she ever realized if he could do something like this.

He didn't even look at Anríq before both bursts combined and smashed him down. They flung him backward and he sprawled on his back on the ground.

Jet after jet of magic spouted from the spire. All those shots pound-ed his body hard enough to make him bounce. He couldn't protect himself.

His eyes fluttered open and he looked straight up at Eliska. His eyes started to lose focus, and in that moment, she recognized the man she loved. Everything about him that she fell in love with came together in her mind.

She gazed down into his eyes the way she'd gazed at him so many times before. The last few days of heartless apathy and cruel dis-gust—they all vanished. He was right there. She loved him more than anything and now he was about to die right in front of her.

She turned back and narrowed her eyes at the Voyant. Destroying this fiend was the only way to save Anríq and for them to finally be together the way they both dreamed.

She couldn't bring herself to hate the Voyant, though. She could see his face from this close range. It wasn't the Voyant or anyone she could hate.

It was her brother, Yann. He was trapped in this disaster as much as anyone and now he was about to die right in front of her, too. Saving Anríq meant killing Yann.

She didn't let herself think about that. She no longer considered herself qualified to make any decisions on what was best for the Coil or anyone else. She just had to end this battle before someone else got hurt, including herself.

She dove for the Voyant one more time, took a catastrophic bombardment from his halo, and swooped in to make her last stand.

She surrounded him with her Darkness, enveloped his halo to hold him in place, and at the last possible second, she dodged behind him and took a flying leap straight for the spire's upper window.

The Shard of Hotha flickered and gleamed right in front of her. She rallied every scrap of magic she possessed to rocket herself there fast enough so Yann wouldn't be able to stop her in time.

She spread her arms and legs as wide as they would go. The arc of her flight would make her fall right on top of the Shard. She would envelop it into herself and this would all be over.

Anríq would survive to walk out of here. He would continue his mission of helping people in the Coil. He would give her up to save her and the Coil from this Darkness. He said himself that he would do it gladly.

Gravity caught Eliska's weight and pulled her down toward the Shard, but at that moment, a hurtling missile of something black and white launched from somewhere on her right.

She had a split second to recognize Marine jumping from one of the nearby buildings. She widened her arms and legs, landed on top of the Shard, covered it with her body, and they both fell down inside the little tower room.

A catastrophic boom detonated in Eliska's face, stripped her away, and sent her cartwheeling for miles across the landscape. The shock-wave slammed her down on the ground with bone-breaking force.

Chapter 47

E liska got to her feet, looked around, and her heart stopped when she saw the city in the distance.

An outward-spreading wave of light translated across the Island from the White Spire in the distance.

The light transformed the city with every block it passed. It restored buildings, caused trees and bushes to bloom, brought people and animals back to life, cleansed all the dirt and dust from everything, and rearranged everything back into the positions they should have been before the instability destroyed the city.

Golden sunshine glistened on thousands of windows. Towering buildings stretched their pointed roofs to the sky.

People, wagons, and carriages bustled through the streets.

A steady river of noise, voices, laughter, and the rumble of activity drifted on the breeze. This wasn't the din of chaos and destruction. It was the steady hum of prosperous, contented, lively people going about their normal business.

A thump and rustling sound drew Eliska's attention away from the city to the hilltop on her left.

She gulped when Anríq pushed himself out of the grass, straightened up, and he stopped dead when he saw her looking at him.

Their eyes met once before she charged into his arms with all her might. She flung her arms around his neck and buried her face in his hair.

"I love you!" Her throat hurt. "I love you so much! I can't live without you!"

His big hand closed on the back of her head as he pressed her deeper into him. She never wanted to feel anything else as long as she lived.

"I love you!" he breathed into her ear. "Don't ever leave me again! I need you!"

She clamped her eyes shut against a well of emotion threatening to break her in half. He was back. They both were.

She fought to contain everything she felt about him. She wanted nothing but to be with him. She couldn't stand the thought of losing him.

They eased apart, but neither would let go of the other's arms while they feasted their eyes on each other.

His features spasmed with buried emotion and his lips trembled, but the radiant smile beaming out of his face brought tears to her eyes.

"Let's never do any of that again," he murmured.

She burst out in relieved laughter. "Yeah!"

She clasped his hands....and then they both turned to stare at the city in the distance.

Birds flocked, swooped, and called in the high blue sky overhead.

The wave of magic kept traveling through the outer neighborhoods, put everything back together, caused grass, plants, bushes, and trees to grow and bloom, repaved the streets, and kept on spreading out into the countryside.

She opened her Coil projection. The wave passed through the whole Coil. The magic stabilized Layers into new Islands that bloomed and thrived with people rebuilding and reconnecting, now that the danger was over.

Her gaze kept drifting back to the city in front of her. It pulsed with color, light, and activity. She'd never seen a more magnificent city anywhere.

"My God! It's so beautiful!" she breathed. "It looks just like the pictures. I never thought it would happen."

"How *did* it happen? I saw you go down on the Shard....and then we were here."

"It was Marine," she whispered. "She took the Shard."

His eyes popped. "She's here?! She's alive?!"

Eliska's gaze migrated back to the White Spire. It glowed blinding white on the horizon. It never looked more beautiful, but it didn't stand alone the way it did before.

An absolutely enormous castle surrounded the spire on all sides. The White Spire was only one of many towering structures among turrets, parapets, side wings, and other spires rising from different parts of the huge, monumental building.

The Shard of Hotha no longer shone in the spire's top windows. They looked out in four directions, but they were empty now.

That little room must be the Sacred Shine. It had been right in front of the travelers' eyes the whole time.

"She's in there," Eliska breathed. "She must be in there with Yann."

"We should go see them. Yann will be King now—which means Marine is his Queen."

Eliska glanced over at him, caught his eye, and burst out in laughter again. She couldn't handle all this happiness spilling out of her right now.

She felt so much happier now than she ever did in the visions of herself taking the Shard.

Yann and Marine were together. Eliska and Anríq were together. None of the four had anything to worry about anymore.

Anríq squeezed her hand again and the two of them set off walking back into the city. They knew this journey so well by now.

They entered a completely different city than the one they left just a few minutes ago.

They kept stopping and getting distracted by watching people working in their gardens and opening shops.

Children played in the parks. Workmen and delivery drivers went into and out of businesses. Longshoremen unloaded cargo from boats along the river.

Tall ships gliding in and out of the port. Wagons and carriages took people and cargo anywhere they needed to go.

The constant back and forth of conversation, negotiation, laughter, and cooperation surged through it all in a symphony of voices.

Anríq and Eliska held each other tightly by the hand all the way into town. She never wanted to let go of him—not ever.

She shuddered at the memory of everything the two of them had been going through these last few days. That quest—or whatever it was—it had been the worst, most painful, most terrifying ordeal of her life.

This moment fulfilled all the fondest dreams and fantasies of her heart. Everything was okay now. Nothing would stand between her and Anríq going out together into the Coil.

They just had to take care of one last important detail first.

They would have been able to find the castle even if they hadn't spent the last week exploring this city. The castle dominated one whole side of town. It towered over every other building and its magical light cast a blessed aura over everything.

The castle covered countless blocks extending outward from the place where the spire previously stood alone. A massive stone wall surrounded the castle on all sides.

Anríq and Eliska followed the main thoroughfare to the castle's huge wrought iron gates blocking the entrance.

Armed soldiers in polished silver armor and gold livery stood guard at the gate, but they didn't challenge Anríq and Eliska when they approached the entrance.

The soldiers bowed low and the Captain of the Guard pushed the gates open. "My Lady.... My Lord.....," he greeted them. "Welcome home. It's so wonderful to welcome you back at last."

Eliska was too stunned to speak. She and Anríq passed through the gates and up a long alabaster avenue leading to the castle entrance itself.

Gigantic slabs of white marble made up the doors themselves. Each one stood taller than a cathedral.

More armed soldiers lined the avenue and surrounded the entrance, but the soldiers all bowed to Anríq and Eliska and greeted them the same way.

All the soldiers welcomed them home and told them how wonderful it was that they were back at last.

Eliska didn't understand any of this, but it all made sense somehow. She was the former King's granddaughter. How else would these people greet her?

She didn't look the part in her ragged clothes. Neither did Anríq.

The doors opened into a colossal hall rising to steep glass windows in the roof. They towered out of sight with blinding sunshine pouring into multiple giant halls angling off in different directions.

Stairways led up from here to dozens of upper stories. Tall, carpeted corridors connected the entrance hall to every other part of this massive castle.

A chamberlain in an elaborately tailored doublet and knee breeches greeted Anríq and Eliska inside the entrance. His outfit, hat, and shoes shone with gold thread embroidered in complicated patterns.

He bowed deeply to Eliska. "It's such an honor, my Lady. Please accept my most humble welcome and consider me your devoted servant in anything you need."

"Um....thank you," Eliska stammered. "I'd like to see my brother if he isn't too busy."

The chamberlain only smiled at her. "Of course, my Lady. Please...follow me. I know he's expecting you."

He beamed at both her and Anríq before he led them off into the castle. Anríq and Eliska kept exchanging amazed glances before they went back to gaping at the surroundings.

The entrance hall led into even bigger, taller, more extravagant cathedral halls, each one more exquisite than the last.

Each of these halls stood tall and empty except for expensive tapestries, paintings, and coats of arms hanging from the walls.

Servants and courtiers passed back and forth in all directions through the castle. They talked, worked, negotiated, and conducted court business with the same energy and relieved enthusiasm as the population outside.

They all bowed to Anríq and Eliska as they passed. No one remarked on Anríq's and Eliska's strange appearance.

The chamberlain entered one of these halls that extended much farther back than anything Eliska had seen so far. It headed away from the castle entrance.

She found it hard to believe that she and Anríq had just stood outside assaulting the spire just a little while ago. It seemed like a lifetime ago.

The chamberlain halted at another set of colossal doors at the far end of the hall. Eliska couldn't tell what they were made of.

Gold leaf covered every inch of detailed carvings all over the doors. Armed guards stood on either side of the doors even though it was in the middle of this enormous castle.

The soldiers pushed the doors open to let her and Anríq through. Blinding light poured from inside. They had to squint and shield their eyes as they crossed the threshold.

As soon as they entered, the light dissipated enough for them to see where they were. The light blazed through giant windows in a ceiling that looked miles above the ground.

The carved golden doors led onto a high terrace carved out of white marble. It overlooked a magnificent garden spreading as far as Eliska could see.

Stands of flowering trees, hedge mazes, sprawling fields of wild-flowers, singing fountains flowing into river channels, chirping insects, and even flocks of birds filled the space with music.

Colorful sprays of flowers spilled from every garden bed, dripped from the trees, and the sun shining on the fountains cast twinkling rainbows in the crystal air.

Long, carved marble staircases curved from this terrace to flagstone walkways passing through the whole garden, but Eliska didn't move. She stood riveted to the terrace staring down at everything.

The light that blinded her and Anríq when they first walked in—it shone on everything with such a blessed light.

This had to be the Hall of Light—and just in case she might have doubted it, she spotted Marine standing down there on one of the sprawling lawns.

A herd of white horses surrounded her along with a few dogs, young fawns, and peacocks. Half a dozen rabbits hopped along the grass at her feet while she petted the horses and fed them from her hand.

Birds of all sizes fluttered around her head, landed on her arms and shoulders, and twittered at her from the nearby tree branches.

The dogs and fawns nuzzled her and then frolicked around playing with each other. They made her laugh when she wasn't too enthralled by the horses.

She wore a full-length white gown that grazed her bare feet. Her long black hair hung loose down her back and washed over the shoulders of her pure, spotless gown.

A simple golden circlet surrounded her forehead. She didn't need any other decoration.

She smiled up at the horses with such a beaming expression of perfect happiness that a lump came into Eliska's throat. She'd never seen Marine so happy.

She looked so much like the princess she was—except she wasn't a princess anymore. She was the Queen in the White Spire.

Right then, Yann called out from the other side of the terrace and strode forward to greet Anríq and Eliska.

He wore a gold, purple, and white doublet belted around his waist with a gold chain studded with gems. Deep purple breeches covered his legs down to his ankles and a decorative sword hung from his hip.

A bigger, fancier crown sat on top of his hair. His hair hung almost to his jawline, but it only made him look dignified. He actually looked like a King even when he smiled the way he used to.

"There you are!" he exclaimed. "I was waiting for you two to show up."

He held out his hand and then waved it away, laughed, and caught Eliska in a hug that lifted her feet off the ground.

"You're all right!" she exclaimed. "You both are!"

"We're fine thanks to you two." He put her down, held her at arm's length, and beamed at her. "It's so good to see you again. You had me worried there for a while."

She turned bright red, but she couldn't stop smiling at him. "We worried ourselves—a lot."

She expected him to make a joke, but when she looked up at him, his smile faded into a more serious gaze of deep love and admiration.

"Thank you," he breathed. "None of this would be possible without you—both of you."

Her eyes darted toward the garden. "Marine......"

"She's fine." A hint of warning in his tone told her not to disturb Marine. "We're both getting used to this. It's all so new, but we're going to be fine. We all are. The Coil is stabilizing. We're entering a cycle of peace and prosperity."

"Let's hope it lasts," Anríq added. "We need to make sure this doesn't happen again."

"It won't." Yann stood back and looked back and forth between Anríq and Eliska. "If anything happens to us, you two might be called on to take the Shards for us."

"No problem. We'll be ready," she replied. "Just let us know ahead of time so it doesn't get as bad as this. Give us some advanced warning if you can."

"I'll do my best."

Yann's eyes drilled into hers from right in front of her. He didn't have to say it.

It was time for her and Anríq to leave. The Hall of Light belonged to the King and Queen—the holders of the Shards of Hotha. Anríq and Eliska didn't belong here.

Their place was out in the Coil wandering from Layer to Layer helping the people who needed them.

She devoured her brother with her eyes. This might be the last time she ever saw him, but that was okay. He was where he needed to be. He and Marine would be happy together.

They would rule the Coil and usher in an era of peace, stability, and harmony for everyone in all the Layers.

His eyes softened just as much when he looked at her. Her chest tightened when she saw him drinking in what might be his last sight of her.

He hugged her one last time. "I love you," he whispered. "I'm gonna miss you."

"You, too," she choked. "I'm so happy for you—for both of you."

He stood back and smiled at her with tears in his eyes. He didn't speak...and then he placed his hand on her forehead.

Powerful healing magic flooded her. It drew all the Dark poison out of her, pulled it up into her head, and drained it through his hand.

His magic left her pure, clean, whole, and healed. Relief and happiness overwhelmed her and tears of happiness streaked down her cheeks. "Thank you!" she whispered.

He smiled back at her, but it was a sad smile. He healed her in ways no one else could. Now she could go out into the Coil without carrying the burden of all that pain.

Her new life waited for her to embrace it and enjoy it for the first time. The Coil offered unlimited possibilities for her and Anríq to build the life of their dreams.

Yann eased back.....and moved his hand down to her chest.

He placed his palm directly over her heart. Searing pain flashed across her skin under her clothes—and she felt the Servant's mark burn into her body exactly where it most belonged.

She couldn't speak to thank him for this last parting gift. His beloved face blurred in her tears. Her heart overflowed with love for him, Marine, Anríq—and all the other loved ones lost along the road.

This moment of restoration somehow gave them back the life they lost on the journey.

All the people she loved were still alive in the Coil to enjoy this moment of victory and redemption.

Their spirits survived to celebrate and to support the survivors in the years of rebuilding ahead.

She could only thank him by raising his hand and kissing the back of his knuckles. He was the ultimate King—a King she would gladly serve as his most loyal subject.

He would rule the Coil the way it needed to be ruled. She trusted him with her life and the lives of everyone else she fought so hard to save.

Yann kissed her on the forehead, stroked her cheeks, rubbed her arms, and then moved over to Anríq. The two men attacked each other in a deep hug that neither wanted to break.

When they finally separated, Yann's voice cracked with strain. "I'm trusting you both to take care of each other."

"We will," Anríq replied. "We'll come back and visit you—maybe when we both have families who can get to know each other."

Yann's lips twisted when he tried to smile. "We would love that."

Anríq took Eliska's hand and pulled her away. "Bye," she whispered.

Yann raised his hand and Anríq and Eliska returned to the big doors.

She paused on the threshold to look back.

Yann didn't stand there to watch them out of sight. By the time she turned around, he was already walking down the steps and crossing the lawn to join Marine.

He put his arm around her waist behind her back and leaned in to murmur in her ear before they both turned to petting the horses.

Magical light shone on both of them. It surrounded the garden in a halo of love and perfect serenity.

Neither Yann nor Marine looked toward the doors again. They existed there in their own private world. No one would ever be able to intrude on their union.

Anríq gave Eliska's hand one last small squeeze and they walked out of the Hall of Light. The soldiers closed the doors behind them and cut off the last thread of connection between Yann and Marine and the outside world.

They passed into another dimension—a dimension reserved only for the King and his affiliate. Eliska didn't want to be a part of that. She didn't want anything to come between Yann and Marine ever again.

The love they shared went beyond words—beyond humanity—beyond time. It bound them together by something more than the human mind could understand.

She didn't need to be a part of it, especially not when she glanced over at Anríq and they both started grinning.

The whole world lay open to them. No one accompanied them back through the castle's many halls, out into the city streets, out into the countryside, and out into the wild Layers where the Coil opened its many wonders for her and Anríq to explore together.

They shared a bond deeper than anything the Shards of Hotha could ever give them. They shared a bond sealed by blood and danger, a bond sealed in service and mutual commitment to the Coil.

They served the Coil the same way Yann and Marine would. Eliska and Anríq just carried out the same mission in a different way.

The Coil was their Hall of Light—their heavenly paradise where all their dreams came true and nothing could ever break that bond as long as time existed.

The End.

Sign Up Once--Get all Theo Mann's free books including brand new releases

S ign Up Once--Get all Theo Mann's free books including brand new releases

With the Corrupted Coil becoming increasingly unstable and the human world torn apart by war, the Barbarians expects their Chieftain's sons to become his greatest warriors and take over his power after him.

When twelve-year-old Anríq's dormant magic comes to the surface, it will destroy everything he knows about his life, his family, and his future.

When those he most cares about turn against him, he'll have to find a new source of strength within himself and the allies to help him do what must be done before it's too late.

Sign up at www.theomann.com to read it for free

About Theo Mann

I write 70 books per year—and yes, before you ask, all these books are my original creative work. Nothing written under my name is AI-generated or ghostwritten because I write better than AI and any ghostwriter out there.

People don't read fiction for entertainment or to escape from reality. People read fiction to see their humanity reflected in another person's character and story.

This is my promise to you. When you read my books, you'll see your own humanity reflected in the characters and stories. I take this commitment to my readers very seriously. My books are an intimate form of communication between us. I would never disrespect my readers by turning that over to a machine or another writer. This is my bond between me and you as my reader.

I write 20,000 words per day as my daily work output. If anyone with a public platform would like to challenge me to prove this in a controlled environment, feel free to contact me on this website's contact page.

I worked as a professional ghostwriter for fifteen years. Now I'm on a mission to set a Guinness World Record by writing 700 books over the next ten years and 1400 books over the next twenty years, all originally written by me. See my website for the full book list.

I'm also the author of *Proof for the Existence of God* and the *Crimes Against Fiction* blog. You can find all my nonfiction work at www.crimes-against-fiction.com.

If you have a story idea, or if you would like me to explore a series in more depth, or if you'd like me to explore a character by writing a spinoff series about that character or world, leave me a message on my website's contact page. I answer all reader emails, so ask me anything, tell me what you liked and didn't like, and let me know where you'd like your favorite series to go. I would love to hear your ideas and find out what you'd like to read next.

Find out more at www.theomann.com.

Also by Theo Mann (so far)